GALENA

Samuel Best

Get Free SciFi Stories!

ISBN: 9798359323512

DEDICATION

For Toccara

PROLOGUE

Hardly any ships those days were built for war. Commercial vessels didn't need weapons and the private sector was so heavily regulated that owners felt lucky to have a ship at all.

A few governments had bolted chain slings to their cargo frigates after the raiding of several trade vessels moving between Earth and Mars ten years ago. Despite the apparent squalor endured by ninety percent of Earth's population, luxury hotels were popping up like mushrooms on Mars and Earth's moon. An underpaid construction foreman commandeered one of his employer's vessels and enjoyed a short-lived career as a pirate, forcing space-borne governments and ship manufacturers to address a sticky regulatory question they'd long been able to avoid.

New laws were passed and harsher restrictions were enacted for private owners, as usual. The end result was the bolting on of the aforementioned chain slings, but no new ships specifically designed with "aggressive offensive capabilities" beyond those commissioned by the World Government Council.

A shame for the other commanders, really, thought Alexander Vola. *I very much enjoy flying a ship with guns.*

He stood on the sparkling new chromed and darkwood bridge of his privately-built warship, the *Morning Sun,* one powder-white hand resting against the back of his command chair. He kept his silky white hair combed back at an angle, and trimmed the sides of his head close to his scalp, as was the youthful trend. Yet even at thirty years of age, his chin and cheeks refused to grow hair.

The snug jacket he wore over his black uniform shirt was real leather, and creaked when he moved. His father's tailor explained this wouldn't happen once he had worn it for a time, but Vola liked the sound. It reminded him that the material had come from a living animal. Instead of his family's company logo, Vola had his own stylized V emblem stamped into the left jacket shoulder. On a whim, he ordered the jacket be dyed a deep burgundy red, which made his ivory skin seem all the paler.

Commander Vola stood tall beside the chair, sleek black highlighted by dark red padding that matched his jacket, its curved back rising higher than his head. At its peak was stitched the burning sun logo of his father's shipping company.

Luciano Vola had started the company with a small passenger shuttle that was decommissioned after Diamond Aerospace had finished building its employee barracks on Mars. Already ten years old when he bought it, the ship could barely hold a dozen of the standard coffin-sized cargo crates. Luciano flew the ship himself, thirty years before Vola was born, shuttling small loads between Sunrise and Tensu stations. During the second year of his modest operation, he was able to buy another shuttle, and then another. Now he owned sixty percent of the trade vessels that regularly made the trip between Earth and Mars.

The *Morning Sun* was a new kind of venture entirely.

Its hull was white, like its commander. Luciano had shunned the traditional aesthetic of most spacefaring vessels that drifted out of the orbital shipyards. The *Morning Sun* had no need for a bloated cargo hold, nor the elaborate docking equipment required to make berth at a dozen different loading stations.

It was broad of wing where most vessels were long and sleek, shaped almost like a wide triangle with rounded corners. From a maneuvering standpoint, the wings were useless without atmosphere. Each was banded fore to stern by three narrow, grooved tracks at five-meter intervals, revealing the true purpose of the ship's broad design.

The ship was fully capable of surface landings and takeoffs, which Vola would test for the first time after he passed through the Rip. The wormhole bloomed green and purple in a small panel of the floor-to-ceiling view screen as the *Morning Sun*'s powerful hybrid antimatter drive carried Vola's crew of twelve rapidly closer.

The newest Rip was exactly where Kellan McEwan's message had said it would be, nearly one AU above the solar system's ecliptic plane, halfway between the orbits of Earth and Venus.

How did that weasel open it without setting off every alarm in the solar system? Vola wondered as he stared into its black pupil ringed by a dancing iris of aurorae. This second Rip was more symmetrical than the one created by detonating Ceres — a near-perfect square with rounded edges instead of a misshapen smear three times as tall as it was wide.

The one Vola approached was a near-perfect square with rounded edges. The hypermass Kellan used to create the wormhole by linking the two identical quantum signatures on separate arms of the spiral galaxy was far more orderly a medium than the dwarf planet had proven to be.

Even at the *Morning Sun*'s current distance from the new Rip, the small yellow speck of the great star Phobis — the last of seven first named when the Rip was opened — could be seen within, beckoning from the other side.

Shunned by his peers and left more often than not to the expanding realm of his own imagination, Vola had obsessed over every little piece of information revealed about the systems beyond the Rip.

He rattled off the names of the seven stars in his mind.

Aegea. Enthos. Tena. Cyphus. Bolon. Neron. Phobis.

The *Morning Sun* made for the system of Phobis, around which Galena orbited, basking in its sun's pale yellow blaze.

The first Rip had been opened between Mars and Jupiter with the obliteration of Ceres, under close supervision of all the world's governments. The blue glory of Aegea could be seen through that Rip, uniting Earth's people in wonder unlike any other discovery in living memory.

Creating a second Rip would have required a

mass detonation no less in magnitude, along with a great deal of subterfuge.

Vola's pale finger stroked a control panel on the arm of his command seat, and he pressed the comms button.

"Prepare to take fire," he announced to his crew.

Hardly any warships these days, he mused. *Yet my pursuers have found several.*

He sat in his command chair and buckled the safety harness over his chest. The four other crew members on the bridge did the same at their workstations, none of them glancing in his direction. Vola liked that about this group. They hardly ever said more than was necessary, and they seemed to pay no particular attention to his unique appearance. He wondered if his father had picked them for that very reason. Surely the tiny fortunes the old man was paying them to crew the first of what he hoped would be a vast fleet played into their deference.

"I want to see them," he told Narienne, his second-in-command.

She had been his father's first choice for Vola's crew, a veteran of his own security force. The shipping lanes upon which he'd made his fortune were not inherently dangerous enough to warrant privatized security, but the political landscape he navigated to keep that fortune was another story.

Narienne's bald head was tattooed with two thick brown lines that started above her forehead and ran straight up over her scalp and down to the base of her skull. Between them were thin-lined glyphic symbols in a lighter shade. Vola often stared at the back of her head as he sat in his chair, wondering at their meaning.

Her workstation was to his left on the oval-shaped bridge, next to the edge of the visual screen that filled the forward wall. On his order, her slender hands moved deftly over the control panel of her station and the wall screen flicked from a multi-paneled layout of ship data and Rip scans to a wide view looking behind the *Morning Sun*.

Three vessels followed at a distance, visibly gaining — three metallic glints in a vast sea of pinpoint stars.

Below two eyebrows like ghostly caterpillars, Vola's pale blue eyes drank in the sight. He'd been itching for a confrontation ever since the *Morning Sun* had blasted free of the lunar orbital station. The foolish commander of the station had actually believed Vola when he claimed to be a political envoy whose ship was in need of critical repairs. The commander even went so far as towing the *Morning Sun* into the station's enclosed shipyard without first running his own diagnostic scans to verify there was a problem.

The plan had worked better than Vola dared hope. He'd been expecting to shoot his way through the shipyard from the outside to get to his prize. Instead, the station commander had delivered him to its doorstep.

His other ship, the dart-shaped *Spitfire*, flew ahead of the *Morning Sun* at the limit of visual range, towing his prize: two metal containers larger than the tallest skyscrapers on Earth.

He'd been uncomfortable with his father's choice of the *Spitfire*'s captain. Marco Mazza was as old as

Luciano, but steady and strong where his father was gouty and prone to tremors. His skin was leathered by the decades he'd spent with Vola's father in the moistureless, sun-pounded soyflower fields outside Rome. He jumped to Alexander's orders far less quickly than the others.

Still, there was no doubting his skill. The *Spitfire* had picked off three defensive cannons stuck like barnacles to the hull of the repair station while *Morning Sun* erupted from its blazing heart. Marco had managed to tether both massive containers to the *Spitfire*'s frame while performing defensive maneuvers *and* providing covering fire for Vola's ship.

"Weapons loose," said Narienne, her hands moving rapidly over her console. "It's an EMP missile."

On the screen, a glowing blue dot took the place of one of the three ships as the projectile shot toward the *Morning Sun*.

Vola *tsk*ed.

"Decoy," he ordered.

There was a soft clank from deep within his ship as a hatch popped open. A tumbling metallic cube appeared at the bottom of the screen, slowly drifting toward the oncoming missile. The cube emitted a litany of signals across a wide range of spectra, all of them identical to what another ship would see if it scanned the *Morning Sun*.

Blue lightning crackled as the missile struck the cube, engulfing it in a net of energy.

"Cut engines!" Vola barked. "All systems off."

His crew didn't hesitate. It was as good a test as

any.

The *Morning Sun* went dark as its systems flicked off, leaving only a small display from a lone heat sensor in the middle of the viewing screen. The vessel drifted free of its course, slowly spinning through empty space.

Vola's three pursuers drew closer, three red-orange blobs on the screen.

He waited, rubbing a thumbnail into the pad of his forefinger while chewing on his bottom lip.

The three approaching ships began to spread apart, close enough that their features were distinguishable even through the heat sensor. Stub-winged and tall in the middle, so their single occupants could pilot standing up.

Council ships, thought Vola. He must have stolen very precious cargo indeed.

"Chains," he commanded.

His crew worked quickly at their stations. Bridge lights blinked back on and a mechanical whir filled the air.

zzzzzzzzPING!

The first chain was away, visible as a silver glint on the restored visual screen as it shot from the left wing of the *Morning Sun*. More of them quickly followed, having gained peak velocity as they zipped along their metal tracks in the wings, counterbalanced by a weight that moved just as quickly on the opposite side of the track.

zzzzzzzzPING! was the sound of their release, and silent was their short journey to the approaching ships.

The three Council ships broke apart as the chains

found their marks, slicing through their hulls like soft fruit. Orange sparks burst from severed cables as the insides of the ships spilled lazily into space.

Vola wondered how the Council would take the loss of three ships, along with their pilots.

Not good, he thought, the corner of his mouth twitching with the threat of a smile.

"Resume course," he said, settling back into his chair.

A moment later, Marco's craggy leathered visage filled the wall screen. Like Nari, his scalp had been shaved smooth. Behind him, the *Spitfire*'s bridge boasted none of the *Morning Sun*'s polished splendor. Marco kept the lights low. After all those years toiling under a burning sun near the smog-belching, cacophonous processing plants, he preferred the dark and the quiet.

"Smartly done," the older man said. His suspicious eyes perpetually squinted beneath well-salted, bushy black eyebrows. "Though disabling them instead may have saved your father a headache."

"My father is no stranger to those," Vola replied. "If I recall the stories, you gave him his fair share."

Vola's father and Marco had grown up together, and often fought like brothers.

Marco *hmph*ed. "True enough. I'll see you on the other side."

He cut the feed before Vola could reiterate the *Spitfire*'s orders for the benefit of the *Morning Sun*'s crew. He didn't like passing up an opportunity to remind everyone who was in charge. A wave of annoyance crested, then passed as he took a deep breath and steepled his pale fingers.

The Rip grew larger on the screen.

Once the ships were on the other side, Marco would take the *Spitfire* to the Ceres Rip with one of the massive stolen containers. Vola would open the other container near this second Rip, the one that opened closer to Galena, deploying its contents to the panicked reaction of the World Government Council, he was sure.

Vola smiled, exposing straight teeth a shade whiter than his skin.

He always lied to himself that he didn't care what the old man thought, and this was no exception. Yet, deep down, he knew his father would be proud.

MERRITT

The soil was improving.

Merritt knelt down and sniffed the ground, which was still wet from last night's rain. Warm water seeped from the soil to soak through the padded lining on the knees of his dark green utility pants.

The rotten smell that had plagued Moyen's field for weeks was gone. He stood, smearing mud across the front of his pants in a vain attempt to wipe them clean. His shirt started out white that morning, but the dirt had made it almost as dark as his pants.

"Seems like the rain flushed out the blight," he told Moyen.

The older man pursed his lips, unconvinced. Wispy white hair floated like a cloud around his head in a hot breeze.

Merritt smiled and slapped the sour-faced man on the shoulder, hoping to cheer him up. He left a wet handprint on his gray coverall.

Moyen and a few of the other aging colonists seemed unbothered by the heat, wearing their sturdier but thicker coveralls no matter the season. Merritt almost always wore utility pants with extra padding sewn into the knees and a loose t-shirt, even during Galena's winter — so long as he was working in the fields. He'd cut his dark hair short in preparation for the hotter summer months and trimmed back his white-flecked beard to stubble.

"Field's gone to rot," Moyen said stubbornly. "How can the blight disappear overnight? Might as well move me again."

"Your stalks are already greening," Merritt replied. "Look."

He used the toe of his boot to disturb soft mud at the base of a tall stalk of soyflower, revealing a hint of green near the ash-colored roots.

Moyen's field hadn't been the only one afflicted by the blight. Nearly a third of the working farms surrounding the colony had reported losing at least some of their spring harvest to an unknown infection, which killed the stalks from the root. Merritt's initial fear was that it could be similar to a bacterium found on the bladeweed plant which was deadly to humans if left untreated. Bladeweed's stiff, razor-edged leaves sliced the skin, allowing bacteria into the bloodstream. The tenacious plant had to be carefully removed from every farm field before each harvest season. He had asked the resident expert on all things flora, Uda Jansen, to run soil samples, but she could find no trace of a contagion. In the eleven years since the colonists crash landed on Galena, she hadn't seen anything like it.

Merritt would have to check the other fields. He sighed internally, dreading the task. His own field was growing wild from lack of attention. It seemed to him he spent all his time those days tending to the problems of others. Uda had more or less lived out of the prefabricated hospital building ever since she took over the role of chief medical officer when Dr.

Leera James returned to her family on Earth. Three years ago, it would have been Uda in the fields on a hot summer day, hunting for rot amongst the roots while Merritt puttered in the shade of his own garden. Instead, more and more farmers looked to Merritt, who some claimed had the greenest thumb in the colony after Uda. Unfinished projects continued to gather rust in his workshop while he made weekly rounds to all the farms.

"We'll keep our eye on it," Merritt said to Moyen. "Still another week or so before harvest. If the rains washed away the rot, you won't have lost much."

The old man had picked off a shoot of soyflower from the top of a stalk and chewed the stem.

"I don't like not contributing," he grumbled.

"I know you don't, Moy," said Merritt, patting the wet handprint on the farmer's shoulder as he walked past.

Most feel the same way, Merritt reflected. *And those that don't have learned other ways to thrive. Just like a real society.*

That last thought brought a half-smile to his lips. The colony had been what he would call cohesive for years — interlocking parts all fitted together, the gears always spinning in harmony. People farmed, they stored what they didn't eat, they traded for what they couldn't grow, and — for the most part — they picked up slack when someone else fell behind. He could think of only a handful of instances over the past decade when one of those who "fell behind" was trying to make a habit of such practice. It usually only took one heartfelt conversation to remind them that every colonist walked the same tightrope. This wasn't Earth. There were no resupply ships. If anyone decided to wobble on the rope, they might all tumble off.

Merritt followed a narrow track between the tall stalks, pausing now and then to wipe away mud from their roots. Most showed signs of healing, though a few would have to be torn up and burned. Moyen didn't grow potatoes or carrots, but Merritt had yet to see signs of infection in the non-soy crops of his own field, nor his neighbors'.

That should make Gavin happy, he thought.

His son's soy intolerance was mostly an afterthought since the farmers had successfully diversified their crops. When they'd first arrived, it was field after field of soyflower, rendering the same protein in as many different ways as you could shape it.

Now the colonists with a chef's gift could offer leek soup and carrot loaf; potato hash with candied turnips; thick vegetable stew and asparagus shoots — all served over a crispy soy steak, if you insisted.

The small pouch Merritt's wife, Emily, had given him before she passed was full of seeds she had modified in her government lab. Galena soil was too acidic for Earth crops, so geneticists like his wife had found ways to tweak the DNA until the plants took root. Most of the seeds from the pouch failed to thrive, but few enough survived to germinate.

Merritt still remembered the wonder on Gavin's face — who was only eight at the time — when he showed his father the colony's first yellow potato.

Part of the reason he'd taken his son and left Earth after Emily died was to find a place where he could finally give the boy some nutrition. The soy mush squeezed out in mass quantities from the processing plants on Earth twisted the boy's insides. Before Galena, he had been frail and sickly, drawn into himself because every day he was forced to eat poison.

It was Emily's dream to come to Galena. She wanted the frontier, and the escape, and the better life for their son. It had taken her death to open Merritt's eyes. He promised her that he would get Gavin to Galena, and he did — but not without trial.

If only I could find him again, Merritt thought as he crested a low hill. The boy was hardly ever home. He spent more time with his friends than with his father, which was to be expected. Yet Merritt couldn't help but acknowledge a nagging feeling of distance growing between them.

Gavin isn't a boy anymore, Merritt reminded himself. He's nineteen. While that may have still been considered young to many back on Earth...here it was different.

His son had been hunting game for years, ever since he'd learned how delicious roasted rock bat could be. He had also taken over fishing duties from Merritt's old friend Willef, who had died three years prior while defending Gavin and two other children from a sky beast. Not a day passed that Gavin's plate wasn't half-covered with meat or fish.

Merritt looked down over the eastern farms, exposed as they were to more sunlight per day than the fields which spread out south and west of the colony center. Large swaths of rich gold hues painted the land as a weathered crop of soyflower ripened toward the first harvest. A ring of trees crowned the hill which hunkered more or less in the middle of the fields like the earthen shell of a great tortoise, several squat prefabricated buildings clinging to its shell. Their own white shells were streaked with gray after so many changing seasons.

"Deciding who you'll send me next time?" spoke a man with a Scottish accent from behind.

Merritt's mouth twisted in a reflexive scowl. He didn't need to turn to know who it was. Kellan McEwan stepped beside him to survey the colony. The man was a head shorter than Merritt, with fiery red hair cut close to his scalp and a thin copper goatee. Three years of exposure to Galena's sun had done nothing to tint his pale skin. It had only seemed to bring more freckles to his cheeks.

"You really haven't done much with the place, have you?" he quipped.

Kellan rested his right hand on his hip and stared at the sky. He was always doing that, as if he expected to see a ship glinting in low orbit. What remained of his left arm hung uselessly at his side, gone just below the elbow. Every time Merritt saw him, Kellan wore the same outfit: long-sleeved dark green shirt, the left sleeve pinned over his stump, faded black cargo pants, and scuffed black army boots.

"We've done enough to live," said Merritt.

He started down the hill, and Kellan matched his pace.

"Samar is fitting in quite nicely," he said to Merritt's cold shoulder. "Supply manager, was he? Good with numbers, but not so good at following orders. Not yet, anyway. I'm happy to take your strays, but I'd like them a bit more pliable."

"Exiling him wasn't a favor," Merritt growled. "He was hoarding the last of the morphine. Tom Wallace died screaming because of Samar."

"That's the man who got drunk and mistook the soy processor for a distilling tank?"

Merritt closed his eyes as the grisly memories flashed unwanted in his mind. Tom had indeed been extremely drunk, having downed nearly an entire bottle of Skip's potato vodka on his own. No one could say why he'd decided to overindulge that day — Tom wasn't known to drink more than he could handle.

The processor was the largest machine in the colony, roughly twice Merritt's height and triple that in length. Most of its parts had survived the crash in a series of containers which were found over the course of a month. Merritt and several others had bent and hammered scrap metal to fill in the missing panels. Gavin had been the one who figured out how to disentangle the machine's guts so it could begin the process of breaking down soyflower into the mush they all knew and loved.

When Merritt found Tom curled up beside the machine one morning, he assumed the man had simply passed out drunk. Then he rolled him onto his back and saw the blood.

A panel on the side of the processor had been forced open, the exposed equipment hissing steam. It was the compressor tank, Merritt realized. If Tom had opened that valve thinking it would dispense vodka, the high-pressure steam would have blasted him square in the face, hot enough and forcefully enough to peel skin from bone.

"He was a good farmer," Merritt said, forcing away the memory as he walked down the hill, "and a good man. He didn't deserve to suffer."

"Sounds like natural selection to me," Kellan replied.

Merritt stopped and sighed, weary of the back-and-forth.

"What do you want, Kellan?"

"Soy steaks and vegetables. My men are hungry."

"We sent you enough to last the season."

Kellan shrugged. "I put no restrictions on what a grown man eats."

"You should if you don't want to run out of food," Merritt told him.

"The colony has plenty in reserve. You don't want my men in these fields picking it for themselves, do you?"

Kellan's "men" were the half-dozen hired goons that had survived the past three years on Galena. Other than his closest confidante, a man named Felix, Merritt didn't know any of their names. He hadn't known any of the other six who had died or gone missing since Merritt and his neighbors joined together and banished the group to their own settlement two kilometers south of the colony.

The one small comfort Merritt took from their infrequent meetings was the fact that Kellan was always in the position of asking for help. Merritt didn't like for anyone to suffer, but penance was a different matter. He glanced up to the sky, at the hazy purple-green outline of the Rip peering down like a misshapen iris. Kellan had detonated a load of hypermass in order to open that Rip, and flaming debris from his jettisoned cargo hold rained down on the colonists below.

There had been a tenuous period of strained tolerance between the two camps after Kellan's wound healed, despite the havoc he'd inflicted on the colony. Merritt still thanked his own good sense in convincing his fellow farmers to confiscate the paramilitary group's weapons while their leader, Kellan, was still recovering in the prefab hospital. Not long after his loyal animals had been declawed, Kellan declared he'd taken all he could of the colonists' ill will and settled with his men permanently to the south.

"I'll send a new crate soon," said Merritt.

Kellan held up a warning finger, but smiled crookedly. "Don't skimp on the vodka this time. My men might take that as an insult."

Merritt was about to tell Kellan where he could stick all of his vodka when a man's distant scream rent the air. Halfway between where Merritt stood and the hill at the heart of the colony, a plume of dirt shot toward the sky, pulled sideways by the wind. A black and sunken pit had replaced most of the farm from which the dirt erupted.

Merritt broke into a sprint, heading for the farm. Kellan laughed at his back, the sound growing quickly fainter.

"Don't forget the vodka!" he shouted as Merritt plunged into a stand of soyflower stalks, following the screams.

GAVIN

He stood still as a statue, staring down into the shallow water near the ocean shore. Sunlight rippled across the waves that gently rocked his raft. His dark green utility pants were dripping with water, and had been rolled up at the ankles. His white linen shirt clung to his skin, still soaked from his swim to the raft. Beneath the lashed planks of spongy tree wood, the closest thing to a fish in Galena's waters darted away when it spied Gavin with his fishing spear.

The traps bobbing nearby on the surface were all empty, and had been for weeks. The small crawling centipedes he dug from the sand at the water's edge no longer tempted the cautious fish. Willef had used them as bait every day. After he died three years ago, Gavin took over most of the fishing duties for the colony.

He welcomed the quiet. Lately, he had been finding it difficult to calm the anger that seemed to so frequently bubble to his surface.

Willef had used the spear when he needed to, but most of the time when Gavin came to the shore, he found the traps already brimming with the slimy gray aquatic animals they called fish.

Each was flat and disc-shaped, with a thin translucent fin wrapping around its body. The ribbon-like fin undulated slowly, propelling them through the waters near the ocean floor. Niku, Uda's partner, had told Gavin that they ate a kind of plankton: animals and plants too small to see with the naked eye. Yet the wriggling worms seemed to be a delicacy to them, and they would rise from the ocean floor to chase them into one of Willef's traps...at least until recently. Niku's guess was as good as anyone's as to why the worms were gone, and even he was stumped. It wasn't seasonal, since they had simply always been there before.

Gavin was starting to think he would need to recruit more people in order to feed so many in the colony. The task of clearing the traps had only taken him an hour every third morning before the worms disappeared and he'd been relegated to using the spear. He did not relish the idea of sharing his quiet time with anyone.

He liked it here on Galena. He had no complaints about living in the colony, but he found it difficult to carve out time for himself. Between his growing responsibilities derived from his innate knack of repairing ailing mechanics and his work on his family's farm, he was rarely left alone.

On the other hand, being so busy had the benefit of distracting him from what he'd seen three years ago, in the alien's cavern.

He had stumbled upon the vaulted cavern by accident, while fighting not to drown as he was pulled along a violent underground river. The alien hung suspended in the middle of the cavern: a hulking, shapeless mass rising higher than he could see, the top of it swallowed by shadow. A web of thick, muscled fibers cradled it like a net, and it was held aloft by thick black tendrils cemented to natural rock pillars. Whip-thin filaments danced in viscous fluid behind its translucent black membrane skin, silhouetted from behind by purple glowing crystals embedded in the walls.

Wordlessly, Gavin had asked the alien to show him the future of the colony...and it did.

Even three years later, his memory of that vision remained vividly clear: his fellow colonists in chains, forced to work the land under looming machines that belched thick black smoke. Soldiers stalked the lines, keeping everyone digging, everyone building, everyone ripping down trees.

Beyond the colony, new-carved roads stretched toward every horizon — the start of the highway network that was to connect four great cities, the first of many, marking Galena's intent to rival Earth as the new capital of humankind.

Shurri was there, standing on weak legs beside a ditch. Her skeletal hand gripped a shovel and she stared at Gavin — the observer of this vision — her black-ringed, empty eyes imploring him to save her. This vision he beheld was only possible because the colonists of Galena were chained, treated like animals, and fearful of their monstrous overlords.

At the head of it all, issuing orders from the top level of a glassy spire, was the chief architect of this dark vision: a young man with white hair and a jackal's smile.

Yet none of it had come to pass.

Gavin had spent the first year after his vision in a constant state of paranoia, watching the skies for a glint of sunlight on metal — of invaders come to subjugate his friends and family. Whatever purpose the invaders had for turning the colonists into a fearful group of forced laborers hadn't been elucidated to Gavin, yet it was plain to see their motivations were evil. He needed only to think about the dead look in Shurri's eyes as her bony hand reached for him in the vision, begging for help, to remember that those events must never be allowed to happen.

Gavin had visited the cavern and its alien occupant many times that first year. It waited there, impassive, its bulk gently pulsing like some massive beating heart, as Gavin asked and asked again if the vision was real. Yet the few warnings he'd received in response were muddled and indecipherable. The alien wanted something from him, he could feel it — though it wouldn't or couldn't elaborate what it might be.

His worry faded as the months wore on, and as thoughts of his life with Shurri filled more and more of his waking mind. He looked to the sky less and less, finding more comfort in his daily schedule — especially since he'd taken up fishing.

The coastline here was a long stretch of black sand that curved in a gentle arc between two points. An hour's walk to the west was the Casmin Sea, a narrow body of water stretching north to south, its gray waters slashed with white by the strong winds that died upon its shores before they could reach the colony farther west.

Gavin's raft was anchored in water less than a meter deep. Fish were plenty in the shallows, but paddling farther out was an invitation to the leviathans that prowled the deeps. The monstrous whales with long rigid jaw cones instantly attacked anything moving in deeper water. Their typical prey was a five armed squid-like creature that burrowed in the sand on the ocean floor. The leviathans rammed the ocean floor with their lower jaw cones, impaling the squids beneath. Yet they had not hesitated to swallow whole the colonists whose escape pods had splashed down into the ocean while the *Halcyon* was falling toward Galena.

A fish swam out from beneath Gavin's raft. He drew back his spear and held his breath. The lean muscles of his arm tensed as he prepared to release. He sucked in a sharp breath, his eyes widened...and someone shoved down on the back of his raft, sending him flying into the air. He splashed down in warm water, scaring all the fish away.

Gavin came sputtering to the surface, searching for his spear. He snatched it up before it could drift away, but the opportunity was gone. He saw no more fish.

The sound of giggling made him turn. Shurri stood thigh deep in the water, covering her mouth with both hands. When she saw Gavin dripping with water, his dark hair clinging to his forehead, she burst out laughing.

At eighteen, she was a year younger than he was, and a head shorter. She wore sun-bleached khaki shorts that had been cut from pants long ago and a plain white linen shirt streaked with old dirt stains. The rays of Phobis had lightened her hair over the years. She always trimmed it when it grew longer than shoulder length, and usually kept it up in a simple ponytail, as she did now.

"You lost your dinner," she giggled.

And yours, he signed, his hands dripping water as they moved to form the words.

"Have you lost the taste for rock bat? I seem to recall two crates full of jerky still collecting dust in your home."

There's a reason for that, he signed, taking a step closer to her. She casually kept the raft between them, circling around it as he moved.

Where's your brother? Gavin asked. Shurri's twin Arthur was usually never far away.

"Helping my mom on the farm."

Gavin glanced back in the direction of the colony as he took another step around the raft.

It's a long walk to get out here alone, he signed. *There are no patches between here and the colony. Dangerous if you get hurt.*

Patches were what the colonists called the groves where flat, rectangular mats of deep red healing moss congregated. The native organisms crawled slowly over the ground and trees in shaded oases, always near a freshwater spring. Gavin would have died after the colonists first arrived on Galena if Dr. Leera James hadn't draped a heavy, sod-like blanket of healing moss over his broken body.

The moss always died in the process of healing, sloughing off as a dried-out husk when all was done.

Shurri's hands moved in response to his warning of danger. *You make the walk all the time.*

I have my machete, and this. He nodded toward his spear, resting in the crook of his arm while he signed, and she laughed. He loved the way she laughed.

"That old thing?" she teased aloud. "It almost breaks every time you spear a fish."

It's enough.

She looked at him without blinking, then signed, *But what if I wanted more?*

He leapt up onto the raft with a big splash and crawled quickly toward her. She squealed and laughed again, then let him pull her up onto the rocking platform. They lay there dripping, drinking in each other's faces with their eyes. His lips found hers, and soon they both enjoyed the warming light of Phobis on their bare skin.

Afterward, they lay on their backs, limbs entwined, staring up at the vivid blue sky.

"Are we out of fish at the colony?" Shurri murmured.

Gavin smiled and shook his head no. His hands moved lazily when he responded.

I just like it out here. It reminds me of Willef.

He remembered the foreman of the Starliner *Halcyon* fondly. Willef had saved Gavin, Arthur, and Shurri from a sky beast — a great winged animal that hunted its prey from the clouds. The one that nested in the twin mountains west of the colony usually flew out well past the shore to rip chunks from the backs of leviathans when their massive golden bulks broke the surface. Yet it had been injured and couldn't take flight. The four of them had stumbled into its new-claimed ground territory, and Willef gave his life protecting Gavin and his friends. In the end, Gavin slayed the beast with the machete Willef gave him, which he always tried to keep close at hand.

He glanced at the shoreline and saw the chrome glint of the blade leaning against the base of a tree.

"It's good to have reminders of those we've lost," Shurri said.

After a long moment, Gavin signed, *I wish we didn't need so many. Are you still happy you stayed?*

Shurri thought about it for a long time, her fingers tracing small circles on his skin.

"I never wanted to leave," she told him, "at least not after you and I truly found each other. But my mother makes it difficult sometimes. She says I'm the reason she had to stay instead of leaving with those other colonists when she had the chance."

It was her choice, Gavin signed.

Shurri nodded absentmindedly, her eyes wide and unfocused on the sky. "And if Arthur hadn't changed his mind at the last minute and decided to stay, mother would've taken him back to Earth without me."

Did you always know he would change his mind? Gavin asked. She claimed to share an unspoken bond with her twin brother — a bond that sometimes allowed them to communicate with a mere glance.

"It's one of the few times I didn't know what he was thinking," she admitted.

Gavin slipped his arm under her neck and drew her closer. He kissed her forehead and she smiled shyly.

I'm glad you stayed, he signed.

"Me, too."

Gavin's gaze drifted to the new Rip. It was no more than a faded purple-green haze outlining a misshapen circle in the blue sky. At night, he knew, the colors would fully bloom to rival the two great nebulae that stretched across the stars.

His father was still mad at Kellan for creating it, claiming it was the most reckless, dangerous, and irresponsible thing anyone's ever done. Gavin often used those words to his own benefit when his father accused him of acting without forethought.

At least I didn't open a wormhole in orbit, Gavin would sign.

He feared he was nearing the end of that defense, however. Last time he used it, his father pointed a finger at Gavin, his eyes flashing a warning, and he said, "You know what I mean."

Why am I thinking about him *at a time like this?* Gavin wondered.

He breathed in the scent of Shurri's hair: clean, with a faint odor of honey. Some of the colonists put small amounts of bittersweet in their bathing water, a sticky syrup derived from the fruit of the bitterbell plant. It overpowered the potent mineral smell of Galena's spring water and lingered on the skin like a hint of perfume.

Shurri craned her neck to check the sun's position, then sat up with a sigh and began pulling on her clothes.

Leaving already? Gavin signed.

She smiled and tugged the end of her ponytail out from her shirt collar. "I've been gone half the day. I promised Arthur I'd help clear the dead stalks. The blight got half our crop."

Gavin looked longingly at the water. It wasn't often he came back to the colony empty-handed, but he wanted to walk with Shurri.

He had just pulled on his shirt and pants when she said, "What's that?"

He stood up beside her, looking to where she was pointing. In the near distance, an elongated shape too large to be one of the plate-sized fish glided silkily under the surface, heading toward the raft.

"I thought you said only fish swim in the shallows."

They do, he thought.

Two long arms extended from the dark shape, moving like gray snakes beneath the rippling surface. It was then that Gavin knew they weren't looking at a fish.

The dark shape changed color to match the black sand beneath it as it shot toward the raft like a missile. Wrinkles of light seemed to flow over its skin, mimicking broken sunlight on the waves above.

Gavin got Shurri's attention, then thrashed the sign for *Swim* with his hands before diving into the water toward the shore. He was glad to hear the splash when she dived in immediately after him.

Wood cracked like gunfire and he looked back. Massive tentacles wrapped around the raft and squeezed until it shattered to splinters. Behind the writhing tentacles and thrashing water, a large eye lolled on a large, fleshy mantle, peering at Gavin.

Despite the water being less than a meter deep, they were still easily ten strokes from shore. Shurri pulled ahead of Gavin, slicing through the water like a knife. She had always been the better swimmer.

The splashing changed tone behind them, and Gavin risked a look back. The squid-like creature was so large that only the lowest portion of its glistening gray bulk was in the water as it pursued. Its roving eyes slid over its mottled mantle and landed on Gavin and Shurri. The sharp lips of its beak *CLACK*ed together and something shot out from its body, a long red rope of muscle that wrapped around Shurri's leg all the way up past her thigh.

She had a moment to scream before she was dragged under water.

SHURRI! Gavin yelled in his mind.

A stream of silver bubbles followed her body as she was pulled along under the water.

Gavin swam after her, his fingertips brushing against the black sand as his arms churned.

The rope of muscle lifted Shurri up out of the water. She coughed and flailed as water sluiced off her clothes.

Water and blood, Gavin realized.

He swam harder.

Almost there.

A thick tentacle snapped around his chest like a whip and *squeezed* the air out of his lungs. His arms and legs beat the cold gray flesh that was crushing his rib cage. Something on the underside of the tentacle burned his skin like fire.

The squid pulled him closer to its beak, which was *CLACK-CLACK*ing in the shallow water. The tentacle flung him back and forth, sloshing the water.

All Gavin could think was, *It's going to snap my neck,* followed immediately by, *Where's my machete?*

His arm knocked against something hard and he grabbed it blindly. It felt like splintered wood.

The raft, he thought.

Part of the wood chunk had a sharp edge. The turbulent waters calmed enough for Gavin to come eye-to-eye with the squid-like creature. Its pale iris was like a runny egg squishing around beneath plastic wrap. It regarded Gavin for a moment with cold indifference, long enough for him to slam the sharp end of his wood shard into the eye, popping the thin protective membrane.

Then he was spinning and falling, his world a kaleidoscope of blue. He splashed down into the water next to Shurri. She broke the surface gasping for air, and blood filled the water around them in a gauzy cloud. Gavin didn't know if it was his or Shurri's.

The creature lurched over the sand in spasms as gray sludge seeped from its punctured eye. Its tentacles flagellated rapidly, slapping the shallow water as it writhed.

Under his torn shirt, Gavin's chest bled freely where he'd been grabbed. A stretched-out oval of ragged lacerations marked where the tentacle's sucker had burrowed into his skin.

He paddled and kicked for the shore next to Shurri. When the water was no deeper than their shins, they crawled to their feet and ran, kicking up fans of water.

The creature's tentacles groped at the sand in front of its mantle, pulling it toward the shore like some lurching chariot.

"It's coming!" Shurri panted, looking back.

Gavin didn't want to look back. He didn't want yet another nightmare image to haunt him when he tried to sleep.

A piercing *SKRAAWWWWK* blasted their eardrums from above. They both doubled over, covering their ears, as a shadow swept across the ground. The squid-creature stopped dead in its tracks, its one good eye swiveling around its fleshy mantle to focus on the source of the shadow. Then its tentacles slid around to the other side of its body and began pulling itself back toward deeper water.

The sky beast swooped overhead, low enough so that Gavin and Shurri could smell the rancid odor of rotting meat that clung to the beast like an extra layer of skin.

Its wide membraned wings fanned out between four clawed legs. It had a body the size of a horse and the loose-skinned head of a vulture, with a sharp pyramidal beak that opened vertically instead of horizontally. Two silvery monochrome eyes were locked on the squid below, watching as its sucking tentacles pulled it through shallow water, toward safety.

The sky beast cried out once more, and tucked its wings to dive. The squid made it to the end of the sand bar and slipped down the ledge, disappearing with a splash. At the same moment, the sky beast slammed into the water, sending a white plume into the air. Tentacles rose from below the surface to wrap around the sky beast's body. Four bony wing-limbs thick with tendons sank into the soft ground, resisting as it was steadily pulled under. Soon the front half of its body was underwater, and only its jointed hind limbs stuck out, dug into the black sand where the ocean floor sharply descended.

It fought to pull its bald head from the water,

snapping its pyramid beak at the fat, crawling tentacle smothering its eyes. With a quick slash of its front talons, the sky beast split open one of the tentacles. The limb opened like a swollen fruit, spilling its pink insides.

The two beasts strained against each other, until they both grew still, frozen in deadlock. Tentacles quivered and made small adjustments, sliding over the sky beast's body and leaving streaks of slimy blood in their wake. The sky beast managed to slide one of its foreclaws back from the ledge and sink it into the sand, strengthening its stance.

"Come on," Shurri whispered at Gavin's side. She touched his shoulder and he pried his eyes from the fighting beasts.

His legs sloshed through the warm water until it was only as deep as his ankles, then he turned back, breathing hard.

The sky beast let out a scream as its claws slipped in the sand. A tentacle slithered around its throat and tightened until the scream cut off. Then the squid yanked the sky beast under the surface in an eruption of white foam.

Gavin stared at the boiling patch of water where the beasts had vanished, his heart thumping in his chest. If the sky beast hadn't turned up just then, he and Shurri would have been the ones dragged to the depths. He wanted to be far away if the squid came back for dessert.

But why had the squid come to the shallows in the first place? he wondered. *Why was the sky beast hunting so close to shore? Would it start attacking the colonists? And what happened to the wriggling worms he used as bait for the fish traps?* He was used to the occasional mystery, but so many at once...

He turned to ask Shurri those questions, but had to look down to find her. She had collapsed onto the black sand in the ankle-deep water, unconscious. It was only then that Gavin noticed how badly she'd been wounded.

Her right leg was a mess of blood. A gentle wave lapped over it and washed enough away to reveal a wide spiral laceration wrapping around her leg from her ankle to her hip, as if someone had peeled off a long, winding strip of flesh. Small bony barbs protruded from the ragged edges of the wound.

Gavin patted Shurri's cheek, but her eyes didn't open. He checked that she was breathing, and felt for a pulse. Relief flooded his tormented mind as he scooped her up in his arms and trudged to the shore, his legs already burning from running through water.

Shurri groaned weakly. Blood seeped from the torn skin of her leg.

Gavin oriented himself toward the colony and ran, dreading the distance, dreading the lack of healing moss, and dreading he might lose her.

AYANI

The shuttle flew low to the ground, skimming claw-like treetops that groped for the craft's underbelly. Instead of metal, the naked limbs caught only a blast of scorching heat as Ayani guided the nimble shuttle across the landscape. The forest she'd been gliding over for twenty minutes suddenly ended at the foot of a small mountain, which she casually avoided.

It was Kellan's shuttle. He'd been forced to give it up when the colonists took away his weapons. His ship, the *Renata*, departed for Earth three years ago, carrying anyone who wished to return, but he, a few of his men, and his shuttle remained. The Envoy, Jeff Dolan, had told her Kellan stayed because he was afraid to go home. He'd stolen a ship and enough hypermass to open the new Rip. Jeff didn't seem to think that would go over too well with Kellan's superiors back on Earth. The man's ploy to enrich the colony to the point where he could barter forgiveness with those who would persecute him had failed the moment he showered colonists with flaming debris.

Ayani made a small adjustment on the controls and slipped out of her safety harness. A semi-circle of control panels crowded the pilot seat beneath a wide, pinched window. She found herself once again struck by the beauty of the untouched world.

Beyond the mountain was a wide tract of flat land, with no obstacles in sight. No signs of animal life, either. The general consensus seemed to be that the migratory hex crabs — moving with shells locked together in a mass that covered half the continent — picked the land clean of any beast that could not burrow or fly during their two-year crawl around the equator.

Ayani leaned forward to look down through the thick shuttle window. Rivers and streams glinted between fingers of verdant, boulder-strewn land. They flowed through shallow valleys and tumbled down sparkling waterfalls below the solid disc of a pale yellow sun, which had traveled two-thirds of the way across a bright blue sky.

The narrow shuttle cockpit was lined with reflective black panels and the occasional control panel. It was large enough to comfortably seat three, but Ayani presently shared it with just one other person.

Henry Tolbard sat on a narrow bench along the padded wall, hunched over a platform table that unfolded down from the wall beside him. His mouth moved soundlessly as his stubby finger traced a line across a faded, hand drawn linen-paper map.

Like Ayani, he wore a dark blue coverall and black boots. A coarse white beard covered his square jaw, and his sun-spotted scalp showed through short white hair. His coverall was unbuttoned at the top, revealing a stained white shirt and a small silver pendant hanging from a tarnished chain.

Ayani kept her coverall buttoned to the collar,

and had clipped a black utility belt around her waist before they'd set out from the colony. Her rifle was secure in a crate near the hatch, but the belt concealed other tools she might find useful in a pinch.

Her long brown hair had proven to be a nuisance not long after she'd arrived on Galena, so she cut it up to her shoulders, and eventually trimmed it until there was just enough of it to tuck behind her ears. This was her third ranging with Henry in six months, ever since Jeff had escaped to Earth without her.

"Recognize anything?" she asked the older man.

He sighed and leaned back against the padded wall, rubbing his eyes. "I'm trying to match your scans with the probe imagery from the shuttle's data banks, but the high concentration of lead sulfide in this region causes the sensors to hiccup. I *think*," he emphasized, wagging a finger, "I *think* we are here."

He pointed to a portion of the map near its edge.

"Almost to the other continent," Ayani commented, studying the map.

Galena was girded by two land masses the size of Australia on opposing sides of the planet. Several seas, two vast oceans, and uncountable rivers, valleys, mountains, and ribbons of land lay between them. A solid polar ice cap cupped Galena at each pole.

Ayani and Henry had been gone from the colony for three days — their longest ranging to date. Usually they departed before sunrise and were back by nightfall, but Henry had insisted they go farther this time. Ayani thought he was searching for something, but he never admitted to seeking anything specific. Yet she had noticed a tremble in his hands as of late, and a malaise that afflicted his thoughts and movements.

They had flown over the Casmin Sea and skirted the edge of the Equatorial Ocean, the largest body of water by an order of magnitude, staying near land in case of emergency. There were no islands to be found in the Equatorial, only the massive triangular waves that never crashed. The Northern Ocean was the only other body of water large enough to not be considered a sea. It was far to the north, on the border of the polar ice cap.

Ayani pulled up an old probe scan on her control panel. They were flying over a spit of land that curled out from the approaching continent like a hook. Beyond the great plain over which the shuttle skimmed was a bay shaped like a knife's blade. On the far side of that bay was Galena's only other continent besides the one upon which the colonists had made their home.

"Look," she said, noticing movement through the wide, thick window.

Henry joined her by the pilot seat, holding its armrest for support.

A flock of enormous winged creatures glided low over the bay, scanning the rough waters with huge silvery eyes. The leathery membranes stretching between their four clawed, bony limbs shivered in the wind.

"Sky beasts," said Henry. "So many. We used to wonder if there was only one."

Ayani's large brown eyes followed one as it tucked its wings to its side and dived into the water, sending up a white splash. A moment later it rose from the surface, its wings beating hard as it took to flight, its black pyramid of a beak empty.

"Maybe it was separated from its group," she offered, "or exiled, like Kellan."

Henry grunted as he returned to his seat with an exhausted sigh. "I wish I could know all the stories this world has to offer. Even without humans, its history must hold wonders."

Ayani couldn't help but smile. She enjoyed the company of the other colonists, but Henry often waxed poetic in a way that painted their excursions in a romantic light. The truth was, much of Galena looked the same once you got far enough above the ground. She needed someone else's eyes to remind her of the planet's beauty. Whenever she began to feel the tug of indifference, she need only mention it to Henry and he would want to immediately set out on a ranging.

She didn't like taking her new home for granted, but she felt she was made to move. Only when she was in the shuttle and mapping new parts of the planet did she feel like she was exercising the right muscles.

My new home, she thought.

It was a bittersweet realization, yet one she had slowly grown to accept. After she and Jeff had discovered that monster in the cathedral cavern three years ago, everything changed. They had come to Galena, she as his protector, under orders to learn what information Kellan had stolen with regard to a top-secret installation in Earth's orbit called Shipyard 6. Once they were on the surface, Jeff sensed the presence of an organism that didn't belong — that was so incongruous with the surrounding oasis of teeming life that it pushed all other thoughts from his mind.

Three years later, Ayani still had to suppress a gag reflex when she thought of the rotten stench in that cavern, of the pulsing blob of a creature suspended within, beating like the torn-out heart of some twisted monster.

Jeff's sole mission since then had been to find a way to kill it. The colonists couldn't help him, nor could Ayani. The alien was three times the size of her shuttle, which was no small craft in its own right — but it wasn't just its size that made Jeff hesitate. It was the fact that it was mostly dormant. The only thing keeping it at bay was a shield of living branches surrounding the cavern, enclosing it in a protective shell — except the shield wasn't protecting the creature from outside attacks. The shield protected the rest of Galena from what was imprisoned within.

There were many things to love about this world, she told herself as her fingers tapped the control panel, checking energy reserves. They would need to land soon to recharge. Galena was beautiful, it was clean, and it was unspoiled. Yet she had spent thirty years on Earth before coming here. She had made friends, had been close with her family, and had a career. Ayani graduated top of her class at the academy, and she didn't mind living in an overcrowded, smog-laden city. Earth's capitals crawled with life — a different kind of life — but that's what she loved about her homeworld.

Yet her mission was to guard The Envoy, to support *his* mission, whatever it may be — and Jeff had decreed they stay on Galena. She had been hand-picked by General Trager himself, the head of operations for the shadowy Global Protectorate, and had successfully completed over half a dozen covert operations before being offered the chance to act as handler to The Envoy. The idea thrilled her.

Every academy student had heard the rumors. The Envoy couldn't die. He could read minds. He was an alien who had taken human form.

Ayani wanted to find out if the rumors were true. Part of her feared she was signing up to be nothing more than a glorified babysitter. Yet that fear was allayed as soon as they stepped off the ramp of his ship, the *Celerity*, onto the soft fertile soil of Galena.

But he abandoned me, she thought acidly. *He left me here to forsake my duty while he flew back through the Rip.*

A yellow warning button blinked on her control panel.

"We need to set down for a recharge," she told Henry. "Should only take a few hours for the cells to fill up."

"Enough time for a nap," he said with a smile. "Would you be opposed to a little walkabout afterward?"

"We didn't come all this way to stay on the shuttle, did we?"

He chuckled. "My thoughts exactly."

Ayani picked an open field dotted by massive silver-gray boulders. Working in tandem with the shuttle's computer, she set the vessel gingerly down amongst the rocks. Its three side landing paddles found the soft ground and sank to rest a meter below the surface. Steam hissed out from the belly of the shuttle as it vented heat, obscuring the cockpit window. Ayani patted Henry's shoulder as she walked past.

"I'll have a look around."

He acknowledged her with a weak nod as he followed her to a narrow bunk set into the wall of a passage leading to the hatch. "You know where to find me."

Ayani waited, fingers drumming against the inner hull, as the hatch lowered to the ground, wafting aside swirls of white steam.

The ground under her boots was just as soft as it was anywhere else, and the warm summer air was no less humid so close to the equator. Phobis was behind her, stretching her shadow across a bubbling stream and onto a large boulder of the silver-gray lead sulfide from which the planet took its name.

An electric hum filled the air as the shuttle's charging mechanism engaged. Flat hull panels on the roof slid back to expose solar cells which fed the core. Ayani checked the counter on her wristpad — five hours to full charge. It would be near nightfall by then. It seemed they would be staying out another day, at least.

Not that it mattered to her. With Jeff gone, her duties had gone as well. The hospital awaited her back at camp, where she'd been shadowing Uda in her spare time. Mending minor wounds and tending to the vats of healing moss was a good way to distract her mind from the constant urge to move — to do something, *any*thing.

Ayani liked the moss, the way it tickled your skin

as it crawled even if you weren't wounded. She'd needed its healing properties once before, when she sliced open her leg in the rocky tunnels below Galena's surface. She remembered picking out a thin strip of the rug-like organism and setting it on her bleeding thigh. Instead of crawling away as she expected, the moss settled closer to her skin with a kind of suction, and went still. When Ayani tugged on one corner, that corner shied away, adhering more tightly to her skin.

A few hours later, the dried husk of the moss slipped from her thigh, leaving only a bright pink line in place of the deep laceration.

Ayani patted her thigh, remembering, as she looked at a distant mountain range.

Why would he leave me here? she wondered for the thousandth time.

Jeff told her he was going back to the *Celerity* to check the most recent set of scans of the cathedral creature. The pair of them had been on Galena for more than two years at that point, and she'd let her guard down. She was starting to feel like he would be fine on his own, unprotected.

Her eyes had traced the bright blue energy arc as the *Celerity* cut through the sky, heading for open space.

Ayani had battled with opposing thoughts for the last six months.

He wouldn't just leave me here, part of her said.

He would if he wanted to keep you safe from whatever he had to do, said another part.

She looked up at the sky, devoid of clouds and birds.

What could be so dangerous that he wouldn't bring me? she puzzled. *I'm supposed to be the one keeping* him *safe.*

Water in the nearby stream babbled over smooth stones. A warm wind rustled her hair as she frowned in thought. Then, very slowly, the muscles of her face slackened as slow realization crept into her mind.

Unless he's going to the only place I'm not allowed to go, she realized. *The most dangerous place that side of the Rip.*

THE ENVOY

Jeff Dolan initiated braking maneuvers as he neared Earth. The sleek hull of his ship, the *Celerity*, spun around until he drifted toward the planet engine-first. After a single long burn, the ship lazily spun back around, aimed like a dart at the brilliant, yet imperfect, blue-green world.

Still beautiful, Jeff thought, captivated by the sight.

Patches of gray smog covered huge swaths of industrialized land, and the west coast of the States was the same dry red-brown it had been since the climate scientists realized that the great transitory drought of the 22nd century was not so transitory after all.

Despite its scars, and the black veins which crawled across its surface in the form of corruption and environmental negligence, from space it was serene.

Atmospheric boosters fired near the slender nose of the *Celerity* and the vessel slowed to a near-stop. Jeff shifted in the pilot seat, the straps of his safety harness creaking. He wore his white Envoy uniform, stained and washed so many times the white material almost matched its gray stitched shoulders and elbows.

Perhaps I can pick up a new one while I'm here, he mused. *Or maybe I can find a regular pair of jeans.*

It was an idle thought, harmless, but it distracted him from the real task at hand. Yet even as he tried to distract himself, his fingers tapped on the control panel, opening a communication line to the white object between his ship and Earth, no larger than his thumbnail at his current distance.

The orbital shipyard was much larger than it appeared now, Jeff knew. He *should* know, because he helped to build it.

A traffic controller acknowledged his request for docking, and Jeff set the *Celerity* on a slow course for the shipyard.

Six of the massive hollow eggs had been constructed by Diamond Aerospace under contract with the U.S. Government. The company at the time was run by Jeff's wife, and he had eschewed every deep space mission he was offered in order to stay closer to Earth and work on the shipyards.

Long enough to hold five aircraft carriers end-to-end, and only slightly less tall, they had churned out thousands of ships in the more than three centuries they'd been operating at full capacity.

Yet only five of them were truly made for the production of spacefaring vessels.

Shipyard 6, toward which the *Celerity* now drifted, was made for quite a different purpose.

It grew in apparent size with each passing minute, eventually occluding his view of Earth altogether. Smaller vessels buzzed around its white exterior. Sentry drones, he knew. Shipyard 6 was operated and guarded by a cabal of military personnel from a smattering of world governments which formed the World Government Council. Jeff had lobbied them for years to give him an official position on the staff overseeing The Weaver's containment facility. He'd heard horror stories about the kinds of experiments they were performing on the alien. That was easy enough to ignore for a time — but then it started reaching out to him in his dreams, reminding him of what happened on Venus...

Within a mountainous hollow pyramid, a sentient cloud of glass shards calling itself the Worldshaper had told Jeff he was to be tested. His unique experiences with The Weaver were molding him to be The Envoy — if he passed the test. Otherwise, he was fit only for obliteration.

Then Jeff met a man from the distant future — *his* future — who claimed to be both Jeff Dolan and The Envoy. He even had the same matching scar on his scalp, and was also missing his left eye.

But my left hand was metal, Jeff recalled as he sat aboard the *Celerity*. He clenched his fist. *At least I still have two good hands. But for how long? Everything else I saw in that pyramid on Venus has come true.*

Jeff saw that man every day in the mirror — the same bitterness in his right eye; the same hard, skeptical mouth.

The WGC eventually conceded they could try a different, less invasive method of communicating with The Weaver. When General Trager's predecessor tracked Jeff down and asked him to act as liaison between the two species, Jeff told him the correct term was Envoy.

He'd been working for the World Government

Council ever since.

A hatch just wide enough to admit the *Celerity* slid to the side as Jeff's ship approached. Six sentry drones flew out through the hatch and surrounded the hull, matching his speed. His control panel lit up under his hands as the ship was scanned.

Jeff took a moment to curse Kellan McEwan and all he'd ever done — or *not* done, in Jeff's case. They had struck a bargain three years ago. Kellan would deliver a load of hypermass to Jeff so he could destroy an organism that threatened the existence of every living thing on Galena, and Jeff would allow Kellan's dream of calling the shots on a new Earth to continue unimpeded. Since Jeff had never received his hypermass, he never saw fit to stand up for Kellan when the short man was ousted from the colony with his pack of hired thugs. After a final visit to Kellan's ragged settlement to ask if the hypermass was forthcoming, Jeff's impatience got the better of him. He climbed into the *Celerity* and blasted out of the atmosphere, straight toward the first Rip. It was farther from Galena, but it also wasn't opened by Kellan. Who could say where it led? Kellan had proved the worth of his promises time and again, and Jeff wouldn't risk his mission by falling victim to yet another lie.

The hatch closed behind him after he was through, and the drones drifted off, joining a cloud of others patrolling the curved inner shell, the opposite end of which was so far away it was little more than a distant fog to the naked eye.

A second shell nested within the first: a sphere suspended in the middle of the cavernous interior. Its shell was black instead of white. Bands of sentry drones encircled the sphere like molecules around a nucleus, and two large warships were parked nearby.

Jeff let the *Celerity* do the flying. He was a steady hand after so many centuries, but even the slightest false movement could unleash an arsenal that would vaporize his ship in a blink. It didn't matter that he was the only living human that could somewhat communicate with the being inside the sphere.

As he drew closer, a docking port distinguished itself from the smooth black shell. He parked the *Celerity* alongside it, unstrapping his safety harness and drifting up from his seat after he shut down the ship's onboard systems. There was a hollow metal clunk from deep within the ship, and a quick lurch. A thin green rectangle glowed around the edge of the control panel, letting him know the hatch seal was secure.

Jeff smoothed down the front of his old uniform and buttoned his collar, then pulled himself, weightless, toward the airlock. Even if he wasn't supposed to be there, he needed to look the part.

When the inner hatch opened, he was greeted by two men in body armor, carrying shock sticks and stun grenades. Projectile weapons were forbidden here, for obvious reasons. Jeff waited for the underfloor GravGens to anchor his feet to the floor, then nodded curtly as he walked past the guards, letting out a quick breath of relief.

They haven't been warned, he realized.

Everyone who worked the sphere knew him by sight. It was perhaps the only place in Earth or orbit where that was the case. Otherwise, the guards would have balked openly at the thick scar that cut a line through his graying hair from above his left eyebrow, up and over his scalp to the base of his skull. They also would have gaped, as most others did, at the teflon eyepatch bolted over the hollow socket of his left eye. And after his visit to Galena, he'd been given yet another unwanted physical flaw — a dim light that glowed within his remaining pupil.

Before he left Earth, he'd kept a low profile for those reasons among others, observing his legend grow as if he were on the outside looking in. Rumors about The Envoy and the contents of Shipyard 6 were as widespread and varied as the peoples of Earth. Occasionally some half-truth would escape the iron wall of security surrounding the operation and take on a new life, evolving as it spread across the land. Jeff hadn't realized it at the time, but being sent to Galena was a blessing in disguise for someone like himself who simply wanted to be left alone.

Yet here I am, right back in the boiling pot, he thought as he walked a narrow metal gangway between walls lined with the barbaric prongs of shock nodes. A dozen cameras tracked his movements. *How long until someone realizes I'm not supposed to be here?* he wondered.

Jeff stopped before a thick metal door at the end of the gangway. A screen silently slid out from the wall and performed a biometric scan. A ghostly X-ray of him was rendered to the screen. As always, he stared at the small black sphere embedded in his skull, near the base. It was an alien object put there by the ring-shaped machines that had brought him back to life after he died on Titan — machines built by the creature he was on his way to visit. Jeff believed his experience on Titan and his subsequent resurrection were what allowed him a small connection with The Weaver. Whenever he remembered to ask the creature directly as to the *why*, he got no answer.

The heavy metal door rose into the ceiling. Hot, sulfurous air pushed past Jeff in a humid cloud, instantly causing him to sweat as he entered the innermost chamber.

Powerful GravGens thrummed beneath the metal floor which encircled the inner wall of the chamber like a viewing platform. The entire space was a hundred meters across, its walls splashed by harsh halogen lamps. Yet most of the lamps were pointed toward the alien prisoner.

The Weaver hung in the center of the chamber, filling half of the space with its bulk. In a resting state, it appeared as a massive burnt black croissant, its tapered ends curled in toward each other. A dull red glow emanated from one of the ends. The Weaver's jailers typically referred to this end as its mouth. The rest of the creature was covered with black rock-textured skin with deep fissures running in jagged lines across the surface. The same dull red light that pooled over The Weaver's "mouth" glowed from within the fissures.

It hung perfectly motionless, like a meteor captured and frozen in place.

Yet Jeff could *feel* its life as he stepped to the platform railing. This was the first time he'd visited The Weaver since before he'd left for Galena three years ago. His visits to Shipyard 6 had occurred infrequently prior to that, only when he was summoned by Trager.

The acrid air burned his eye and nostrils, but that was easy enough to ignore. He walked along the platform, following the inner wall of the spherical prison, heading for the extendable gantry. Robotic arms hugged the wall, syringes as large as swords in their metal grasp. They would detach from the wall several times a day to inject The Weaver with a cocktail of suppressants powerful enough to put half the Earth's population into a deep sleep. While Jeff had worked on the shell of Shipyard 6 — at the time believing it was meant for building spacecraft — he had no part in its interior. The engineers involved had isolated some kind of energy pattern emitted by The Weaver. They quickly discovered they could construct a prison that emitted a negating signal to keep The Weaver at bay.

Jeff was alone in the chamber. He had been inside when the place swarmed with scientists and military personnel. That had been near the beginning, when they'd first captured the dormant Weaver near Venus.

If it had been awake, they never could have taken it, Jeff thought.

The Weaver hibernated while its mechanical creations and resurrected human drones toiled on the surface of Venus, forging a new homeworld for their displaced master. All progress had stopped when The Weaver was snared in a tensor net and hauled back to Shipyard 6. Centuries later, the military still kept a close eye on Venus, though the terraforming process had frozen mid-stride. City-sized buildings of material so black it swallowed the light remained half-finished, the hovering human drones that guided the process stuck like flies in amber all around.

Now the chamber was only busy when he was summoned, when there was something Trager and the others wanted Jeff to communicate to The Weaver in the hopes of gleaning some critical intelligence.

Why did it send the meteor shower that poisoned our soil? Are there any others like it? Can it open more Rips? Why will it only talk to you?

Jeff was hardly ever told the reasons for his summons. He was given a set of questions to ask, and he did his best to ask them.

"Ask" was a bit of a misnomer in that regard. Communing with The Weaver was so far from having an actual conversation that Jeff considered it a positive experience when he had even a single bit of information to report.

Sometimes the committee seemed satisfied with his findings, but more often than not, they wanted *more*. More and more...always more.

He reached the gantry and stepped over the railing onto its grated metal platform. It extended from the wall-hugging platform by a long arm which slowly brought him closer to The Weaver.

When Jeff had first set foot on Galena, his normal vision had been overtaken by what he came to call *life-light*. On that planet, solid beams of multicolored light rose from every living organism, from the massive to the microscopic. Each one had a kind of crystal resonance, a faint song that hummed inside the light as it rose toward the sky. The larger the animal, the wider the beam, but all of them faded as they reached toward the sky. Even the upside-down trees emitted their own special light. The underground canopy had turned out to be perhaps the most complex organism on Galena. Jeff often felt as if he were walking on a net of light whenever he strolled through the forest. The flying sky beasts were, to him, soaring rainbow ornaments, a thousand pillars of light bursting from their bodies.

He had not seen The Weaver in such a manner, until now.

Its life-light was solid red, and did not take the shape of solid beams, as did the creatures of Galena. This light was a million crystal shards bursting from its black skin like spikes, red as garnet. Tiny points of brighter light drifted slowly from the bottom of the spikes to their sharp tips, then flowed into the air and vanished.

The light songs of Galena's organisms were a mixture of tinkling glass and high-pitched buzzing. The Weaver's song was a deep *thrummmm* that vibrated Jeff's ribcage and made the sphere inside his skull tingle, as if a low-grade current were passing through it.

The massive alien twitched internally, and Jeff grabbed the handrail of the moving gantry as he twitched at the same time, linked to it somehow — yet The Weaver did not move.

It knows I'm here, he thought.

The deep thrum grew louder as the gantry came to a stop mere meters from a deep fissure splitting the rocky black skin of The Weaver. Jeff reached out for one of the myriad crystal spikes covering the alien like a second skin. His fingers touched air while his eye saw them pass through the glowing razor edge of garnet light.

Then he closed his one good eye, and waited.

The deep thrum vibrating his ribcage was not only an aural representation of The Weaver's life force — it was the pathway to connecting with it. Jeff let the sound consume him. It flowed into his veins and inside his skull until he was a part of it, carried along its steady wave onto a plane outside of his own senses. His consciousness dipped into an endless void, where it floated in calm nothingness.

Endless quiet.

Jeff smiled.

Another presence bloomed to life before him, dark red in its nascency. Here, in this place, he still had both eyes, and more besides with which to see. The light formed the shape of The Weaver, not contracted in forced dormancy, but unfurled to its full length.

Yet Jeff was unafraid. He had been to this place at least a dozen times over the years, and he was never in danger because his corporeal self was someplace else, standing on solid ground.

Usually, he started his feeble attempts at cross-species conversation by asking for knowledge. This time, however, he simply needed to talk.

He spoke without words, unspooling images from his mind, which seemed to enshroud his weightless body like a gauzy nebula. Pinpricks of lights were his thoughts, and they flashed as he formed the images he wished to convey to The

Weaver.

It was taxing work, and seemed to take ages. Yet time meant nothing in that realm, he had learned. Whenever he communed with this alien intelligence, he always returned to his real body moments after departing — though at times he felt as if he'd been away for years.

Jeff conveyed images of the cathedral creature on Galena, suspended by thick black tendrils above a platform piled high with a gelatinous mass of putrid black muscle. He tried to capture the essence of its life-light, tainted by darkness, unlike the other organisms on Galena. The colony world was 10,000 light years distant, burrowed within a different spiral arm on the far side of our galaxy, yet in that moment, on that plane with The Weaver, Jeff could feel himself back inside the cathedral cavern. He could hear the throbbing pulse of the alien; could see the whip-like filaments inside its body. The filaments were silhouetted against its translucent black membrane skin by dim purple light, their shadows swaying back and forth inside the shapeless sac that was the creature's body — a sac held aloft in the cavern by an encasement of thick black rope-like muscle in the form of a net.

After the last image was pushed beyond the veil of Jeff's consciousness, he waited. Days? Months? Years? He couldn't tell. His thoughts flowed like cold mercury. They crept over the past, seeped into the dark cracks of forgotten memories.

He recalled a vision that had been relayed to him over four centuries ago, while he was aboard a ring-shaped machine called a torus. He was shown a recreation of The Weaver's homeworld. It was a volcanic, primordial place. Red clouds covered the sky — clouds swollen with the black ash of countless eruptions. Lava belched from the planet's rocky surface, the ground shook from the incessant quakes, and Weavers drifted like stone-skinned blimps above the chaos.

Yet there was another presence there...something that didn't belong.

The cathedral creature was a wolf amongst sheep, drifting between them almost casually, engulfing the small Weavers with its long black tendrils, pulling them in close.

When it was finished with its prey, the tendrils uncoiled, spilling lifeless remains to the strong winds, which tumbled the corpse as it fell to the riven surface below.

That memory now seemed as fresh as if it happened yesterday, yet Jeff hadn't thought about it in years.

Silence deepened in the void. The manifestation of The Weaver slowly lifted one end of its long tapered body, and red light flashed across the garnet crystals sticking out of its skin like spikes.

Jeff saw the Earth in his mind. It spun along its orbit in a cloud of glittering metallic debris — enough to be the remains of ten thousand ships. The cathedral creature was somehow as large as the planet — no, *larger* than the planet. It settled onto the surface as gently as falling snow, smothering a quarter of the globe. Tendrils crept through the oceans as they enwrapped the Earth — once, twice, a third time. Continents broke in half as the monster *squeezed...*

Jeff stumbled on the gantry and groped for the handrail. He missed and fell hard, cracking his temple on metal before his knees absorbed the fall. Groaning, he leaned against the rail, clutching at his pounding heart while panting like he'd nearly drowned.

"What do I...do?" he croaked hoarsely. He swallowed hard, his throat dry as powdered ash.

Slowly, keeping the heel of one hand pressed to his throbbing temple, he climbed to his feet. He was back to just the one eye again. The Weaver still boasted its phantom armor of red crystals, but now a light was strengthening within the deep crevices that gouged its skin.

A waking light, thought Jeff.

Another vision flowed into his mind, though this one was gentler than the first. It was little more than a vast and empty room. In the middle of this room hovered a grid of large black objects the size of city buses in the shape of medicine pills.

Hypermass, Jeff knew. *The Weaver is showing me how to destroy its enemy.*

As plainly as if he'd been born with the knowledge, Jeff saw what he must do. For a brief moment, he wished Ayani was there beside him.

I didn't want to put her at risk, he told himself. Even though that was the very essence of her assignment, Jeff had known from the beginning that there was a very real possibility he would die before he ever made it back to Galena.

That fear cut him like a sharp blade when an alarm klaxon blared within the hollow prison sphere. Red and yellow strobe lights flashed against the inner walls.

Trager knows I'm here, thought Jeff, *and he knows I wasn't summoned.*

"What if I'm too late?" he bellowed over the alarm, directing his question at The Weaver. "It almost escaped once already." The *Celerity* was a fast ship, but it would still be at least six months before he made it back to Galena.

A warmth blossomed inside his skull, just above the tip of his spine. Knowledge flooded his mind as if it were thick oil being injected by a syringe — knowledge that was archaic and undiscovered all at once, known to half the universe and to none of it, two sides of the same coin flipped around and melted together.

The Weaver's grip on his mind slipped away. Jeff didn't understand any of it, not yet — but now he knew where to find a trove of poorly-guarded hypermass.

Then he was running along the gantry, ignoring the pain in his skull as he leaped over the platform handrail and raced back to his ship.

MERRITT

The screaming grew louder as Merritt ran through a field of soyflower stalks. Yellow-green leaves longer than his arms slapped his face and neck. *Whose field am I in?* he wondered as his boot snapped a fallen stalk in half. *Uda's? No, that was before.*

He burst from the tall stalks and skidded to a halt in loose soil at the edge of the crop field.

I'm in Daren's field, he realized, panting. *That means...*

Merritt ran again as the scream peaked, then faded to silence. He leapt an overturned crate that had spilled dirty potatoes. His heel squashed one and ground it into the soil as he passed.

A two-story home with sheet-metal siding loomed ahead. Its corrugated blue roof and two empty windows that gave it the appearance of eyes confirmed that the surrounding field torn by screams belonged to the Cohens.

"Shurri!" Merritt shouted as he ran. "Arthur!"

He went around back, past a row of well-used farming tools and then he was past the wall, sliding to a halt at the edge of a pit twice as wide as he was tall, his arms pinwheeling to keep his body from tumbling over the side. His heel slipped over the edge and he stumbled back as a fresh cascade of soil fell into the pit.

A scream crawled out from the pit, much weaker than before...and far more distant.

He wasn't alone. Several other colonists stood far from the edge, talking in low tones and gesturing to the pit.

Arthur Cohen exploded from the front door of his house, frantically coiling a long rope around his torso while trying to keep hold of a stunner staff taller than he was. His dark blue coverall was streaked with dirt.

The teenager was twin to Shurri, and both were close friends to Merritt's son, Gavin. They shared the same straw-colored hair and lighter complexion, but Merritt had noticed a timidity in the brother that he never observed in his sister.

Until now. It was fear he saw in the young man's eyes, but not meekness.

"I-i-i-it got Dale," he stammered when he saw Merritt at the edge of the pit. "P-pulled him in."

His shaking hand rattled the stunner staff when he stood beside Merritt, gaping into the hole.

"What happened?" Merritt asked quickly. "What got him?"

"I d-don't know," Arthur replied, "but I saw him fall down. I was upstairs when he...when he screamed."

"We need to move fast," Merritt said. He sat on the edge of the hole and nodded at the stunner. "Do you have any more of those?"

Arthur shook his head, then offered the stunner to Merritt. He grabbed the staff and dropped a meter to the hard floor of the pit.

Not a pit, he realized. *A tunnel. Why didn't we know this was here?*

Sure enough, a rock-walled tunnel slightly taller than Merritt extended in both directions beneath the Cohen home. Sunlight spilled through the hole above in a bright circle, making it impossible to see what could be waiting beyond the glare.

Arthur hopped down beside him. He adjusted his belt holding up his dark green field pants, then tightly squeezed the coiled rope around his torso with both hands. The shirt beneath was once light blue, but had turned a mottled gray over the years.

After the first few months on Galena, the colonists would experiment with different methods of washing clothes. Often a new soap derived from a local plant would be tried. Many of the experiments served only to infuse the clothing with peculiar stinks and permanently alter their color. Eventually it was discovered that a sticky sap could be rendered when you boiled the outermost layer of porous "wood" from one of the ubiquitous Galena trees. The sap had a sweet smell, proved to have antibacterial qualities, and became soapy after whisking. The only trick was finding a tree that had naturally fallen or was already dead standing up, because chopping into the living wood was an invitation for an undesirable reaction from the underground canopy.

Merritt led the way out of the circle of sunlight, moving at a brisk pace in the direction he'd last heard the screams. He blinked as cool air rushed past him, then shivered. His shirt was soaked with sweat, and clung to his chest.

"Where's your mother and sister?" he asked quietly.

"Mom's at the market," Arthur whispered. "I don't know where Shurri went. She wouldn't tell me."

Probably to find Gavin on the coast, thought Merritt. He and his son spoke more infrequently those days, it seemed to him, but at least Gavin had scribbled a note in the dirt outside their home that morning for Merritt to find later: a cartoonish fish with an X for its eye and a hook in its mouth.

The market was held every few days, or whenever enough farmers requested it. They would gather on the hill near the center of the colony and trade food and supplies to supplement their own stores at home. Sometimes someone would lose their crop of carrots, or their soy jerky would sour and need replacing before the next harvest.

"He's a good man," Arthur said suddenly. "Not like the others my mom…spent time with."

Merritt knew a little about the Cohen family struggle. The twins' mother, colloquially known as The Widow Cohen, had never wanted to stay on Galena longer than it took for her warden husband to complete his brief tour. Yet she was stranded here along with everyone else when their ship crashed. Shortly after, her husband was poisoned, leaving her to care for two children alone.

Gavin mentioned to Merritt that she had been icy by nature, but her circumstances hardened the few soft edges that remained, turning her into a spiteful, bitter woman. The few love interests she'd become involved with in the ensuing years had done little to bring her peace.

Until Dale.

“He’s nice to me and Shurri, and he helped mom fix up the farm,” said Arthur.

"Fix up” wasn’t quite the way Merritt would phrase what happened. The Widow Cohen had never attempted to work a functioning farm. She had squatted on the land meant for harvest and refused to vacate so someone else might produce a crop. Over the past year, however, since she invited Dale to share her home, the field was cleared, the tools repaired, and the stands of soyflower stalks seemed healthy enough to be cut for the next harvest.

“He’s a good man,” Arthur repeated sullenly. He kicked at the floor, scuffing the soul of his boot. “He doesn’t deserve to die in a worm pit.”

Merritt thought back to the hole, and the thick, broken roots lining its edges. Their ends had been dry and brown, as if they’d been dead for a while. It wasn’t the worm that had burrowed its way to the surface. Perhaps Dale had been walking over a rotting patch of ground the whole time he’d been helping at the Cohen farm, and it had finally given way beneath him.

...but a simple fall didn’t account for so many screams.

Merritt shivered again, but not from the cold. He remembered all too well his near-death encounter with a cave worm shortly after the *Halcyon* had crashed into Galena. He was separated from the other survivors, and had been forced to find a path beneath the mountains blocking his way.

A light bloomed behind him and he looked back. Arthur clipped a small palm-lamp to his coil of rope and let it dangle there, bouncing with his footsteps. The young man had his own encounter with a cave worm, Merritt remembered. He was with Gavin and Shurri at the time. They found a colonist named Ahmed still asleep in his stasis tank in an underground cavern piled high with the dead exoskeletons of hex crabs. The only reason they were still alive was because they had the good sense to run and jump into an underground river, which carried them out to sunlight.

Arthur's eyes were wide with fear, but he kept close behind Merritt.

"Mr. Alder," he said, gulping, "will that stunner stop a worm?"

"I hope to not find out. Might not be a worm at all."

Yet even as he said it, Merritt knew that couldn't be true. These round tunnels didn't form all by themselves. The cave worms chewed through rock and soil to form their winding pathways which seemed to criss-cross beneath half of Galena.

A faint scream echoed toward them from the darkness, and Merritt broke into a jog. He paused at a junction, waiting, trying not to breathe too hard. When the next scream came, he bolted to his left, descending on a gentle grade. His boots slipped on wet rock and he braced himself against the smooth walls. The tunnel became more of a ramp aimed deeper into the ground.

Arthur whooped in surprise as his feet slipped out from beneath him. He kicked Merritt behind his knees and they fell together, splashing in a shallow trickle of water. The tunnel surface was slimy with mold, and Merritt couldn't get a grip enough to stand. Arthur slipped on his attempt to get up and bowled into Merritt, sending them both sliding down the descending tunnel.

Arthur's light strobed against the shining walls as he tumbled, flashing against his boots, Merritt's legs, the tunnel, the rope, Arthur's scared face.

They spilled out onto a flat surface in a rush of water.

Something screamed again, this time loud enough to nearly pop Merritt's eardrums, but it was no man.

He stood in a low cavern and bumped his head on the wet ceiling. As far as Arthur's light could show him, the cavern extended away in all directions, its floor a shallow lake of icy water.

A series of purple pinpoint lights blossomed in the distance, illuminating in a line from left to right. A second line of lights appeared above them, and then another below. Three rows of stacked purple lights that twisted in unison. Half of them lifted higher, and glowed so brightly they lit up the cave worm's head and its slavering circular jaws which gnashed in Merritt's direction. In the dim purple glow, a man's bloody legs could be seen on the ground nearby.

Merritt flicked on the stunner and twisted the dial to full charge. The staff thrummed in his hands, vibrating his bones.

"Here!" he yelled.

"What?" Arthur whispered in surprise.

"Back the way we came," Merritt told him. "Now!"

Arthur didn't need to be told twice. He turned and fled, the sound of his boots echoing away down the long tunnel.

Merritt walked slowly backward, following after him. An arc of blue lightning spat from the end of his stunner when he touched it to the wall.

The cave worm forgot Dale and launched toward the intruder. It slid like silk over the cavern floor, without friction, gliding as if it were being pulled by some invisible force.

Merritt wasn't prepared for how quickly he moved. He tripped and fell, landing hard on his back. The cave worm was suddenly over him, its teeth swirling in a serrated circle in its jaws. It had no eyes, but didn't need them down there, in the dark. A thick tongue lashed side to side behind its teeth as it lunged for Merritt.

It got a mouthful of his stunner instead. Electricity surged from the pronged tip, crawling into the worm's mouth like snakes of lightning. The beast howled and slammed its head back and forth against the tunnel walls, shaking the ground. Merritt scrambled away, but the worm quickly recovered and resumed its pursuit.

I won't make it to the hole in time, Merritt realized.

He stumbled to his feet and turned back to face the oncoming worm. In the light of the crackling electricity spitting from the end of his stunner, the monstrous mouth was bathed in a harsh blue light.

It spread its jaws wide as it fell upon its prey. At the last moment, Merritt braced the butt of the stunner against the arch of his boot and ducked, keeping one hand on the bottom of the staff so it pointed up at an angle, like a spear.

The long weapon punctured the back of the creature's mouth. Merritt heard a wet pop of flesh as it burrowed deeper into its body.

Then he flicked the switch.

The worm thrashed within the narrow confines of the tunnel wall, heaving its bulk up and down, twisting in place like a corkscrew, and screaming — the screaming was worst of all. Merritt could not flee, he could only cower in the darkness and shield his ears from the crumbling, ripping, screeching sounds of chaos.

Finally, at long last, the beast went still.

"Mr. Alder?" Arthur said hesitantly from behind. "The screaming stopped."

Merritt slowly lowered his hands from his ears. They rang from the aural assault, and he couldn't shake his head to clear the high-pitched *skreeee* that plagued them.

Two more colonists had come down with Arthur. A middle-aged woman, Beth, held a solar lamp and carried a knife with a long blade. Behind her, a wiry man in his fifties with a stringy goatee and receding hairline bounced from leg to leg impatiently, waving a machete.

"Saved some for us, I hope," Skip declared.

"You like worm steak?" Merritt replied as Beth and Arthur helped him to his feet. "Thank you."

"Is it dead?" Arthur asked, staring in disgust at the worm.

Thick, clear jelly dripped from its limp mouth.

"I'll carve it up, just to be sure," Skip assured him.

"Haven't tasted worm yet."

Merritt patted his shoulder and smiled.

"Let's get Dale out of here, first."

It was good to see his oldest friend in the colony again. Between Skip's six children and his wife who felt only the dead should be idle, and Merritt's growing responsibilities to the colony as a whole, the two rarely had the time to speak.

Maybe it's more my fault than Gavin's that we never see each other anymore, Merritt thought. It was the first time such a possibility had occurred to him.

Skip considered the worm for a moment. "We supposed to push this thing out of the way?"

Merritt took careful notice of the narrow space separating the worm from the tunnel walls.

"I can squeeze past."

Arthur unclipped his palm-light and handed it to Merritt. After a nod of thanks, he flattened himself against the tunnel wall and squeezed next to the worm's body. The stench of vinegar and alcohol assaulted his nostrils, making tears fall from his eyes.

"If that thing wakes up, it'll squash you 'ginst the wall like a slug," Skip said.

"Then stick that machete in its mouth and kill it again."

He pushed against the worm's sticky skin, wriggling deeper into the tunnel. Its bulk pushed against him like a heavy blanket covered in slime, but it was not enough to smother him. A meter beyond the head, a hard black rod blocked his progress. It protruded from the worm's flesh, an obsidian barb as long as his leg. Merritt looked farther down the length of its body. Countless more barbs kept the worm's bulk from sagging against the tunnel wall. Its skin was covered with them.

Merritt shoved against the one blocking his passage. With a wet sucking noise, it folded back against the worm's body. When Merritt slipped past, it snapped back to full extension, cracking against the tunnel wall.

It was slow, wet, sticky progress, but he eventually popped out of the tunnel and fell into the cold, shallow lake of the cavern. Half of the worm protruded from the tunnel mouth. Water dripped down upon its motionless corpse from above.

Long beast, Merritt thought as he slowly got to his feet. With a groan and a wince, he cracked his back, knowing his body would be sore for days after this encounter. That was the first time he noticed the burning sensation in his right forearm. He looked down to see blood dripping from a long, thin cut in the meat near his elbow where one of the worm's teeth had sliced him.

Guess it wasn't such a clean victory after all, he mused.

He heard a moan from a distant part of the cavern and hurried toward the sound, Arthur's palm-light bouncing wildly.

Dale lay on his back in the shallow water, his limbs outstretched. His clothes were shredded and deep lacerations marked him from ankle to shoulder. His swollen eyes were little more than thin slits in his bruised face. Merritt shuddered to think about how much blood the man must have lost.

"I'm here, Dale. You're not alone."

Dale opened his bloody mouth to speak, but only

a faint whisper escaped his lips. He lifted a feeble hand.

Merritt shined his light toward the worm. Those black spikes sticking out from its skin seemed to only bend one way — away from the creature's head. There was no way Merritt could haul Dale back through the tunnel and manipulate the spikes.

He shined his light on the ceiling instead. Most of it was rock, but he saw soft patches as well. If some of it was as soft as the land under the Cohen farm, he might be able to dig a hole wide enough to lift Dale up to the colony.

There was a wet slurp as Skip popped free of the worm.

"Yee-*uck*," he said with disgust. He brushed goop from his arm and flung it down into the water with a light splash.

Arthur emerged a moment later, his face twisted in revulsion.

"Beth wanted to go get Uda," he said.

"Good," Merritt told him. "He needs to be at the hospital."

"How you gonna squeeze him past the worm?" Skip asked, jerking a thumb back at the beast. "Can't imagine that jelly on its body is good for open wounds. Probably not even good *period*."

"Check the ceiling near the walls," said Merritt. "Anywhere you can climb. Even if we have to follow a different tunnel, we need to find a soft spot where we can dig to the surface."

"What if there are more worms?" Arthur asked, looking around warily.

"Then we run." He checked Dale's pulse. Red

foam bubbled from the corner of his mouth. The look he shared with Arthur and Skip spoke the words for him.

He doesn't have much time.

GAVIN

Shurri's head bounced against his chest as he ran. Her blood ran down his arms, the arms that carried her, and that now shook from exhaustion. Gavin felt as if his muscles would betray him at any second and spill her to the ground. The wound on her right leg was — it was too much to look at. In his periphery, he glimpsed a solid sheet of red draped over his arm, limp like the rest of her body.

He had made his stumbling way from the ocean shoreline, past the southern tip of the Casmin Sea, and into the sparse woods that marked the easternmost edge of the colony. Gavin had stopped only once, when his bare toes kicked a rock and he fell to his knees, screaming without sound at the sky — screaming from the pain, for his weakness, for Shurri.

By the time he finally made it to the hospital prefab on the low hill at the center of the colony, Shurri's skin was paler than the moon. He took the metal steps to the raised building two at a time, suddenly unable to recall the journey. It had to have taken hours to run the long distance, but it seemed that one instant he was scooping her from the black sand on the shore, and the next he was lowering her with shaking arms onto a cold metal table in the hospital.

Uda's soft words were unintelligible to Gavin's ear as he stepped back from the table, his legs shaking like jelly. He heard his own ragged breaths, and the pounding of his heart. The back of his legs bumped against a short stool, and he plopped down onto it. Her blood dripped from his fingertips to the clean white floor. Gavin looked down at his quivering fingers with unblinking eyes. A rectangle of light from one of the hospital's many glassless windows made the blood shine.

Uda sluiced purified water over Shurri's leg, washing away the dark red crust that had dried to her skin. Fresh blood welled from the spiral wound that encircled her leg from ankle to hip.

Uda said something else as she inspected the cut, but Gavin didn't hear. Then she was standing at his side, shaking his shoulder. He forced his eyes away from Shurri and looked up at Uda.

"What was it?" she asked.

His red hands formed the word, *Squid*. If she was surprised, she didn't show it.

"There are barbs stuck in the skin," said Uda. "We need to get them out quickly so we can heal the wound with moss. Do you understand?"

Gavin's understanding came slowly as he looked from Uda to Shurri and back again. He felt cold and weak...helpless. Finally he nodded.

Uda snapped to the task, her hands moving quickly but deftly. First, she sprayed both their hands with a fine mist of disinfectant from an aluminum bottle, then she set a metal tray on the table next to Shurri and handed Gavin a simple pair of pliers, gesturing toward Shurri's ankle.

The work was distracting, for which he was eternally grateful. When he leaned in close enough to the hideous wound, he couldn't even tell it was Shurri. His pliers picked barb after barb from the pale skin edging the laceration — small white hooks with tips so thin and sharp they were translucent.

After more than a hundred of the hooks filled the metal tray in a film of pink water, Uda declared the task finished. She took Gavin's pliers and washed the wound again. As she poured water over Shurri's knee, the leg twitched.

Shurri lurched forward into a sitting position and sucked in a gasp, but her eyes were still closed. She flopped onto her side and convulsed, her body shaking violently and her head banging against the metal table.

Uda grunted as she forced Shurri onto her back, pinning her down at the waist and shoulders.

"Help me!"

Gavin ran to her side, and Uda didn't waste a second. She bolted for the back of the room, toward a row of bubbling gestation tanks. Shurri started to twist sideways again, so Gavin leaned over her, keeping one arm across her shoulders and the other across her waist.

He didn't often curse his muteness, but he did then, with more fury than ever before.

I can't even tell her I'm here, he thought. Rage battled sadness in his mind, and he wanted to rip the whole building down on their heads...but more than that, he wanted to see Shurri open her eyes again — to hear her laugh at him, even if was a tease.

Uda ran back to the table with a rectangular

carpet of healing moss draped over each arm, still dripping from their tanks. They were smaller than what Gavin was used to seeing, as if they hadn't had time to reach maturity. Uda slapped one on the metal table and used both hands to gently cover a portion of Shurri's wound with the other. The laceration was as wide as Gavin's palm at some points, and what remained was never thinner than two fingers pressed together. Both pieces of moss combined weren't enough to cover more than half her leg.

He looked at Uda, waiting for her to run back for more, but she didn't.

So he did.

Uda yelled after him as he went to the tanks. They stood in a row beneath the back windows, gurgling quietly, the fat, silvery bubbles churning thick water in which the healing moss floated. Yet two-thirds of the tanks were empty, and the ones that were occupied housed pieces of moss smaller than the ones Uda had retrieved.

Gavin popped the lids of two tanks and plunged a hand into each one, ignoring the icy white mist that swirled on the water's surface like a sentient cloud. Each hand was able to grab two pieces of moss. He ran back to Shurri's table, trailing a line of water that poured from the textured moss. Their small soft legs tickled his wrists and forearms.

Uda was still shouting at him, but he didn't listen. Too roughly, he pushed the moss at Shurri's wounds, forcing it down into the corkscrew valley that had been carved into her pale skin. The moss flattened as its corners crept up the walls of the laceration. The patches Gavin added helped to cover all but the topmost edge of the wound.

He stepped back as the moss fluttered, then went still.

"Oh, Gavin," Uda said quietly.

He didn't understand why she sounded so sad. Wasn't she there to *help* people? Why hadn't she given Shurri more of the moss?

There was a shout from the door, and the sound of boots clanging up the metal stairs. His father burst through the door, covered in dirt and blood, a wild look in his eyes. He carried an unconscious man under the arms. His father's friend Skip, no less filthy, had the man's legs.

"Moss!" his father shouted as they struggled to carry the man inside. "Uda, moss!"

Arthur ran in after them, a rope coiled over his shoulder. His face was streaked with dirt and a thick jelly-like substance. He skidded to a stop and froze when he saw his sister.

Uda helped carry the man to a table next to Shurri's. Gavin's father set the man down with a grunt, then noticed his son. Confusion flashed across his face, and he looked down at Shurri. His mouth hung open in shock.

"Help me with his clothes," said Uda.

Her hands moved quickly, snipping at the unconscious man's torn shirt with chrome scissors. Skip tugged off the man's boots and began peeling down his ripped pants. Gavin tilted his head to better see the man's face.

Dale, he realized with sinking horror.

Arthur slowly walked to his sister's side, eyes wide and unblinking. He bit his lip and picked up one of her pale, limp hands, then pressed it between his own. His gaze slipped over to Dale, then back to his sister.

Arthur and Shurri were very fond of Dale, Gavin knew. He was the first of their mother's suitors they not only approved of, but whole-heartedly welcomed into their home.

Beneath the clothing, Dale was a ruin of rock shards and red flesh. Uda froze when she saw him in full, her hands filled with the ribbons of his shirt. She glanced over at Shurri, and at the heeling moss compressed against her skin.

Gavin realized what he had done.

Healing moss couldn't be removed once it contacted a wound. It bonded with the epidermis, became a part of it until the process was finished and it became a hollow, chitinous exoskeleton and sloughed away. Removing it before then would mean ripping off even more of Shurri's skin.

Uda quickly regained her composure and began cleaning Dale's wounds.

"Skip," she said, "two trays of water. Fresh towels from the back."

He moved with a purpose, hustling to the back of the long room.

"Merritt, that syringe." She nodded to a neat row of medical instruments on her work table, and Gavin's father grabbed one of the three syringes that waited, already filled with a pale yellow painkiller.

Dr. Leera James had synthesized the drug after her first year in the hospital. Not much in the way of advanced medical technology had survived the crash of the Starliner *Halcyon*, but Leera had said that the toaster-sized synthesizer was the most valuable.

Skip shuffled back to the table, water sloshing from the sides of the two metal trays he carried. It sloshed like the water at the ocean shore, when the squid was pulling Shurri toward its mouth. Gavin swallowed and took a step back, feeling lightheaded. His hands shook with a steady tremor. All the blood had drained from his limbs and he felt dizzy.

"Gavin," Uda said calmly as she injected the thick fluid into Dale's arm. He shuddered and went still, his breath coming in shallow gasps. "I need your father's help, alone. You and Arthur wait outside."

I want to stay, he signed weakly.

His father wiped sweat from his brow, streaking his filthy skin. He gave Skip a helpless, imploring look — but when he glanced at Gavin, there was fear as well.

"Best if we don't crowd them," Skip said amiably enough.

He draped a thin arm over Gavin's shoulders and guided him toward the door. Gavin didn't protest. He let himself be pulled along as if in a dream, his feet moving by themselves, taking him farther away from Shurri. He looked back as he stepped out of the prefab, but all he saw were the backs of Uda and his father as they hovered over Dale's table.

Arthur was already outside, hands on his hips as he stared up at the blue sky. He squinted in the sunlight. The courtyard at the flat crown of the hill was otherwise empty.

Gavin took two steps down and his legs buckled beneath him. Skip helped him to sit, then patted his back kindly. He opened his mouth to say something, then closed it again. After a long moment, he returned inside.

"My mom isn't a happy woman," Arthur said. "Not since Dad died." He rubbed his palms on the dirty chest of his coverall. "Well, she *wasn't* happy. Then there was Dale. I don't know what this will do to her." He paused a moment, then added, "They wanted to get married."

Before Gavin could process the words, Arthur had wandered off, kicking at the wet soil with his hands in his pockets, his neck bent so he could stare at his feet.

Someone shouted in the distance, but it was a happy shout. A child, perhaps. The colony had been blessed with several births over the last few years; a stark protest to the dangerously anemic birth rates back on Earth.

Metal clinked from inside the hospital, and Gavin turned his head just as his father walked outside, wiping his hands on a rag. His left arm had been bandaged from wrist to elbow, but already the red was seeping through. He sat next to Gavin with a heavy sigh, his hands shaking when he rested his arms on his knees. They looked toward the afternoon sun together.

His father handed him the rag, but there were no more clean spots on it. Gavin held it limply in his blood-stained hands, his gaze a thousand worlds away.

What happened to him? Gavin signed.

"A sinkhole at the Cohen farm. There's a worm tunnel underneath."

They sat in silence for a long time.

"Sometimes it's hard to know what to do when someone you love is hurt," his father said at last. "And even harder to predict the fallout of your actions."

Gavin swallowed hard. His skin felt cold despite a warm, gentle breeze crossing the hilltop.

"But it's not your fault, son. No one told you our supply of healing moss was running low. The nearest oases are empty. Weston and his rangers had to travel half a day to find the little ones on Shurri's leg. They won't propagate in the tanks like they used to."

Is Dale going to die? Gavin signed.

His father hesitated, then nodded. "He's lost too much blood. I couldn't get him here fast enough."

Gavin's hands moved quickly in response. *Put him in the hypergel tank until I find more moss. It helped Kellan.*

"The *moss* helped Kellan. He only lost half his arm. Hypergel is antibacterial. It has no healing properties. Putting Dale in the tank might clog his wounds and stop the bleeding, but it can't fix what happened to him."

The pit of Gavin's stomach sank lower, into his bowels. He shifted uncomfortably on the metal step. Then he looked behind him, inside the hospital. Uda was bent over Shurri's leg, gently poking at the edges of the wound the moss couldn't cover. Dale lay outstretched on the next table, as if he'd already been forgotten, his chest no longer moving up and down.

Gavin looked away slowly, fighting the urge to be sick.

We could use Kellan's machine, Gavin signed. *To bring Dale back.*

He had remembered the bulky device when his

father burst into the hospital — but he hadn't been considering it for Dale at the time, only Shurri.

His father's face hardened to stone. "I've already said it will never be used."

Gavin's hands jerked with frustration as he signed, *Why keep it, then?*

The large machine sat shrouded under a blanket at the back of his father's work area in their home. No one had looked at it in years, not since he had taken it away from Kellan. His father told Gavin that Kellan baited him with the promise of using the machine to bring his mother back to life. It was some kind of human growth tank. All it needed was a LifeScan of the person's mind and a cocktail with all the necessary ingredients to create a perfect clone.

His father sighed wearily. Gavin had never seen him look more sad.

"I was tempted, at first," he admitted. "To allow Kellan to bring your mother back. He had her DNA on his ship, before it went back through the Rip, along with a hundred others. It was the reason I agreed to guide him to the field where he opened the new Rip." He looked up at the sky, then down to his open palms. "You never saw your mother when she was sick. I had to keep you hidden because of all the snatchers. If I brought you to the hospital, someone would have followed us home and stolen you away. I try to remember her before...before she was sick. I can't. But if she was brought back...it wouldn't be her. Not really, no matter what Kellan says. When a person dies, they are gone, Gavin. Even your mother."

She doesn't have to be! he wanted to scream.

His father called after him as he stumbled down

the steps to the soft ground, his bare feet kicking up soil as he ran for home.

Someone shouted to him as he ran through long rows of soyflower stalks, following the narrow paths between farms, but he ignored them. Only a few people in the colony knew sign language, and with his blood running so hot, he didn't have the patience to pantomime for anyone else.

Gavin made a sharp turn past Uda's farm and jumped a thin dike onto his own land. His home sat in the middle of a field divided into four parts. Soyflower stalks covered two of them in a neat grid, and the others were for the vegetables Gavin was able to eat without his stomach cramping.

The repurposed roof of an unused grain silo capped the top of his and his father's dome-shaped house. Rough corrugated metals lined with ship's insulation formed the walls, out of which had been cut two windows and a doorless entryway. In the winter, his father would secure a piece of insulation to the opening to keep out the cold, but lately they welcomed any breeze they could get. Gone were the days of artificial air regulation to your perfect desired temperature. Gavin rarely missed anything about his pre-Galena days, but he could remember the pleasant feeling of an air-conditioned room on a muggy day.

He would have kicked in the door if there'd been one. Instead, he burst into his house and swiped at the first thing he saw, which was a cup of screws and bolts sitting on his father's work table. The contents went flying, clanging and tinging against half-finished machinery — pet projects of the Alders. His father often told Gavin that he was gifted with machines. He seemed to know just the right panel to open, just the right wire to snip or bridge, just the right replacement part to make a machine hum again.

Gavin crouched down and yanked the dusty blanket off Kellan's machine, coughing and waving a hand in front of his face against the ensuing cloud.

It didn't look like it could grow a human. Part of it beneath a thick pane of filthy plexi might have been long enough for a person to sleep in, but they would have to be in a fetal position.

Maybe that's how they're grown, Gavin thought, the gears in his mind turning. *Like babies.*

This thought experiment was a soothing distraction.

He studied the machine, following its curves and joints, trying to work out how it functioned. The portion that wasn't a hollow tank was shielded by a metal panel with a lined vent, like an exhaust.

Heat sink? thought Gavin. *What's the power source?*

He swiped his palm across the lone, dirty control panel, smudging the blank screen. Two orange buttons flanked each side of the panel. Gavin depressed each one with a loud click, but the screen did not wake. He tried to open the tank, but the plexi lid wouldn't budge. Finally he got his fingertips under the edge of the metal panel and *pulled*.

His fingers slipped and he fell back with a thump. A moment later, he was on his feet, silently raging, hitting objects of the work table then flipping it over with a terrible crash.

He stumbled back a step, breathing hard, and waited. The room came back into focus. He saw the table on its side, the mess he'd made of his and his father's tools.

Slowly, defeatedly, he righted the table, then closed his eyes and bent forward until his forehead thunked against its gritty surface.

Shurri, he thought helplessly.

A gentle vibration coursed through the table, tickling his skull. Gavin stood sharply, eyes on the doorway. A shadow blinked across it. The vibration became a rumble, and the ground shook as he ran outside, into the late afternoon sun.

A ship in the shape of a round-cornered triangle hovered above the colony. At Gavin's distance, it didn't look like a big vessel — perhaps three or four times the size of the shuttle Ayani and Henry had taken on their ranging. Three bands of metal around each broad wing glinted in the sunlight, and its white hull brilliantly reflected the rays of Phobis, casting a pale golden light onto the fields below.

It had already flattened the spread of soyflower stocks below, its atmospheric wash blasting down to flatten the soil. Now it set them alight as it fired its parking boosters and dropped to the surface, perched on three arcing landing legs. Smoke billowed up around its white hull, but was momentarily pushed aside as a long ramp descended near the nose.

A man walked down the ramp, but Gavin was too far away to discern much detail. He could tell he wore a red jacket and black pants, though, and that the hair on top of his head was white as snow.

AYANI

She leaned back in the shuttle's pilot seat and crossed her ankles atop the control panel. After yawning for what seemed like half a minute, Ayani laced her fingers over her chest and lazily glanced back at Henry. He was still doing his thing with the maps. They surrounded him like a nest, covering his lap, the bench, and the table on which his current source of interest was subjected to the smudged black tip of his stubby index finger as it traced the inky outlines of rivers, mountains, and valleys. The old man seemed to be looking for something, but would only smile secretively when asked.

The landscape flowed languidly beneath the shuttle as it flew near the surface. Rivers glinted gold in the afternoon sun. Between them, verdant mossy fields stretched between short, boulder-strewn hills. There hadn't been a single tree for more than an hour. According to the shuttle's navigation system, they were only a tenth of the way across the continent, heading east from the shore of the Equatorial Ocean.

A red warning rectangle flashed on the control panel. At the same time, Ayani's wristpad beeped. She tapped the screen to clear both messages — the shuttle's fuel cells were almost empty again. Henry had talked her into taking off prematurely after their last stop, with only sixty percent of their reserves. He was eager to press on, he told her, to get to their turnaround point. Apparently he had *some* destination in mind, though Ayani couldn't see how there was anything else out here but more fields, forests, rivers, and mountains. It was fair to say her wanderlust had been sufficiently satisfied over the past two days. She was ready for her cozy bunk in the small farm shed she'd been given when Jeff left for Earth. It was far more comfortable than the hard cot on the shuttle, or even one of the cramped wall cutouts aboard the *Celerity*, where she'd spent her first year on Galena, and where Jeff had slept for all three.

If she landed the shuttle within half an hour, there would be enough remaining sunlight to fully charge the cells. She glanced at her wristpad again, wishing she had some way to contact the colony. One of the many luxuries the colonists had never been able to manage for themselves was long-range communication. There had been some equipment to manage just such a task in the beginning, shortly after their ship crashed, but it was destroyed.

Once you left the colony, you were on your own. The shuttle could scan for signals sent by other ships, and even detect a signature in orbit, but she and Jeff were the only ones with wristpads for shorter range comms, and he was back on Earth. The homing beacon he had linked between their two wrist units had a much greater range than voice comms, but it was useless if one of them was on another world.

"Trees," said Ayani, gazing through the narrow cockpit window. She sat forward in her chair to get a better look. "A *lot* of trees."

Henry grunted as he slid out from behind the thin table and extricated himself from his nest of maps. He stood beside the pilot seat and stretched his back, sighing with pleasure after three loud pops.

"They are closer together than the ones near the colony," he observed, squinting out the window.

The riverlands seemed to end abruptly at the border of a vast forest. Henry was right — the forest was incredibly dense, much more so than the comparatively spacious groupings of trees on the other continent. Here their trunks were almost touching, forming an impenetrable mass of light gray sentinels. The three identical branches crowning each tree — jutting from each trunk at a ninety degree angle and bending up again halfway along its length to point toward the sky — created a near-solid plateau of gray spikes.

"It runs north-south, but not east-west," Henry said, leaning forward. "How very strange."

"It does," Ayani corrected. She pointed far to the north. "Look, it curves there."

The forest swooped west at the edge of her vision and disappeared back the way they'd flown. She swiped through several screens on her control panel and called up an old drone scan of the region. There had been a similar map in Henry's pile, she remembered.

"Here," she told him, hovering her fingertip over the panel. The forest only covered a north-south portion of the continent for thirty or so kilometers before both ends turned abruptly west, heading for the ocean shore. On the map, it formed an enormous sideways U.

Henry hurried back to his table and shuffled through his maps.

"Ah," he said, smiling. He swiped the table clear and spread out a wrinkled linen-paper map, its edges frayed and colors faded. Ayani joined him at the back of the cockpit. She had to bend her knees slightly to not hit the top of her head on the ceiling. "That forest runs along the northern and southern borders of the Equatorial," he explained. "I thought it was two separate forests. Both tracts run across the riverlands all the way to our continent...and to our colony."

He beamed at her, nothing less than victory shining in his eyes — yet Ayani couldn't guess why.

"What does that mean?" she asked.

"*Look!*" he said, pointing to the window.

A mountain rose in the distance, straight up from the heart of the dense forest.

Not a mountain, Ayani realized. *A pyramid.*

She couldn't discern a color from that distance, but she would have guessed black or slate gray. Its edges were perfectly flat, rising from the forest at perfect angles to meet at a sharp point several hundred meters above the plateau of spear-tipped branches.

"That isn't a natural structure," she whispered.

"No!" Henry said gleefully. "It's the source. I knew it. I *knew* it!"

"What source?" was all she had time to say before the cockpit lights flicked from sterile white to caution yellow and the control panel lit up red. A warning alarm blared from speakers embedded in the soft padded ceiling.

Her brow furrowed as she stared at the panel, not believing what she was seeing.

"Ships," she said softly, returning to her seat. She quickly cleared the warning boxes and silenced the alarm. The lights in the cockpit remained the same harsh yellow, bathing everything in a sickly glow.

The shuttle's radar was reading five independent signals on an intercept trajectory. Tracing their energy signatures, she knew they had come from orbit. Yet there was something odd about the signals she was reading. There was an additional wavelength buried in the stream, something she wouldn't see in a scouting vessel.

"Attack drones," Ayani said suddenly. The extra signals she detected were their weapon systems, already at full charge. "Strap in!"

She tightened her safety harness and activated the shuttle's defense mode, authorizing the onboard computer to do whatever it could to shake the drones. Behind her, she could hear Henry fumbling with his own harness.

Ayani worked the control panel, searching for options. They were in a transport shuttle — the only thing that could be considered a weapon was the heat from their exhaust housing.

And that's not going to stop an attack drone, she thought grimly.

"Are you sure they're enemies?" Henry asked from the back of the cockpit. "Could they be an escort?"

The dead mouse waits to see if the hawk is truly diving, her trainer at the academy once told her. *The smart mouse runs as soon as it sees the wings tuck.*

Of course, that reference had only made sense after she visited the library archives to refresh her grade school lessons about the many now-extinct, but once-prevalent, animal species of Earth.

The shuttle banked unexpectedly, throwing her into the side of her chair as a blinding orange firework exploded against the shuttle's underbelly, sending a shower of sparks up past the cockpit window.

She watched the blips on her radar. The five points converged on the shuttle's tail and sped forward, closing the gap and leveling out once they reached a similar altitude. Then they fanned out again, aligning into a half-moon configuration as if they meant to surround the shuttle.

More weapons fire thudded the air to port and starboard, rocking the shuttle side to side. The yellow lights flickered and Henry let out an involuntary yelp.

Ayani flicked through her panel screens in a flurry, hunting for anything she could use as a deterrent, angrily dismissing entire useless sub-interfaces.

Exhaust Venting, Waste Removal, DHSJ.

No, no, and...she tapped on DHSJ.

Damaged Heat Shield Jettison. The display on the screen showed a wireframe representation of the shuttle from the side. Four large hull panels just aft of the nose pulsed deep red.

Why would a shuttle need a heat shield? she wondered distantly as she tapped again.

SHIELD NOT DAMAGED, the interface spat back at her. *PROCEED WITH JETTISON?*

Ayani pounded the YES button with her fist.

There were four loud *TINGs* as the heat shield panels released from the hull. Ayani called up the rear view on her panel to see them tumbling wildly in the shuttle's wake. The five attack drones were glimmering diamonds against a bright blue sky, their outlines obscured by heat from the shuttle's engine wash.

Two red-orange explosions bloomed against the blue sky, and only three blips remained on her radar. In response, tiny pinpoints of fire blipped from each of the three drones in rapid succession. Tracer bullets zipped past the shuttle's hull.

Ayani had to stifle a shout as the shuttle's defense autopilot twisted the vessel into a corkscrew spin and rose higher, angled toward the sun. Bullets flashed past the cockpit window. Several loud metal thunks reverberated from the rear hull as some of the projectiles found their mark. The control panel lit up red again.

"What do we do?!" Henry shouted.

Ayani glanced back, her head bouncing against her chair as the shuttle swerved and evaded. Henry sat with his eyes clenched shut, his head pressed back against the padded wall, and his bloodless hands crossed over the straps of his safety harness.

Turning back to the control panel, Ayani saw the drones separate. One moved to either side of the shuttle, and one approached from behind.

This is it, she knew.

"Hold tight!" she yelled.

With a few taps, she disengaged the autopilot and took control of the shuttle. Manual controls flashed onto the screen and she immediately took the shuttle into a sharp dive. Henry groaned as he was pushed sideways on his little bench, squashed against the straps of his harness. Ayani felt the strain on her chest as she pulled up the nose to level out.

The drones dropped down to match her altitude. They had stopped firing bullets for some reason — a reason Ayani was sure not to like.

Ahead, the dark pyramid rose from the forest floor.

"What are you doing?" Henry called weakly.

"Trying to keep us alive," she growled through clenched teeth.

A blue lightning bolt licked across the outside of the cockpit window. Electronics in the padded walls snapped and crackled, spitting streams of black smoke. The yellow warning lights blinked out.

Energy weapons, thought Ayani. She knew of them from her years in uniform, had actually held one that could fry anything smaller than a car — but they weren't legal in flying vessels. Not even the military installed them in their patrol craft.

Sunlight flashed off the polished walls of the pyramid, making her squint. She accelerated to maximum, the impact padding of her chair swallowing her back, and headed straight for the structure.

There has to be something, she hoped, straining to look out the window.

Another bolt of blue lighting snaked across the hull, and the engines cut out. Ayani smelled smoke from deep within the shuttle. Frantically, she paged through the warning screens and initiated the reboot procedure. A moment later, the engines belched exhaust and roared to life once more, jerking Ayani forward in her seat.

She turned the shuttle in a wide arc around the pyramid, tilting one wing down to get a better look. The drones followed.

The base of the pyramid seemed a perfect square. Ayani maintained a steady descent as she passed the first three sides. There was nothing she could hide behind, nowhere to shield the shuttle from the drones. Perhaps she could nose-dive into the trees. They were so close together there would only be a minimal opening in the branches. She and Henry could scramble free of the wreckage before the drones got too close. The drones could fry the shuttle, but at least she and Henry would be safe.

And trapped on another continent with no way back, she thought, not liking the idea of that one bit.

Blue light flooded the cockpit as a net of lightning crackled over the cockpit window. Her control panel flicked to black and the engines cut off.

The shuttle was dead weight. It dropped sickeningly without the engines to keep it aloft. As the blue lightning faded, Ayani saw the fourth side of the pyramid. A wide, rectangular opening stretched across most of its base, almost touching both edges of the triangular wall.

Something whirred within the shuttle, and there was a metallic groan as failsafe aileron flaps extended from the blunt wings to help guide the shuttle to the surface. They responded to changes in altitude and wind direction, and were impervious to EMP-style weapons, containing only simple gyroscopes and an attitude indicator.

Ayani felt useless in the pilot seat. The control panel was blank and there was no way to manually force the shuttle toward the pyramid opening. An explosion just above the ship knocked it lower.

Her entire world was shaking.

Do something! her mind screamed at her.

She popped her safety harness and was thrown from her chair as the shuttle lurched sideways. Sunlight beamed through a jagged hole in the roof. Flames roared past the opening.

We're on fire, she thought with absurd calmness.

A drone buzzed past the cockpit window, its faceted metallic body reflecting daylight like a mirror. Something small and cube-shaped detached from its hull and *clunked* onto the shuttle's nose.

There was a blinding flash of white and a resounding *THOOOM* as the nose exploded into a circle of peeled metal. Wind ripped into the cockpit through the large opening. The impact sent Ayani tumbling backward. She slammed into Henry's table and spun sideways, coming to a violent stop next to the aft passageway.

She caught a quick glimpse of Henry as she flew past: eyes closed hard, his face frozen in a pained grimace.

Hand over hand, she pulled herself toward the front of the shuttle. The control panel had been ripped away, along with the window and the entire nose. Her seat was all that remained at the edge of the ragged hole. It rocked back and forth madly in the wind, offering a front-row view to the vast forest below — which was quickly rushing toward the shuttle.

Ayani looped her arm through a metal bar at the base of her rocking seat and pried at a wall panel with her free hand. She had to brace her foot against the padded wall to get leverage, but the panel popped free at last. A blue-and-white logo on the underside read *Diamond Aerospace*. The panel flew to the back of the cockpit when she let go to reach inside the wall.

Inside were the manual override controls. She had been trained on a wide array of both smaller and larger craft during and after her tenure at the academy. There were always differences between companies and their proprietary ship designs, but federal regulations mandated that certain safety equipment be standard no matter who made the vessel or where it was built.

Manual override controls were always right where she found them.

She didn't have a free hand to swipe her hair back. It whipped around her head, blocking her vision. She grabbed hold of the handle connected to the left wing (*Please be the left wing*) and twisted, but it wouldn't budge. The handle vibrated in her hand as the wind fought her control.

Ayani screamed, but the noise was lost to the roar of wind and the rattle of the failing hull.

The handle budged, and the view outside the open cockpit tilted a little sideways. She pushed against the handle, bracing her feet against the base of her shaking chair.

A little farther...

Her hand slipped as the handle moved another finger-width to the left and the wind caught her, sending her spinning backward. This time she fell into the passageway, through darkness. She smacked flat on her back against the airlock door. The back of her skull banged against metal and she went limp.

The last thing she saw as her vision shrank to a pinpoint of light was the wall of the pyramid rising up to meet the shuttle.

MERRITT

He didn't see the ship at first.

The roar of water pouring through the hydroelectric dam drowned out all other sound. Merritt had stood there for long minutes, watching the river thunder through the apparatus that kept so many little lights glowing in their homes; kept the moss tanks gurgling and the crab sticks charging. Metal bars plunged into the raging waters from a low metal bridge, the foundations of which were sunk deep into the soft ground on either bank.

Gavin had fixed the hydroelectric dam more than once, and it seemed to be a place of comfort for him — a place to go when he needed a distraction. Merritt had expected to find his son here after their talk at the hospital, yet Gavin had gone somewhere else. Perhaps he went home after all, though Merritt had initially doubted he would. Gavin tended to find any excuse possible to stay out until he fell exhausted into bed without a word to his father.

Merritt wasn't ignorant of the fact that the dam held some special significance for Gavin and Shurri as a couple. He had once spied them from a distance many months ago while on perimeter patrol, two silhouettes in the moonlight, sitting atop the dam, their shoulders touching. Perhaps Gavin liked that his way of communicating was a boon near the rushing water instead of an obstacle to be overcome with the other colonists. Even if you shouted, your voice was drowned out by the river — but that didn't matter if you knew how to sign. It put him on more equal ground, or maybe even superior ground, since others wouldn't be able to communicate at all.

Shurri was a good girl, Merritt knew.

Young woman, he corrected himself. *And your boy is a young man now.*

He'd never had any misgivings about their relationship, and it wasn't as if the two of them had a lot of other options near their age. Fate had intervened and made them extremely compatible, for which Merritt was ever grateful. He saw a happiness on Gavin's face when he was with Shurri that he had never seen on Earth, nor in the early years of the colony.

His heart ached to think of her in the hospital, and for the pain his son must be feeling.

He turned away from the dam to go home, hoping to find Gavin there — and that's when he saw the ship.

It dropped from the sky like a stone in a ball of fire, brighter than Phobis. A kilometer above the surface — above the heart of the colony — atmospheric thrusters fired, slowing its decent, and its triangular shape became discernible in the flames. Three thin silver bands wrapped around each wing shone like mirrors.

Merritt took a hesitant step toward the colony, his mind reeling with possibilities. The last time a ship had arrived, it brought Kellan McEwan, and he had opened a new Rip amid a slew of broken promises — promises of nurturing the colony toward a new and thriving phase of expansion, regardless if his plans went against the colonists' wishes.

Yet Kellan was a fugitive from Earth, having broken promises with and stolen government property from powerful people he could only escape by remaining in exile on the other side of the galaxy — on Galena.

In short, Merritt's doubts regarding the altruism inherent among new visitors outweighed his idealistic notions of like-minded farmers.

He had just made the decision to run back to the colony when he heard a faint whistle overhead. The whistle was joined by another, amplifying the first, and those were joined by more until the sound was a chorus, a scream, and he had to cover his ears as he looked to the sky.

Metal darts bigger than an escape pod fell from the sky, their whistles peaking just before slamming into the river bank in violent eruptions of soil and rock and water.

Merritt fell to his knees as the debris shot past him — and against him. Rock shards pelted his thin shirt and utility pants. When the soil and rock settled back to the ground, he stood slowly, lowering his dirty arms.

The metal darts were half-buried in the soil. They were as thick around as a garden shed, with smooth, seamless exteriors — all except their tapered tops, which were an exposed tangle of coils and rods.

Merritt looked down the river bank. The objects were placed at identical intervals as far as he could see, perhaps twenty meters apart. At the edge of his vision, he could see they arced away from the river, as if to encircle the colony.

He took a step toward the nearest fallen dart, wanting a closer look. An electric buzz filled the air and his hair stood up straight. Static shock snapped between his fingertips and blue lightning erupted from the top of the dart. The lightning burst to both sides like twin ropes as thick as his arms and connected with the streams of its nearest neighbors.

One of the beams licked out and punched Merritt in the chest. There was a physical force behind the attack, and he was thrown backward to the ground. Amid coughs and smoke, he rolled onto his side. The lightning formed an unbroken beam connecting the tops of the metal darts — a barrier that extended in both directions.

It's surrounding the whole colony, Merritt thought.

The smoke was coming from his shirt. He poked his chest gingerly inside the ragged hole the energy had burned in the cloth, and his fingertips crunched against charred flesh.

Groaning, he climbed to his feet — and quickly collapsed to his knees. The blue lightning was blinding. He turned away and crawled for the trees. The soil near the river bank was softer than on his farm, and his hands sank up to his wrists as he crawled. One of them closed around a large smooth stone the size of a bitterbell fruit.

He undertook the exhaustive effort of standing once more, this time steadying himself against a tree trunk to keep from collapsing. Walking slowly back toward the blue energy barrier, he weighted the stone in his hand. When he thought he was close enough, Merritt held his breath, painful as it was, and threw.

The stone soared unmolested over the wavering, electric blue snake connecting the tops of the darts.

Idiot, he scolded himself as he took a step closer to the barrier. *Don't be a fool.* Another step. He reached out, needing to know; needing to see if he could break it. *Don't be a—*

The lightning snapped out like a whip and smacked his hand. He drew it back sharply with a curse, blowing on his smoking flesh. A thin trail of black skin traced a wavy line over the back of his hand.

He would have to come back with something more powerful than his curiosity, Merritt realized.

Then he remembered the ship.

Each breath burned like fire in his lungs as he trudged through the forest, toward the colony. An invisible knife continuously cut into the flesh of his burned hand, stabbing down with every rapid heartbeat.

He had to stop several times to catch his breath as he leaned heavily against a hard, spongy tree trunk. The summer heat plastered his short hair to his forehead, and sweat stung the wound in his chest.

Eventually he came in sight of the low central hill and the prefab buildings perched at the top. Black smoke billowed from a soyflower field near the hill.

Moyen's place? Merritt wondered, breathing hard. No, too close. *Maybe the Perdillos? It's Lysette.*

Perched amidst the pillowy clouds of smoke was

the triangular ship, blunted nose pointed toward the sky. Several people, dressed in mostly white and red, stood near a ramp that had extended from the hull. The colonists that had gathered in a ragged semi-circle around the visitors were easily discernible in their earthen tones, and Merritt recognized most of them at a distance.

The three or four colonists he couldn't identify were on the ground near the visitors, splayed out and unconscious.

He left the protection of the forest and hurried across the farm fields, ignoring the searing pain in his lungs. Merritt stumbled and fell when his foot found loose soil where vegetables had recently been harvested, but he quickly picked himself back up again.

He must have made quite the sight when he burst panting from a stand of soyflower stalks to join the colonists near the ship. Whatever conversation they'd been having ceased abruptly as everyone stared at him, sweating and out of breath, the arm with his burned hand held protectively over his burned chest.

His eyes locked instantly on the young man he pegged for their leader. He stood more rigid than his companions, with his hands clasped behind his back. His stark white hair was combed back, the sides of his head shaved. There was more than a little of the predator in his sleek features when he met Merritt's stare with pale blue eyes. His skin was the chalky white of talcum powder, and he wore a dark red jacket over his black pants and shirt, as if to further highlight his lack of pigmentation.

His two companions, standing slightly behind the pale young man at the edge of the ramp, were no less memorable.

The man was older, perhaps in his late fifties, but he had the hungry look of one who spent most of his time brawling. He was bald, and wore black utility pants and boots, and a sleeveless black shirt that clung tightly to the muscles beneath. Thin scars like stab wounds covered almost every inch of skin that wasn't under his uniform, including his face. He glared at Merritt with white-hot hatred, breathing hard through flared nostrils as his empty fists opened and closed, opened and closed.

The woman beside him was a head shorter than the pale young leader, but twice as broad in the chest and legs. She was also bald. Twin brown tattooed lines ran up her naked scalp, small glyphic characters between them. She held a thick white rifle-style weapon in her two strong hands, its bulbous tip emitting a thin stream of white smoke. Her gaze was cooler than her scarred companion's, but no less malignant.

Merritt looked to the colonists on the ground.

Lysette was there, sprawled face-down, her blonde curls tumbled around her head. Beside her was Ahmed, curled into a fetal position. Gavin and his friends had found the young man in the worm cavern three years ago, still in his stasis pod. He lived alone on the neighboring farm.

Last was Skip. He lay closest to the visitors, also face-down, his arms outstretched toward them as if he'd been reaching...reaching just as Merritt had reached for the electric barrier.

Merritt ignored the visitors and dropped to his knees beside Skip. He gently turned his friend on his side and felt for a pulse. It was there, but so weak Merritt almost missed it.

He could guess what had happened. The three colonists on the ground were among those he would have expected to resist at the first sign of trouble.

The three visitors from the ship waited patiently as he checked Ahmed and Lysette. They were alive, and there was no blood, but they were out cold. He eyed the chunky white rifle in the woman's hands as he painfully got back to his feet.

Without taking his eyes off the visitors, Merritt gestured for the other colonists to move back. He could hear the shuffle of their boots against soil as they obeyed. When the shuffling stopped, he gestured again, and he heard them retreating through the tall stalks of soyflower, the long leaves whispering as they moved farther away. Merritt's eyes darted around nervously, hoping Gavin hadn't seen the ship yet. Doubtless he would waste no time coming to investigate. Hopefully he was back at the hospital, with Shurri...

"Who are you?" Merritt growled, his voice raspy with pain.

The pale young man grinned sharply.

"Commander Alexander Vola," he answered, his voice crisp and clean.

Vola, thought Merritt. The name sounded familiar. "Shipping company," he rasped.

"My father's," Alexander said with a sigh. "Mine, eventually. No one lives forever...a maxim you should remind your friends of when they wake."

He gently tapped one of Skip's outstretched hands with the toe of his black boot.

"We have nothing but food," said Merritt, stumbling forward to plant himself between Vola and Skip. The bald woman's grip tightened on her rifle. "If that's what you want, take it and go."

"You know who my father is, and you think I came here for food?" the young man said, his voice dripping with contempt. He turned to his companions with a half-smile. "Narienne, tell me. How did they survive so long with wits like this?"

"There *is* nothing else," Merritt spat defiantly.

"Not yet," Vola replied. "But there will be. Ah, speak of the devil."

At that moment, Kellan McEwan emerged from the same wall of soyflower from which Merritt had burst onto the charred field.

Kellan's face lit up with sheer triumph when he saw the three visitors. He was just as sweaty as Merritt, his cheeks and neck flushed. The fold of sleeve covering the stump of his left forearm had come unpinned and flapped undiplomatically as he spread his arms wide.

"I knew you'd come! As soon as I saw the ship, I knew it was you. Well, I thought it was your father, but one Vola's as good as the next, eh?"

"I certainly hope not," Alexander replied coldly, clearly no fan of Kellan's. "My father's pronounced girth makes travel...cumbersome. Yet he was quite taken with your proposal."

"Proposal?" Merritt said, his thoughts thick with confusion. "We can't send massages through the Rip."

"You can if the message is on your ship," Kellan

quipped, "and you send your *ship* back through the Rip."

"The Renata," said Merritt quietly. "When some of the colonists went back to Earth. That was three years ago."

"A bloody long time to wait for a response, I agree," Kellan admitted, frowning at Vola. The bald woman, Narienne, took a step closer to him, brandishing her rifle. Kellan smiled and held up his remaining hand in concession. "But better late than never, I suppose."

"It takes a long time to build illegal warships," Vola stated. His pale eyes roamed the landscape, never once deigning to land on Kellan. "Longer still to hire a crew who won't spill your secrets to the highest bidder. And longest of all to test the veracity of a claim made by a man with nothing to lose."

His gaze found Kellan then, settling like heavy weights. Kellan swallowed thickly and cleared his throat, then managed a shaky smile.

"Yes. Well. As I said in the message, the possibilities are endless. Control of the colony, control of its exports, absolute rule over the cities. The patents and technologies derived from the plant life alone would far exceed your father's shipping profits. They have a healing moss that—"

Vola lifted a ghostly hand and Kellan immediately stopped talking.

"Don't presume to know our family business. You have been out of the loop for quite some time."

Kellan cleared his throat again, growing more nervous. Merritt could tell the meeting was not going as well as he'd hoped. "Yes, of course not. There is also the *other* thing I mentioned in my message, the real prize."

What prize? Merritt wondered. He wanted to leave, to find Gavin and gather as many colonists as he could, but he wouldn't leave Skip, Lysette, and Ahmed at the feet of these people.

"And have you discovered the *location* of this prize?" Vola asked. "Your message was quite vague."

"Not yet, no. The Envoy fled before I could pressure him into telling me, and the boy is cleverer than he looks. Every time I try to follow him to the location he slips away." He shrugged helplessly and laughed, hoping to make light of his statement, but Vola was not amused.

Boy? thought Merritt. Surely he didn't mean Gavin.

Vola's eyes were back to studying the surrounding farms. "Are they the only two who know?"

"I think so, yes," Kellan answered quickly.

Vola nodded briskly. "Then we will proceed with my father's plan." He turned to Narienne. "Round up the colonists. Bring them to the top of the hill and line them up for orientation."

"No!" Merritt yelled, bulling past Kellan.

The scarred man placed his meaty palm against Merritt's burned chest and shoved, sending him back as hard as if he'd been hit by a rolling boulder. Merritt lay on the ground, moaning, his eyes clenched against the pain.

"Yes," Vola corrected, stepping closer to Merritt as he writhed on the ground. He studied him as if he were observing an organism in a petri dish — with detached superiority. "After orientation, put them to work," he told his companions while staring at Merritt. "Roads don't build themselves." He tapped the sole of Merritt's boot with the tip of his own, then smiled at the scarred man. "I don't think he likes you, Henrik. If he steps out of line, kill him where everyone can see."

Kellan moved quickly aside as the three visitors swept past him, their boots thudding hollowly on the ramp.

"I don't know if I'd call it redemption, exactly," Kellan said to Merritt with a sigh when Vola and his companions were well out of earshot, "but it sure beats rotting like a second-class citizen in the shadow of your primitive colony. If only you'd worked *with* me instead of against me, I wouldn't have needed to call on Luciano Vola. His son and I will mold this place into the metropolis it was meant to be. You don't have *vision*. That's your problem, Merritt. If you hadn't saved my life three years ago," he added wistfully, "I think I would have strangled you in your sleep by now."

He walked away before Merritt could respond. Black smoke continued to billow upward from beneath the ship as Lysette's crops smoldered. Merritt crawled over the soil and collapsed next to Skip. Talons of flame clutched his lungs, squeezing the breath from his chest and clouding his vision with pain.

He was still in the soil next to Skip, drifting in and out of consciousness, when thunder boomed across the land — only it wasn't thunder. It was the sound of boots pounding the metal ramp as soldier after armed soldier marched from the ship and stepped onto Galena soil.

Merritt heard a swishing noise from the wall of soyflower nearby, but when he looked, he only saw a few bent leaves moving slowly back into place.

He hoped it was Gavin. He hoped his son saw what was happening and was trying to get as far away as possible.

THE ENVOY

There was a good reason hypermass was only manufactured in one place in the solar system. Each "pill" — as the individual units were called — was the size of a city bus and extremely volatile up until the final stage of creation, possessing enough raw explosive power to rip open half an orbital shipyard.

The Korolev crater on Mars was far from the bustling luxury hotels built by Diamond Aerospace and other private companies, and far from the precious shipping lanes. Its ice-covered floor tempered the fickle nature of the dense materials fed into the great machines that produced solid cubes of hypermass the size of a three-story building. The cubes had to be brought to orbit immediately, before they settled, or else, as some feared, they would sink so far into the Martian surface it would disrupt the core.

In the vacuum of space, the cubes compressed into themselves, eventually firming into the pill-shaped objects which gave them their name.

Many of the materials were derived from the outer ring of an alien artifact known as a torus — one of a fleet of identical artifacts with which Jeff had an intimate history.

They'd asked for his help on that project, he

remembered as he tightened his safety harness in the pilot seat of the *Celerity*. His wife, Kate, had just turned ninety, and was on her death bed at the time. A century later, without his input, the first hypermass object was hauled into orbit from the surface of Mars. He'd never known them to be put to any practical use, but he had big plans for the one he was now towing toward the Rip.

It was just sitting there like a ripe fruit, Jeff thought. *Just where The Weaver said it would be.*

Fully aware of a single pill's destructive capabilities, he was surprised when The Weaver showed him that one was in the cargo hold of a vessel anchored to the outside shell of Shipyard 6. Later, as the computer aboard his *Celerity* forcefully overrode the safety protocols of the lesser automated transport tug, he learned that both ship and cargo were destined for an undisclosed location above the ecliptic plane.

He hadn't even needed to leave his ship to hook up. Once the hold on the other vessel had been opened remotely, he guided one of the *Celerity*'s tow cables into the locking bracket on the outside of the pill's cube-shaped radiation shield.

Then the drones showed up.

Word had apparently passed high enough up the ladder for someone, probably General Trager, to realize he'd made an unauthorized visit. Jeff didn't think the general would order the drones to fire on him right out the gate — especially not after he saw what trailed behind the *Celerity* from a thick white cable.

Jeff was correct on that front, but not for long. As

soon as he put a little distance between himself and Shipyard 6, the drones fired warning shots across *Celerity*'s nose — silent streaks of orange against the deep black of space. Trager had even tried to contact him personally, but Jeff flicked off the screen as soon as he saw the general's stern face.

There were ten drones tailing the *Celerity*, moving into a constellation configuration to surround the ship.

Part of him felt like he didn't owe anyone an explanation. He'd been alive more than four-hundred years and had earned the right to not be questioned. The other part felt guilty about the theft. Trager could have remanded Jeff to a research lab when his predecessor disclosed what he was...and what he could do.

It was a long haul to the Rip from Earth's orbit, and Jeff couldn't make the run with attack drones — and soon their bigger, crewed siblings — dogging his heels all the way.

Eventually they won't miss on purpose, Jeff knew.

It happened sooner than he'd expected. A dull metallic thunk sounded from elsewhere in the ship, and he dismissed the alarm that popped up on his control panel. The drone had targeted a non-essential part of the *Celerity* and merely punctured the cargo hold.

He closed his right eye and felt a surge of electric warmth inside his skull, emanating from the small black sphere near the top of his spinal column. His hollow left eye socket tingled behind its teflon patch, and the thick scar running up and over his scalp from atop his left eye burned as if it had been cut open by a dull blade.

The surge dissolved just as quickly as it peaked, and he opened his eye.

The drones were gone.

Jeff double-checked he wasn't venting oxygen from the hold, then set his autopilot course for the point where Ceres used to be before it was blown up to open the first Rip. He unstrapped his safety harness and drifted to the cockpit window, looking out at the stars. After so many years, the sight never ceased to impress.

The drones weren't *truly* gone, of course, at least not in the literal sense. In the instance of space that overlapped the one in which Jeff and the *Celerity* occupied, there was a very good chance they were still moving right along with his ship, their collective mechanical minds clicking to figure out why there was a void where a moment before there'd been a ship.

For that was Jeff's gift — the gift given to him by machines left behind by an extinct alien species. The small black sphere he'd seen on an x-ray inside his skull after he was resurrected by a torus allowed him to access and manipulate something called fold space.

The way he'd described it to Kate all those years ago was clumsy, but she'd understood — even more clearly once he'd demonstrated.

Imagine a small, empty room. The concept of fold space tells you that the room can be stacked — an endless number of identical rooms occupying the exact same space and time can be created by one who possesses the ability — a process called mapping. The Weavers were either born with the knowledge of how to create and travel between these rooms at will or discovered it sometime early in their existence.

Once that small room is mapped by stacking a chosen number of identical instances, you can flick yourself between them at will without ever stepping beyond those four walls. If you enter the room with a friend, then flick to another instance of that same room, your friend will vanish. You will seemingly vanish to their eyes as well, since you have physically moved yourself to another instance. Yet you will both be reunited if you step out into the hallway.

Anything you bring into one instance will remain there, which once made Jeff's car keys very difficult to find. The tori — ring-shaped machines created by the Weavers before their extinction — used fold space to grant themselves endless storage rooms inside their hollow rings. Jeff had used it to stack several instances of his cramped broom closet.

His brain mapped new spaces almost as an afterthought these days. He could feel it happening as a background process when he entered a room, or a new ship, or even a field. The open spaces were the hardest to map. Four walls, a floor, and a ceiling meant physical boundaries — simple delineations for mapping new instances. His first attempts at mapping borderless areas resulted in imperfect stacks with amorphous edges. He had to be in the middle of the space to flick between them or risk popping out of a misshapen edge back into a situation he'd been trying to escape.

Yet Jeff was growing more adept at mapping an area without volume. The disappearance of the drones proved it. Eventually they would fly out of their separate instance, but Jeff expected to be through the Rip by then.

As he drifted back to his seat and strapped himself in, he remembered his old friend Tag Riley, commander of Jeff's first mission to Titan four hundred years ago. Riley had died first, and been brought back, the same as Jeff. Before he'd been swallowed by a comet, he had used fold space to flick a nearby starship into another instance, saving its crew. Perhaps it was the adrenaline in his system from being so close to death, but Riley had managed to flick both himself and the comet to another instance — a feat Jeff had so far been unable to reproduce with even the smallest object.

And now for my next trick, he thought, sinking deeper into the padding of his seat.

The Weaver had granted him a vision during his visit, which was rare, but not unusual. What *had* been unusual was the flood of extra images that followed the vision.

Images is the wrong word, Jeff thought, frowning. *It was knowledge.*

The Weaver had injected someone — or some*thing* — else's knowledge into Jeff's mind.

It occurred immediately after he expressed concern that he'd never make it back to Galena in time. The months-long voyage negated his urgency.

The first drone popped back into existence next to the *Celerity,* quickly followed by the other nine. Alarms blared as they opened fire, but Jeff ignored them. He closed his eye, and pictured a point along his trajectory — not too far distant, just a few hundred kilometers. He could *feel* its texture in his mind, could sense the walls of his ship surrounding him in this new location.

The *Celerity* rocked as projectiles glanced off or sank into its hull.

Instead of the electric warmth associated with mapping new instances of fold space, a deep hum reverberated inside Jeff's skull from the small black sphere embedded there. It sounded like a single, low-pitched note hummed by a choir of a thousand monks.

The hum clipped off to silence, there was a blinding flash of white, and the *Celerity* skipped across space and arrived at the point he'd visualized. The drones disappeared once more, but they weren't in another instance that time — they were a few hundred kilometers behind him. Everything else looked the same through the cockpit window.

Space is space, Jeff had once heard a long-haul shipping captain declare with a shrug. *Of course it looks the same.*

He worked the control panel to verify the hypermass object was still in tow, and grinned when he saw the aft visual feed. Its cube-shaped radiation shield followed the *Celerity*, attached by its long cable, intact.

Jeff scanned the local region around his ship and detected no signs of other vessels. The mapping system told him he was still three months from the Rip at max velocity.

Let's change that, shall we? he thought.

Three more skips of equal distance were enough to convince him that the ship wouldn't break apart, the hypermass object wouldn't detonate, and he was ready to try for more.

In less than an hour, he was staring at the Ceres Rip, its wavering edges stretching out of sight above and below the cockpit window. A marble of blue light glowed in the center of the murky darkness — Aegea, the first of seven stars in the nearest systems beyond the Rip.

Jeff shook his head in amazement as the wormhole's purple-green aurora washed into the cockpit. Few things were novel enough after four hundred years to warrant his stupefied appreciation, but skipping was one of them.

I can go anywhere, he suddenly realized. The vast impassable distances that had kept humanity pinned to their own corner of the universe even before the Rips were opened no longer meant anything.

Then he remembered the cathedral cavern beneath Galena's surface, and the creature trapped within.

He piloted the *Celerity* toward the Rip, not daring to use his newfound skipping ability to quicken the journey.

It is already quick enough, he told himself. *And what if I skip into the entrance and bypass the exit altogether? No one truly knows what's inside the passage...or what happens if you get trapped.*

The lights in the cockpit dimmed and blinked out as the *Celerity* entered the Rip. Purple-green light danced over the walls.

White stars that hadn't been visible a moment earlier filled the cockpit window. They moved slowly into the distance, pulled toward a single point in the void as the universe slipped away. The stars joined into a spinning white sphere the apparent size of a golf ball.

Streaks of white light shot toward the sphere from all directions and was absorbed. The sphere swelled.

It filled the cockpit window, becoming a rectangle of pure white light...then it imploded upon itself in a microsecond, plunging the universe into darkness.

Jeff squinted into the darkness. His arms drifted above the arms of his seat. He knew what came next. Many times he'd been asleep in a hypergel tank during his previous Rip passages, but that had been from a sort of chronic malaise brought on by the endless drudgery of days unending as opposed to appreciation of the experience.

For some reason, he found himself more taken with the journey than ever before.

He shaded his right eye when a spinning quasar apparently no larger than his thumbnail flickered into existence.

A ring of expanding light bloomed from the quasar, moving quickly outward. It washed over the *Celerity* in a blinding flash, rattling the ship's interior. The dampeners installed in newer Rip-capable vessels had come a long way since the clunky installations on the larger Starliners a mere few decades earlier.

Ships with active GravGens lost gravity at this point of their passage, Jeff remembered. Here was the true void; the space between spaces.

The quasar exploded into a universe of electric colors — beams of light dancing around a central core, which expanded to swallow the light, an ever-widening rectangle that stretched to infinity, its inner walls awash with the swallowed colors.

Jeff sucked in air, feeling as if he'd been holding his breath for an hour.

The space beyond his cockpit window was calm and featureless, save for the distant blue spark of Aegea, the nearest star.

He ran a cursory check of the ship systems, finding nothing out of the ordinary. The radiation shields were soaked to maximum, but that was standard after passing through the Rip. His cargo seemed no worse for wear. The aft visual showed it drifting along behind the ship as the Rip slowly receded into the distance.

Jeff was just thinking about taking a quick nap before skipping the rest of the way to Galena when the ship's proximity alert blared throughout the cockpit. He silenced the alarm with the swipe of a finger and scanned the vicinity.

There was a box in his path, long and rectangular, some fifty kilometers out. The *Celerity*'s computer told him it was twice as large as the *Celerity* itself...and there was another ship alongside.

They couldn't have beaten me through the Rip, Jeff thought. Granted, he had given little thought to how quickly his pursuers would follow him to this side of the Rip even if he'd used his hybrid antimatter drive, but seeing as he'd skipped through the five month journey in a matter of hours, he was hoping to have plenty of time to probe the depths of his willful ignorance.

The man's face that popped up onto his control

panel a moment later was none too friendly. He was older, but exuded strength simply by the way he carried himself. Deep crags formed shadowed lines on his weathered face. The dim lights of his ship's cockpit reflected faintly on his bald head. Two caterpillar eyebrows moved expressively when he saw Jeff.

The *Celerity*'s computer immediately began spooling data in a long stream next to the image:

Marco Mazza

72 YO

Employer: Vola Shipping Corporation

Residence: Earth, Rome

Arrests: 3

Pre-adult record: Expunged

"The Envoy," he said simply, his eyebrows twitching. "I bet they'll miss you when you're gone."

His image vanished from the control panel before Jeff could respond.

In its place, the *Celerity* flashed a record of Marco's ship it had gleaned from a shipyard database, one of the many archives it kept tucked away in its circuits. Jeff frowned as he paged through the record. It was vastly incomplete, as if it had been pieced together from fragments or deliberately redacted.

A wireframe model of the ship expanded on the control panel, rotating in a sequence to show every angle. It wasn't as long or sleek as Jeff's ship, but there was a certain rugged beauty to its gentle curves and short, blunted wings that hugged the back of the ship.

Name: Spitfire

Class: Unknown

Captain: Marco Mazza

Build Date: Unknown
Origin: Unknown
Armament: 4 Chain Slings, 2 Unknown
Armor: Unknown
Rad. Shield: Standard

Big help you are, Jeff grumbled internally as he swiped away the information.

He saw the box in the distance, and the toy-sized ship beside it. Marco's welcome had been less than warm, so he decided not to linger. He shut off all incoming comms channels and dampened his energy signature, then veered off-course, moving parallel with the Rip.

Closing his eye, Jeff pictured a spot in the void ahead, somewhere, anywhere to get him away from the *Spitfire*. His own ship was a fast cruiser, with two small projectile cannons — no match for a vessel that had clearly been designed for battle.

He waited, but nothing happened.

There was no hum from inside his skull. There was no tingling sensation in his fingertips that signaled the impending skip. Jeff opened his eye to find he was exactly where he had been — only now, red lights were flashing in the cockpit.

The *Spitfire* had launched a volley.

Jeff's instincts took over. His hands blurred over the panel as he swiped to the manual control interface and dipped the nose of the *Celerity* while firing a burst from all three engines.

He braked after the burst, forward thrusters firing, then spun to angle his cannons toward the *Spitfire,* strafing sideways as the computer kept him locked on to his target. There was a sudden jerk as the tow cable attached to the hypermass cube snapped taut. The ship compensated with a metal groan.

The distance between the vessels was too great for his projectile cannons to reach anything close to accuracy, and he hoped the *Spitfire*'s weapons were the same.

Something *TINK*ed against his port side, and a red box flashed on the control panel.

So much for that notion, Jeff thought. Either Marco's ship had long-range weapons, or he was a blessed good shot — or both.

Jeff throttled toward the threat and switched his cannons from burst to open fire. They spat tongues of orange flame that vanished in a microsecond as the *Celerity* roared onward under full thrust, dull *thud-thud-thuds* in the hull signaling the counterbalanced recoil of the two weapons.

Marco's ship peeled away from the drifting box faster than Jeff expected, flipping sideways to drop out of sight below the edge of the *Celerity*'s cockpit window. Jeff tracked the vessel on his control panel, watching its little red triangle swing wide under the belly of his ship as it moved closer.

Jeff had shortened the gap between them by some thirty kilometers, and Marco seemed intent on crossing the remaining distance as fast as possible.

More impacts rocked the hull of the *Celerity* from below.

Should have put my suit on, Jeff scolded himself as he banked hard to port, veering out of Marco's line of fire. *But it wouldn't do me any good this far from Galena if my ship broke apart.*

No one was likely to pass through this section of

space for a long time — not with the *Spitfire* guarding the Rip.

Jeff squinted at the drifting box when it flashed past the cockpit window in the distance, his ship still banking. He braked hard, reoriented the *Celerity* on a collision course with the *Spitfire* as another volley raked his starboard side, then maxed out the throttle. The hypermass cube swung wide, threatening to carry him along its trajectory, but the *Celerity*'s engines roared, negating the opposing force. He loosed another dozen rounds at Marco's ship, which was on a direct course for a nose-to-nose impact, spinning like a corkscrew.

Two blips of orange flashed on *Spitfire*'s hull. A moment later, titanium chains ripped through the starboard side of the *Celerity* before Jeff could peel away. Marco juked just enough at the last moment and the ships came within meters of each other.

A klaxon blared and the control panel warned Jeff that the ship had lost aft cabin pressure. One of the engine icons blinked red on the screen. The computer quickly sealed the rear cabin and cut the line to the damaged engine. Outside the cockpit window, the stars spun in a lopsided circle.

Jeff forced himself to take a deep breath. He closed his eye and tried to wake that part of his brain which allowed him to skip across such a vast distance in no time at all.

Nothing.

Was he no more than a drained battery? His manipulation of fold space had never worked that way before. He had always been able to stack rooms and move between them, almost without trying, whenever it suited him.

Ripping holes in space-time might be a bit more strenuous, genius, he chided.

He tried to slow his corkscrew spin but the computer spit back an error each time. Only the starboard-side thrusters were working, along with two of the rear engines.

Marco had turned his ship and was in pursuit. Long tracer projectiles flicked silently over the *Celerity*'s nose.

Ahead, the long metallic box spun dizzily in Jeff's view. He considered it a moment, then plotted a course that would take him directly past it. Perhaps it would absorb a projectile or two before the *Celerity* was finally ripped to shreds.

As he spun closer, however, the box began to open.

It unfolded gracefully, its sides aligning on the same plane to form a long platform.

That's a sentry wall, Jeff realized. Fear was usually a hazy memory for him, but it gripped his heart in that instant with an icy fist.

Sentry walls had been outlawed by every government on Earth after one was deployed by the Martian Consulate along the Earth-Mars shipping lane during the Union riots over a century ago. Still in the experimental phase, its software wasn't able to properly distinguish between military and civilian threats. Any vessel within a certain range that moved a millimeter in the wall's direction was turned to Swiss cheese by the reciprocal barrage.

They had come to be called kamikaze walls because anyone who approached must have been seeking death in the first place.

Marco fired at Jeff's ship as he drew closer, but the attempts seemed almost perfunctory. Suddenly, the *Spitfire* broke off pursuit and rocketed away, putting distance between itself and the sentry wall.

He needs to get clear before the wall is fully active, Jeff realized.

The unfolded box rotated, small puffs of white visible along its edges against the spinning starscape behind. Jeff had long since cut power to the starboard thrusters, but he couldn't slow his inexorable spin. He mashed the controls for the forward thrusters, but they were unresponsive.

As the *Celerity* spun, the sentry wall grew larger through the cockpit window. Jeff could now see the forty-meter-long mini city of weaponry stacked on what used to be the inner walls of the box — a cluster of thin skyscrapers glinting with ice crystals. They were gradually orienting themselves toward the *Celerity*.

He could no longer call up the aft visual. If the hypermass was still back there, it had a better chance of killing him when it came under heavy fire than the wall did.

Marco's weathered face popped up on the control panel once more. It took Jeff a moment to realize the computer had probably turned on the incoming comms as a safety measure when half the ship stopped working.

"I was going to ask if you wanted to surrender," the older man said, his left eyebrow arching in amusement, "but maybe you're too busy."

Jeff ignored him, instead choosing to swipe

through the myriad errors constantly spooling from the ship's computer onto his control panel. His hand paused over a flashing red square with a block of text inside.

It couldn't be that simple, he thought in disbelief.

"The sentry wall is almost at full power," Marco was saying. "We are all trapped on this side after. And if anyone comes through the other side, well..." He shrugged.

Jeff opened the sub-menu linked to that particular error message and found a bright red radiation shielding schematic. Heavy plates covered most of the ship, and were at their maximum load of absorption. The rads needed shedding, which usually happened in orbit after a ship passed through the Rip.

"Very aggressive, this wall," said Marco, almost to himself. He frowned and nodded. "If I were you—"

Jeff swiped the screen away, dismissing it. He called up the override for the rad shield system and rapidly tapped through all the requisites for jettison. A wireframe model of the *Celerity* showed a flashing encasement of thick plating.

VERIFY blinked a large yellow button. Jeff pushed it and thirty dense hull plates soaked with Rip radiation *PING*ed away from his ship. A countdown timer took the place of the button, running backward from thirty minutes.

Jeff's brow furrowed in confusion as he stared at the decreasing numbers. The readout told him that was the remaining time before deep space radiation penetrated the inner hull.

I dumped my protection with that plating, he knew in that moment. *All of it.*

He had once been exposed to the naked vacuum of space with no other protection than his power-drained space suit, adrift for hours and hours. When he was finally rescued, he'd been on the verge of death for half a day — yet he'd survived. His cells regenerated at a remarkable rate, the doctors had told him afterward. Not only had they kept his organs functioning while he was floating in space, they would also keep cancer from ever ravaging his body.

Sitting in the *Celerity*, it wasn't the radiation he was afraid of soaking into his skin, it was the cold that would freeze his limbs until he could no longer control the ship.

He watched the spinning sentry wall as his ship flew toward it like a missile. The tops of the glinting skyscrapers erupted in short-lived fireworks as the weapons fired.

Jeff closed his eye once more.

This better work, he thought.

Free of the tainted radiation shielding, he could feel his mind unfetter as if a binding had been cut free. It mapped the surrounding area, creating stacked instances without thinking. Jeff accessed the newer ability buried within the small alien sphere at the back of his skull, the deep hum, and let it build until it was a full choir belting out a single, eardrum-shattering bass note.

He envisioned the space around Galena, its safe orbit, far, far from the Rip. The alarm blared louder now — impact imminent.

Jeff's fingertips tingled, and he skipped.

GAVIN

There were at least ten of them, Gavin observed from a distance, all wearing protective body armor and carrying the same heavy white rifle as the tattooed bald woman, Narienne. She and the other two men who had been talking with Gavin's father before he collapsed retreated back into the ship, and the soldiers had descended the ramp.

They fanned out across the scorched ground in the middle of Lynette's soyflower field, moving into the neighboring farms.

Gavin crouched behind a wall of soyflower stalks, using their broad leaves for cover. He had run north from the landing site when his father collapsed, then cut directly east, in the direction of his own home. Gavin had wanted to burst from his hiding spot in the soyflower stalks when he saw his father's injuries. His chest looked as if a fire snake had slithered from shoulder to hip, his shirt in tatters.

Then he heard what Kellan said to the man named Vola, and he fled.

He has tried to follow me before, Gavin thought, *when I visited the cavern.*

He felt a wave of gratitude for a simple bit of advice he took for granted when it was given. Shurri was the only other one who shared his secret of the alien creature under the surface, in its cave of purple crystals. She warned him not to go back. When it became obvious to her that he would, she warned him not to go too often. And when that urging went unheeded, she at least cautioned him to take precautions on the journey.

Afterward, he always left under the cover of night, and took a different route each time he made the three-hour trip to the mouth of the underground river, pausing often to make sure he wasn't being followed.

Kellan knew something was out there — something powerful, or worth a lot of money, or both.

And he knows I know where it is, thought Gavin.

He crept slowly through the crop of new soyflower stalks, staying low to shield himself from view, looking around to catch his bearings. Where had he ended up? Was this Niku's farm?

Gavin turned to angle himself in the direction of his home, his thigh muscles aching from walking in a crouch.

There was shouting far away, and he froze. Then he heard an electric crackle, and a scream. Silence followed. Gavin held his breath as he crept forward, the only sound the rustling of broad green leaves.

Why should I care if Kellan finds the creature? he wondered. *So what if he sells it or tests it or whatever else he wants to do? If it makes the soldiers leave...*

Yet something nagged at the back of his mind. After every visit to the cavern, Gavin spent the following days vacillating between believing the creature truly wanted to help him protect the colony from future threats and attempting to grab hold of the slippery feeling that he was being manipulated.

The thought of a man like Kellan getting his hands on an alien that could grant visions of the future disturbed Gavin greatly.

There has to be another way, he thought as he paused to catch his breath. *Maybe it can help me.*

The thing had shown him a vision of the future, of his fellow colonists in bondage. Yet how had that helped him prepare for such a day once it finally came?

I should have done more, he thought, shaking his head. *It's my fault.*

Perhaps the creature would tell him what to do next.

He reached the border of Niku's and Uda's farm, having swung wide around the house, and peeked out of the edge of the soyflower field. The bald man with a thousand scars, Henrik, was stomping around the outside of Gavin's home in a red fury, his fists opening and closing like he wanted to hit something. He roared and kicked the corrugated metal wall next to the open door, leaving a deep indentation. Then he stormed inside, and Gavin heard the sound of equipment being thrown around the room.

He carries no weapon, Gavin noticed. *He must not need one.*

Henrik reemerged and stood in front of the doorway, frowning as he scanned his surroundings. Gavin sank lower behind his wall of cover, holding his breath again. For half a second, Henrik's eyes landed on the section of soyflower stalks behind which Gavin crouched...then moved on. He stormed off to the west, heading toward Niku's and Uda's farm.

Niku was most likely still at the Casmin Sea. He probably didn't even know a ship had landed. *But what about Uda and their son, Toma?* Gavin wondered.

He couldn't fight a man like Henrik with his bare hands, so he turned away from the direction of their farm after Henrik moved out of sight, and ran for his house.

Gavin burst into the relative coolness of his home, breathing hard. Sunlight beamed in through the two front windows, falling in harsh squares across the floor and his father's work table.

Food, he told himself. *Weapons.* Water he could get from a spring.

He found the machete Willef had given him leaning against the wall near his hammock — the same machete that had killed a sky beast three years ago. The beast's blood had stained part of the blade, making it ripple with darkness in a certain light. Gavin sheathed it and shoved it into a pack, then tossed in several sealed cans of dried rock bat jerky and the precious few potatoes and carrots that hadn't been added to the storehouse out back. He eyed a sealed bag of soy jerky, deciding if the stomach pain would be worth not dying over if he couldn't find anything else. Then he remembered Shurri and added it to the bag.

Shurri.

The thought of her stopped him in his tracks.

How am I going to get her out of the hospital? he wondered. *They must have posted guards.* Then a darker thought occurred to him. *What if they keep her on their ship? I'll never get her out.*

But why would they? He had no idea what they intended to do, just an indication they wanted to find whatever was inside the cavern.

Don't be stupid, he told himself. *You think all those weapons they're carrying are for a fireside chit-chat?*

Gavin heard footsteps outside and immediately put his back to the curved wall of his dome-shaped house. He shuffled sideways, toward the door, as a shadow crossed the entrance. Reaching into his bag, he silently unsheathed the machete and drew it out.

A man ran inside and stumbled at the door. He lost his footing and fell forward, collapsing to his hands and knees.

Gavin dropped the machete and ran to his father. He helped him back to his feet and guided him out of view of the doorway, glancing outside to make sure no one else was there. His father winced in pain as he eased himself onto a short supply crate, then groaned as he stretched out his legs.

He was filthy, sweaty, bloody, and the burn mark on his chest oozed a thin black fluid down his chest between the frayed hole in his shirt.

But for all that, he smiled as wide as Gavin had ever seen when their eyes met.

"I looked for you...at the dam," he panted, struggling to get out the words. "Glad you...came home." He coughed and wiped his mouth with a shaky hand.

How did you get away? Gavin signed.

His father shrugged, then made a face like it was a mistake. "Soldiers...left. I crawled."

Gavin's hands moved. *What do they want, Dad?*

His father closed his eyes weakly, and shook his

head. "Everything. They'll put us to work." He grunted and picked up a clean cloth from a nearby stack, then pressed it to his chest. A scream started to escape his mouth, but he bit it off. "Roads. Cities. More farms."

How can they do that? Gavin asked.

"Who will...stop them? Water. Water, son."

Gavin hurried to find a dented metal canteen he knew his father kept on the work table. Henrik had thrown it clear across the room along with so much else. He helped his father take a long swig, then set the canteen on the floor beside him.

When he stood back up, his father was staring at Gavin's pack, and the machete.

I'm getting Shurri out, Gavin signed firmly.

"Son, you can't—"

Gavin's hands forcefully formed the words. *We're leaving!*

His father smiled, exhausted. "I'm not here to stop you. I came to...help you. Just glad I...caught you in time. They..."

He sighed, too exhausted to speak. Instead, he signed the rest with shaking hands.

They put a barrier around the colony. That's what did this to me. He gestured toward his chest. *You have to go another way.*

There isn't one! Gavin signed. *We have no ships. Ayani took the shuttle.*

Not over, his father signed. *Under.*

Gavin's eyebrows rose as realization struck. *The tunnel under Shurri's farm.*

His father nodded. *Won't be easy. They're gathering everyone at the courtyard. Hopefully that means the pit isn't being watched.*

But the courtyard is right in front of the hospital! signed Gavin.

His father reached out and Gavin took his arm, helping him to stand. He took a deep breath and stretched a little taller. "I think I can do something about that."

He seemed to find more strength after they left their home and began working their way through the fields, jogging across the open spaces between the acres of tall soyflower stalks to move closer to the central hill.

When they stood among the stalks of the last farm before the hill, Gavin's father rested a hand on his shoulder and guided him down until they both squatted in the dark, rich soil.

Up the low rise, three lines of a dozen colonists each stood shoulder to shoulder, facing a group of soldiers. White-haired Vola paced before the colonists, speaking. Gavin saw Shurri's mother, nervously twisting the hem of her shirt. Uda was there, holding her five-year-old son, Toma, to her chest. Even at a distance, Gavin knew the look of Uda's fury when he saw it. Try as he might, he couldn't spot Arthur. Hopefully he was still in the hospital with Shurri.

"Not even half the colony," his father whispered, though he didn't seem happy about it.

Maybe they got away in time, Gavin signed.

His father shook his head, but didn't reply. Instead, he said, "It was your mother's dream to bring you here. I resisted until after she passed. Then it became..." He paused, searching for words. "It became almost a duty to see it through."

Gavin had heard similar speeches before, usually after his father indulged in a cup or two of Skip's homemade vodka.

I can't remember her face, Gavin signed without thinking. He'd never told anyone.

His father smiled at him. "Neither can I. But I'll see it again. I don't regret bringing us here, son. This is our home." He patted Gavin's shoulder. "You wait here. Get Shurri out when it's time and head for the sinkhole. There's a panel in the floor at the back of the hospital. You can't open it from below, but you can drop through it if you're already inside. That will lead you straight down the hill."

Gavin grabbed his father's wrist as he made to stand, then signed, *You're coming, too.*

"No. I want you to get as far away as you can. Head for the twin mountains, there's shelter. I have to find a way to stop this, or get our neighbors out."

How will I know when it's time to move? signed Gavin.

"Oh, you'll know." Gavin saw his own features in his father's face in that moment, as he so often did when he looked into a mirror: square jaw, trusting face, melancholy brown eyes. Usually he disliked the fact they looked so much alike. In that moment, crouching in the soyflower field, he felt proud.

I love you, Dad, he signed.

It had been so long since he'd said it, his father seemed taken aback. Then he tousled his son's short hair.

"I love you, too, son. Stay low. Get Shurri out of here."

Then he was off, pushing through the last of the

soyflower stalks to emerge in full view of the hill. The soldiers were too focused on the colonists in front of them to notice.

Gavin crept through the field, angling for the back of the hospital. He would be able to climb the hill unseen, using the large white prefab building for cover.

"You won't kill us because you need us!" his father bellowed behind him.

Gavin turned to look, but his view was blocked, so he continued on, moving closer toward the hill. The last farm closest to the back of the hospital ended fifty meters from the base of the low hill.

"And you need us for your roads!" his father continued. "Your mansions!"

Gavin caught a glimpse of him through a break in the stalks. Three soldiers had separated from the group atop the hill and approached his father, who walked toward them with his arms raised.

Just a little farther, Gavin thought as he crept. He was almost directly below the hospital now.

"Uda!" his father shouted. "Moyen! Hanna and Luis! Don't listen to the lies he tells you. He—"

The speech cut off abruptly.

Gavin risked standing up to see what was happening. His father had started running parallel to the hill, leading the three soldiers away from it before they could get too close to him. Vola said something Gavin couldn't hear, and three more soldiers left their pack and hurried down the gentle slope.

Everyone was watching his father.

Gavin ran, too.

He ran up the hill and leaped over the side railing

of the front steps, grabbing the lip above the doorway before his boots could hit the floor, then he swung inside, releasing at the last moment to land on the metal floor with a soft thud.

Gavin quickly spun sideways and pressed his back to the wall, his heart pounding like a fist in his chest. He waited, and waited. There was an electric crackle from outside, across the courtyard.

"Now that's out of the way," Vola said crisply, "we'll continue."

Dad, thought Gavin.

He wanted to poke his head out the door to see. Instead, he moved as quietly as he could to Shurri, who still lay on a cold metal table, her injured leg covered in healing moss.

The moss was a pale red, and sickly — a far cry from the rich, deep red it boasted before attaching itself to a wound.

Shurri moaned when he wiped a sweaty strand of hair back from her forehead. Her eyelids fluttered, then she went still.

Metal clinked behind him and Gavin whirled, grabbing for the machete in his pack.

Arthur sat huddled under a table in the corner, continuously trying to slide himself deeper into the feeble shadow. His eyes were vacant. Gavin went to him quickly, kneeling down to his level.

"I hid," he whispered, not meeting Gavin's eyes. "They came in here and dragged Uda away, but I hid, and they didn't get me. They didn't even care about Shurri."

Gavin snapped his fingers in Arthur's face. The boy was the same age as Shurri, but his fear made him look ten years younger.

There's a way out, Gavin signed. *But you need to help me.*

Arthur blinked, then something seemed to click behind the fear. He nodded and tried to stand, but Gavin put a hand on his shoulder to stop him.

Your mom is outside, he signed. *If you see her, you can't go, or we'll be caught. We'll come back for her and the others.*

Arthur nodded again, and Gavin helped him out from his hiding place.

As they walked to Shurri's table, Gavin signed, *She has to wake up soon. The moss is almost done.*

"Yeah but it didn't even cover half of it," Arthur whispered.

Gavin had been trying not to think about that. He made a cursory check of the back of her leg, his gaze constantly flicking to the front door. Uda had done a good job cleaning the small barbs from the ragged edges of the spiral laceration. She had sewn up what the moss couldn't cover, but the wound was still fresh and oozing clear pink serous fluid.

There was a stack of gauze and tape on a shelf under Shurri's table. Gavin scooped it into his pack and put it on over his chest. He got to his knees, gesturing for help transferring Shurri to his back. Then he grabbed her wrists as Arthur grunted to slide her off the table. He twisted her at the waist as she dropped, and Gavin pulled her arms forward over his shoulders, carrying her piggyback.

They moved to the back of the hospital, Arthur bringing up the rear.

Panel, Gavin spelled out with one hand, already

feeling the strain of Shurri's weight. He lightly stomped the floor with his boot, and Arthur seemed to understand. They looked together, wandering in separate directions. Gavin was near the gurgling healing moss tanks, nothing within but thick liquid.

"Here!" Arthur said a bit too loudly.

A square panel half-covered by a rolling equipment rack had two silver handles embedded in its surface, flush with the floor. Gavin slowly rolled the rack to the side while Arthur knelt down and got his fingers under the handles. He yanked hard, and the panel lifted with a loud pop.

They froze, waiting for the inevitable sound of boots on the metal stairs outside. When it didn't come, Gavin motioned for them to continue. Arthur set the panel aside and hopped down through the hole.

"It's the ground," he said in surprise. "It goes all the way out the back of the hospital."

Gavin went to his hands and knees next to the hole and gently lowered Shurri to the floor. Arthur took her under the armpits and pulled her down. Her feet slipped over the edge in a blink, and Arthur fell on his backside with an *oomph*, his unconscious sister on top of him.

Gavin hopped down beside him. Standing meant bending over double below the hospital. It was cold and damp in the dark, and the soft ground under his boots was wetter than elsewhere, almost like mud. The prefab building was raised on a grid of thick pillars. Stacks of empty supply crates had been piled in the open spaces, blocking most of the underside from view. A narrow path ran between the crates from the opening in the floor to the back of the hospital, and out onto the back of the hill where Gavin had climbed a few minutes earlier.

Help me carry her, he signed.

Arthur grabbed Shurri's arms, and Gavin got her ankles. His right hand touched the corner of a piece of healing moss, and its brittle outer layer flaked off in the dark.

They grunted and struggled, shuffling half bent over, to get her into the sunlight. Arthur collapsed as soon as they cleared the underside of the hospital. Without waiting for him, Gavin pulled Shurri onto his back again and trudged down the hill, heading for her farm. Arthur appeared at his side a moment later, dirt smeared on his cheeks. His sandy hair hung limp on his forehead.

"I heard the man say he put an electric fence around the colony," he said. "What does he want?"

Gavin shifted Shurri a little higher on his back. He had to walk slightly leaned forward so she didn't slip down. Her injured leg bounced freely against him, flaking off more of the healing moss.

He remembered what his father told him when he asked the same question.

Gavin leaned forward farther and released Shurri's wrists so he could use both his hands to sign the word, *Everything*.

AYANI

A voice called to her in the dark. It was distant and weak, but it pierced the heavy shadow that smothered her like a blanket.

Ayani opened her eyes, but couldn't see.

Am I dead? she wondered.

She wiggled her toes, then her ankles. Her fingertips tapped against hard, cold metal. Her left shoulder felt sticky with blood.

Not dead, she concluded. *Might be easier if I was.*

Something heavy pinned her thighs against a twisted piece of what used to be the shuttle. The sharp stench of burnt plastic made her sniff.

Someone called her name again, this time closer. When she opened her mouth to call out, pain welled up from her chest and clogged her throat.

Bile, or blood, she knew. If it were blood, that meant her chest cavity had been punctured. There was a particularly sharp pain in her back, over the left side of her ribcage.

Her left arm was pinned as well, trapped under a heavy weight, but she had limited range of motion in her right. Ayani rapped against metal with her knuckles — a feeble sound, but it was all she could manage.

A thin shaft of light knifed down from above as a

thin square of metal sheeting was pushed aside. Henry stood there, smiling down at her, his fuzzy head limned by sunlight. A long cut trickled blood on the left side of his face, and his dark blue coverall was torn down one side, but at least he could still walk.

Ayani wasn't so sure about her own ability in that regard.

"*There* you are," he said. With a grunt, he shoved aside the metal sheeting. A burst of sparks assaulted him from the side, and he shielded his face as they fell and winked out. "That seems to happen a lot when one crashes," he observed.

Kneeling down, he tried to pry up the heavy black rod that lay across Ayani's thighs. While he groaned and grunted, she wiggled her left arm free of the wall panel it was under.

She lay on a mound of wreckage in a vast, empty room, its ceiling twenty meters overhead.

Empty except for her, Henry, and the wrecked shuttle.

We're in the pyramid, she realized.

Her last-ditch attempt to manually veer the craft into the opening at the base of the structure seemed to have worked. Her eyes traced the smoking black track where the shuttle hit the floor of the room on its way in. A chunk of ceiling material had been chipped away above the track at the top of the wide entrance, indicating they had most likely come in a little too high, caromed off the top of the opening, and slammed into the ground. The impact became a hundred-meter slide, and the shuttle broke to pieces on its way to its final resting position beneath her.

She looked to the opening, and couldn't see it all

without turning her head. It stretched the full length of the base of the pyramid. The inner walls, floor, and ceiling were all made from the same blue-gray material, making it difficult to tell where their corners met.

The opposite end of the lower level was lost in shadow. Sunlight spilling in from outside only reached a little farther than the ruins of the shuttle.

Something hissed deep within the mound, there was a pop, and the whole thing shifted. Henry let out a yelp and lost his balance, rolling to the side and slipping partway down the hill of debris. He bumped against a broken piece of the outer hull.

The shift was enough to free Ayani's legs. She wriggled loose, trying to ignore the acid pain in her ribcage.

If there's something stuck in my back, she thought as she twisted, *I'm certainly not doing the wound any favors by moving so much.*

Then she was free, and pulling herself hand over hand on her belly toward Henry. Her legs were numb from the pressure of the rod, and she didn't trust standing on such unstable ground.

"You've got something in your back," Henry told her when she reached him. He craned his neck to get a better look. "Mostly superficial, I would say."

She arced an eyebrow. "'Mostly'?"

"Do you want to pull it out, or shall I?"

"Where? I can't feel it."

"Under your left shoulder blade. There isn't much blood..."

She sighed and relaxed her body. "Be my guest."

He stood up and brushed his palms against his

coverall.

"One," he counted, "two..."

He ripped it out, and Ayani screamed.

"You see?" he said, smiling and showing her the triangular shard of metal. He tapped one bloody corner. Her blood covered no more than a finger's width.

He chucked it aside and it landed with a hollow clonk. Metal creaked and the mound shifted again. Henry whooped in surprise as he was knocked off-balance. A curtain of sparks showered them both as they tumbled down the side and smacked against the hard floor.

It felt like cold slate. Small ripples in the surface formed stone streams that criss-crossed over each other, as if the entire inner surface of the pyramid was some giant topographical map. Henry was entranced. He sat with his legs spread apart, both his palms spread against the floor between them.

Ayani fought back a shout as she boosted herself up to one elbow. Her legs were dead weight, unable to even feel the cold emanating from the floor. Her wristpad beeped, letting her know she had sustained injuries.

Gee, thanks, she thought.

The small screen was cracked in one corner, but seemed functional. She tapped through the menus until she got to the homing beacon linked to Jeff's own wristpad, then activated it with no small amount of skepticism. It wouldn't work as far away as he'd traveled, but maybe the signal would be picked up by someone at the colony.

How? spat a voice in her mind. It was the same

sharp voice that had driven her through her academy training all those times she'd wanted to quit. *How will they pick up the signal if they don't have any equipment?*

Ayani didn't feel like arguing with herself just then. She forced the challenging voice away.

"The drones," she whispered, not wanting to risk the effort to speak any louder. Her stomach roiled, threatening to send up everything inside if she made the wrong move.

"They won't come inside," Henry said absentmindedly. "Perhaps they can't see it."

That didn't make any sense to her. "Can't see it?"

He reached into his pocket, but his hand came back empty. After patting around his other pockets, he found what he wanted inside a flap over his left thigh. He waddled over to her with one hand pushed into his lower back and the other holding a woven linen-paper map. He gave it to Ayani, and she unfolded it on the floor.

"This is where we are," she said. "But I don't see the pyramid."

"None of the maps show the pyramid," he told her.

"But...how old are the maps?"

He shook his head. "Not that old. Unless this structure sprang up from a box, I would have seen it being built, at the very least." She slid the map toward him, and he tucked it back into his pocket. "I don't think this place was scrubbed from official records, either," he said, staring up at the ceiling. "I think it's made of some kind of material that optical cameras can't see."

"Then how did you know it was here?" she asked. "You seemed pretty sure of it before the crash."

"Are you able to walk?"

"I have no idea. Why?"

His knees popped as he stood. "Because we can't go back outside, so we must go farther in, to look for another way out. It's a long walk to the back of this room. Plenty of time for explanations."

Ayani massaged her thighs, then bent her legs at her knees. She couldn't feel them, but they worked. Awkwardly, she got to her feet and stamped her boots against the floor, trying to shock some feeling into them.

A shadow flitted past the sunlit entrance a hundred meters from the wreckage. The drones were still hunting.

But why? she wondered. *Why target our shuttle? Who sent them?*

That line of questioning raised even more regarding the colony.

Had whoever sent the drones landed at the colony? What could they possible want with a bunch of farmers?

She turned away from the opening, wondering what the drones made of the void where the pyramid should be in there scans, if what Henry said was true.

"It started with the hex crabs," he said as they walked slowly away from the shuttle debris. "I had decided to map their migration patterns. Little more than idle hobby, I confess. But over the past few years, I've found I'm not so stable in the wilds as I used to be. Though I suppose seventy years of adventure is more than most could hope for."

The numbness in Ayani's legs became a stabbing sensation as thousands of invisible ice needles danced on her skin. Her stomach was calming, but her shoulder and back throbbed with raw, painful weakness.

"I hadn't gotten very far in my study when I noticed something odd about their timing," Henry continued. "They circle this planet once every two years. Yet, based on their speed, they could make the same journey in one." He wiped at the cut on the side of his face, and his hand came back bloody. "So I began to wonder."

"Where do they go the rest of the time?" Ayani asked.

"Precisely. Perhaps they hibernate. Perhaps they spawn, and grow large enough for their migration the following year. Or, perhaps they go somewhere else entirely."

Ayani frowned. "Here?"

"The opening behind us is wide enough to admit thousands of the crabs side-by-side. The forest surrounding this pyramid extends unbroken around the globe, mostly following the equator. Hex crabs only travel in or near the forests."

"Following the underground canopy," Ayani added.

That much she'd learned during her stay at the colony. Uda had explained how their barbed, segmented legs churned the soil above the canopy for nutrients shed by the tangled web of thick, buried branches, enriching the soil at the same time.

"And while this pyramid doesn't show up on any drone scans, guess what does," he said.

"Hex crabs."

He nodded proudly. "I followed their migration using a series of drone scans a decade old. They group together in the millions, did you know that? When their shells are linked, they can cover half this continent. In my search, I noticed one section of the planet where they seemingly vanished in plain sight. On one scan, they smother the continent. Three days later, poof. Vanished without a trace."

"They come here for a year," said Ayani. "Why?"

"We may just find out."

The stone floor drank the sound of their boots as they walked deeper into the cavernous room. There was almost no sunlight on their backs now. Ayani looked back. The low mound of shuttle wreckage seemed tiny in the distance, silhouetted against the solid yellow rectangle of the structure's opening. She guessed they were about halfway through the pyramid.

"I can't see anything ahead," Henry admitted, squinting. "Can you?"

Ayani's eyes took a long moment to adjust to the approaching darkness after glancing at the opening.

"Not a thing."

They were so far in that she could no longer see the ceiling, either. She wished she had a light.

Are we supposed to keep stumbling blindly ahead? she wondered.

Just at the edge of absolute darkness, the far wall materialized before them.

"This isn't the other side of the pyramid," she noted, pressing her palm to the cold wall. "We're only about two-thirds across."

Henry regarded her thoughtfully. All she could see of him were two shiny spots representing his eyes.

"I would guess the same," he said. "You have a remarkable gift for spatial awareness. That was obvious in the shuttle, when you knew exactly how much to angle the shuttle to fly inside the pyramid instead of dashing us against the wall."

Ayani looked away. "That was blind luck."

"Oh, hardly. Maybe there was no forward thought put into it, but your instincts saved our lives. Thank you."

She nodded, but doubted he saw the gesture in the gloom.

"I myself acquired the knack for it on the moon," he continued. "Earth's moon, I mean to say. There was only so much space to fit all those buildings, and you wouldn't believe the regulations involved with their construction. My architects and I had to be most creative. And I had to see it all in mind beforehand, no less. Imagine if I had raised two buildings side by side only to discover the promenade of one ran through the concert hall of the other!"

Then he clapped his hands, startling her.

"Back the way we came, I should think," he said.

"There might be a door in this wall."

"It occurred to me that many of the interesting things happening on this planet are below ground. The place seems designed for caverns, aquifers, and tunnels. We certainly can't reach the ceiling, and I don't relish the thought of walking into that forest. I'm not sure we'll find a more suitable door in this pyramid besides one that leads..."

He pointed toward his feet.

"Down," Ayani finished. "If we're looking for a panel or opening in the floor, we should spread out."

"Agreed. At least we'll be walking back toward the light."

The next few minutes were spent in silence as they slowly moved back in the direction of the opening, their eyes focused on the floor.

Any echoes that might have followed Ayani's voice when she next spoke were swallowed by the floor. "You were talking about Avalon and Haven."

She was starting to wonder if Henry heard her, or if he was choosing not to answer, when he called back, "The Twin Pearls, my wife used to call them. The first two cities built off-world. It was more her doing than mine, but I saw it through."

"You were famous for a time. My mother told me she watched the advertisements as a girl. 'Life is brighter, life is lighter, life is better on the moon'."

"That I was, that I was," said Henry. "Though fame drained me of my other pursuits. I spent all my time traveling, but not for reasons I loved. Too many hands to shake, too many contracts to negotiate. But my wife...my wife loved it. I placed flowers on her headstone the same day they placed the final stone on Avalon's great Central Hall. I sold my shares and never went back."

"I've watched you," Ayani confided, not sure how he'd take it. "You're not like most others in the colony. Some have grown to find happiness here. Some do little more than they need to survive. For some it's duty. But this life, on Galena...it suits you."

In the growing light, she could see his smile. "I've

been happier here these past eleven years than anywhere else since I said farewell to my wife. Every self-proclaimed explorer should be so lucky to see what I've seen."

He stopped suddenly, staring down at the floor. "Here, now, what's this?"

Ayani walked over to him, pounding the sluggish muscle in her right thigh with her fist. A wide square had been cut into the floor. Both of them could easily stand next to each other inside its border.

"All of those crabs couldn't fit through here," she said, tapping the seam with the toe of her boot. "If it even opens in the first place."

"They could if they weren't in a hurry," Henry replied. "Or if there is more than one square." He pointed to a spot on the ground nearby and walked outside of the square in which they both stood. "Look."

Ayani could see the faint line of the square-shaped seam in the floor. She hadn't noticed them on the way in because they'd been looking everywhere but down.

As she knelt down on the square beneath her, the downward motion seemed to transfer into the floor, depressing the area between the bordering seam ever-so-slightly. The square cutout was no longer perfectly flush with the rest of the floor.

She jumped. When she landed, the square noticeably dipped a little lower in its setting.

"It's a pressure plate," she explained when Henry looked over at her, confused. "I bet there are hundreds of them in here."

"The hex crabs are not large creatures," said

Henry, "nor are they particularly heavy. They would have to be stacked floor to ceiling to create enough weight to move the plates as much as you just did."

"You said there were millions. Imagine them all here, crowding in through the entrance, boiling on top of each other when they reached the dead end. Eventually they *would* stack up that high."

Henry walked back to her. "This is absolutely remarkable, Ayani. If only we—"

He stepped onto her square and it lurched downward, then stopped when their hips were level with the floor.

"Get out," said Ayani. "Now!"

They scrambled over the ledge onto the floor — but the floor was moving, tilting up at an angle that would spill them back into the hole.

Across the entirety of the lowest level of the pyramid, countless square pits had been revealed. The floor around each had separated into four large triangular sections, like pieces of a pie around the square openings in the middle. The sections lifted from the back, creating ramps angled down toward the pits.

Ayani clawed at the rising ramp, but slipped slowly backward. Henry rolled onto his back and slid back into the pit, shouting. His shout became a scream and fell away quickly as a square pillar of white light shot up from the pit. It dissipated into shadow halfway to the high ceiling.

The vast room was filled with them. It had become a grid of square pillars marking hundreds of openings in the floor.

The ramps continued to rise.

Ayani lost what little grip she had and slid down into the pit, over the edge, and into nothingness, falling, falling, falling…

THE ENVOY

His ship was falling.

The radiation shielding he'd been so quick to shed exposed the secondary heat shield, which the *Celerity*'s computer had been screaming at him couldn't take any more of what it was designed to deflect since he plunged into Galena's upper atmosphere.

Jeff's last skip had plunked him into the twilight between sky and space. Through the tinted face shield of his helmet, he could see both at the same time: brilliant blue gradating gently to a star-studded infinite blackness. He lifted his sun visor to see it more clearly.

His cargo was still dragging behind him by a tow line, a ball of fire in its own right. Jeff lowered his sun visor and silenced the shrill alarms. His fingers were clumsy in the thick black gloves of his space suit. He held on to the sides of his quaking chair, listening to the rattle of loose ship parts and watching the flames lick up over the nose of his vessel through the cockpit window.

Then they were doused, and the cockpit fell silent. Jeff let out a breath he didn't know he'd been holding and plotted a course on the nav screen.

As the *Celerity* sluggishly responded to his

commands, it began running self-diagnostics. Jeff was skeptical those reports would come back in his favor. He settled back into his chair, enjoying the familiar sensation of gravity pulling down on his body, and watched the landscape of Galena unfold below.

From his altitude, rivers were thin ribbons wending into lakes and out again, crossing each other in a loose weave of glimmering water. Mountains were anthills, and the trees were ash gray toothpicks stuck in the smooth surface between the rivers.

It only looked smooth from up here, Jeff knew. Tiny silver-gray dots were actually boulders as large as his ship. They dotted the surface in multitudes. He had always found it impossible to walk in a straight line any meaningful distance without at least a dozen of them blocking his path.

The control panel beeped and a flood of information lit up the screen, including details of his journey through the Rip.

On the subject of distance... he thought as he scrolled through the data.

He'd traveled from the Ceres Rip to Galena's orbit in less than ten minutes, using only three skips. The last time it had taken him just under two months. His plotted trajectory showed as a dotted line on the control panel screen, yet there were three green blips along its length that indicated where his skips had landed him, and where he'd vanished again.

Not knowing the *how* of the process troubled him somewhat. Granted, neither did he know what he was doing — what kind of universal laws he might be breaking — every time he manipulated fold space, but that was less about transporting his person across vast distances than it was stacking closets to get more storage space.

Jeff conceded he would probably need a room full of people a lot smarter than he was to scratch the surface of that problem.

The rest of the ship reports were as he'd expected: the hull, minus its thicker outer shell, was nearly soaked through with cosmic radiation, and had taken a beating punching through the atmosphere. Two of the *Celerity's* three engines were operating at forty percent capacity. The third wasn't registering as being there at all. He'd lost cabin pressure in all but the cockpit during his dogfight with Marco Mazza and the *Spitfire*. Most unexpected was the disconnect between his ship and the detonator for the hypermass. The control interface for the timer was blank. It blinked a yellow error box at him every time he tried to call it up. Even the command to open the cube to expose the pill was grayed out.

That means manual trigger, he groaned internally. *Or firing on it from a distance. Wonderful.*

Jeff himself was no worse for wear, he just felt ten years older. His joints ached and his leg muscles constantly teetered on the edge of cramping.

A trend that's not likely to stop any time soon, he thought. He had escaped death on both sides of the Rip, but he was heading toward another kind of danger altogether.

He glanced at the brief line of text regarding the scan of his cargo. The shield cube around the pill-shaped hypermass object was undamaged except for some superficial scorching. Apparently it maintained more heat shielding than the *Celerity*.

Perhaps I should climb inside, Jeff mused. *Depending on how this landing goes, it could be much safer.*

He had pulled on his all-black multipurpose space suit after surviving his first skip after the Rip. The Constellation Mark VIII line was military-issue only, reserved for drop crews and covert operations.

Jeff had stolen one before he left Seattle.

He smiled fondly as he remembered the garish orange suit they'd given him for his first mission to Titan. That one wasn't overly large, but it seemed like a nylon balloon compared to the fitted woven-fiber of the newer Mark VIII.

The *Celerity* planed out as it neared the surface, its engine wash slicing down into the churning gray waters of the Casmin Sea. On a southward trajectory, the colossal triangular waves which never broke appeared as monstrous knives jutting up from the white-slashed surface. Seen from the east or west, they were pyramidal in shape, with broad faces of choppy water.

His ship avoided them easily, and soon the southern shore of the Casmin came into view. Jeff thought he saw the brief flash of a yellow tent erected on black sand, but it was gone just as quickly.

The engines slowed when he was in range of his target landing zone. Metal groaned inside the walls of his ship as the landing gear cranked out from the hull. A panel above his head burst downward, cracking against his helmet in a shower of sparks. Condensed air hissed from a ruptured line. Jeff ignored it all as the *Celerity* gently set down on the surface of Galena.

He had to force the failsafe hatch at the rear of the cockpit, which had slammed shut when the aft cabins lost pressure. It groaned in protest when he rolled it to the side. The ramp at the back of the small cargo hold was no different. It lowered haltingly at first, then lurched to a stop halfway to the ground. Jeff got on his stomach, turned backward at the lip, and dropped down to the wet soil. He peeled off his helmet, sucking in a deep breath of the warm, earthy summer air.

Celerity's hull hissed and popped. White ribbons of smoke rose lazily from countless sources. He patted the landing gear as he walked past, silently thanking the ship for holding together.

It had delivered him to the exit of the underground river which led down to the cathedral cavern. Water roared from the mouth of the cave to become a lazy flow that burbled over stones as it snaked off into the distance. Wet stone teeth lined the upper jaw of the cave. Beyond them was darkness.

Feeling parched, Jeff was tempted to kneel at the side of the river for a drink. All the flowing water on Galena's surface had proven to be pure enough to drink without filtering, but he didn't trust this river knowing what rested below, deeper under the ground.

The water from his suit supply that fed up to the drinking tube in his helmet had a sterile, unsatisfying quality. Carrying his helmet in one hand, he flicked the straw idly with the other as he followed the thick white snake of the tow cable to the shield cube, within which rested the hypermass.

Standing next to its charred and pockmarked

exterior, he had to crane his neck back to see the top. The cube was roughly the size of a two-story building.

He made a slow circuit of it, searching for a control panel. Three huge circles lined the bottom of each side, filling the space from edge to edge. Their color seemed to shift between dark gray and solid black. Jeff touched one with his gloved hand, and a viscous ripple crawled across its surface.

Some kind of inertial dampener, he thought. *No wonder it didn't drag me down as soon as I breached the atmosphere.*

The bones in his hand began to vibrate so close to the circle, and he stepped back abruptly.

It was evidence of yet more technology derived from the ring-shaped tori. The hull of a torus was so black it seemed to absorb all nearby light. An amorphous shadow slid slowly across its outer ring — the hatch. Jeff remembered approaching a torus near Titan...a very long time ago. When he got too close, it seized him, paralyzed him, and pulled him closer. His vision blurred as his skeleton shook from some subsonic vibration, his teeth clacked together so hard he thought they would shatter, and his heart...his heart pounded so quickly it seemed one long, painful beat.

The sliding shadow had rushed up to meet him, and then he was on the floor of an alien hallway inside the torus, gasping for breath while his lungs fought the heightened gravity.

Jeff gave the cube a wide berth as he searched for a way to open it. When he walked back around far enough to see the river cave, he paused, staring at it.

Two sets of eyes had been there watching him,

just inside the cave, only a moment before.

"Come out of there!" he shouted. Suddenly he wished Ayani was there with him. His helmet fell to the ground with a soft plop.

He'd had minimal interaction with only a few of the colonists, preferring to sleep aboard the *Celerity* while he learned more about the alien. That had contented Ayani for a while, but she became restless. To be honest, he never expected her to keep quiet as long as she had. Ayani was made to move, and he'd tethered her to a mission with hardly any motion. Jeff told her she didn't have to stay on the ship, that the only threat to him was in the cave. She made him promise he would never go in there without her by his side.

Jeff sighed when no one appeared at the mouth of the cave. He couldn't detonate the hypermass with someone inside, now could he?

He took a step toward the cave and his wristpad beeped. Jeff tapped the cracked screen. He didn't remember that happening. A text box flashed, flickered, and vanished. When he looked up, two teenagers were standing near the mouth of the cave.

Ayani would know them, he thought.

They looked like siblings, of similar height, with straw-colored hair and fair skin.

"You're the man in the ship," said the girl. She stood slightly in front of the boy, protective. He watched Jeff warily over her shoulder while she did the talking. "The Envoy."

Her left leg was a ruin of fresh stitches and dried blood. Much of the spiral wound that wrapped up her leg from ankle to the hem of her stained khaki shorts had been partially sealed without glue or stitches — most likely from the native healing moss, Jeff guessed. The moss hadn't finished the job, though. The girl wasn't bleeding freely, but her leg needed to be wrapped. Then Jeff noticed the stack of gauze in the boy's fist, and the roll of tape in his other.

"Jeff," he told them. If they were unnerved by his scar, eye patch, or glowing pupil, they didn't show it. He glanced back at the cube, uncertain. It had been so long since he'd spoken with anyone other than Gavin or Ayani. "Do you need help with your leg?"

"Are you with them?" asked the boy.

"Them, who?"

"The other ship. The man with the white hair."

"Vola," said the girl.

Jeff's face darkened. "Vola? You're sure?"

The girl nodded. "That's what Gavin said."

"What does he look like?"

"He's young, with skin white as powder and white hair."

The younger Vola, then, Jeff thought. For some reason, that fact disturbed him more than if the father had come himself. The Vola name was infamous within Earth's own solar system. Luciano Vola had built his successful shipping corporation from a single vessel.

Jeff met him only once, by chance. Luciano had been a member of a political entourage touring one of the orbital shipyards. The leaseholders of Shipyard 4 were hoping to lure prospective new clients, and it was said Luciano was looking to expand his fleet. In the end, he walked away from their offer, but not before Jeff had a chance to realize that the plump, clever elder Vola was no ordinary man. His blood ran as cold as the water beneath a glacier. There was no humanity behind his eyes, just a vast abyss that made Jeff shudder to think about. If the stories were true about what dark fates befell his captains who tried to unionize, and if the son took after the father even the slightest...

Was the family looking to expand their enterprise to Galena? he wondered. *Why would the greedy old man send his son? Does Kellan have something to do with this?*

"No," Jeff said. "I am not with him."

After a nervous pause, the girl nodded toward the boy. "That's Arthur. I'm Shurri."

Twins, Jeff thought. Hr tried to smile to show them he wasn't their enemy, but it died on his lips. Nothing was going the way he'd wanted. "Where is Vola?" he asked.

"At the colony. He's going to put everyone in chains. Gavin saw it in a vision."

The boy looked behind him, at the cave.

"Is he down there now?" Jeff asked.

The girl crossed her arms. "Are you going to help us beat them?"

Jeff blinked. "*Beat* them? With what?" He gestured behind him, at his sad excuse of a ship. "I barely escaped my last encounter with a friend of his."

"What's inside the box?" she asked.

"A weapon," he replied curtly, turning away.

I warned the boy to stay away, he thought angrily as he stalked back to the shield cube. *I told him not to go near it!*

"You have an hour to get him back to the surface," he called to the twins. "The three of you can either stay here when I unload my cargo or you can come with me back to the colony. I suggest the latter if you don't want to be vaporized."

"We can't go back!" the girl shouted. The effort made her sway, and she put a careful hand on her wounded leg. "We can't," she added weakly, exhaustion evident in her voice. "He'll capture us, too. You have to...you have to help us."

"I can't," he said quietly. "Do you know what's beneath us, under the river? Have you seen it?"

Shurri shook her head.

"It must be destroyed."

"*Then* will you help us?"

As Envoy to The Weaver, Jeff was mandated to avoid conflicts which might embroil him in politics or wars unrelated to his defined purpose. As a human, Jeff said, "I can drop you near the colony. That's all I can promise." *For now,* he added silently.

The girl wasn't satisfied with his answer. Jeff wouldn't have been, either. She turned away and sat on the ground with her back to Jeff, and crossed her arms while Arthur gently pressed gauze into her wound.

"One hour," Jeff reminded them.

She flashed a rude gesture over her shoulder, and Jeff sighed.

He and Kate never had kids, and the ones he'd met so far on Galena did little to make him regret it.

Gavin wasn't so bad, he supposed. Stubborn, but bold enough to be a leader if he could learn to temper his opinions with the wisdom of others. Jeff continued his inspection of the shield cube, wondering about the boy's father.

They'd briefly spoken on one of Jeff's few visits to the colony. Most of those had been undertaken as cover so that Jeff might talk with Kellan, to press him about why he still hadn't sent the promised hypermass to Jeff.

Gavin took after his father, Merritt. They both had the same dark hair and brooding features — but there was a light in Gavin's eyes that had gone out in Merritt's. Or perhaps it had merely been dulled by years of duty.

The ever-dimming light of youth, Jeff thought. That's what it was.

Merritt was polite enough, though curt. He and Jeff had shared only a few words before he excused himself to return to his farm.

Would he resist Vola? Jeff wondered. *Could he?*

He pushed the thoughts from his mind when he finally found a small black panel hiding in a scorch mark on the outside of the shield cube. The interface was so heat-blasted it didn't respond to his touch.

Jeff tapped the screen of his wristpad, hoping he could link the two systems and control it from his own device. He saw a flashing red exclamation mark at the bottom of the screen and tapped the icon.

It was Ayani's homing beacon.

It's been sending for hours, he realized, his stomach dropping. He remembered the blip on the small wristpad screen right after he landed. The *Celerity* was trying to relay the signal even then, but there must have been a disconnect.

He looked up at the shield cube, then back at the

twins, and the river cave behind them.

Jeff scooped up his helmet and ran back to the *Celerity*, hopping over the tow cable as it snaked over the wet soil.

"Where are you going?!" Shurri hollered after him.

Jeff climbed up the nearest landing gear truss and opened a panel in the hull. He twisted a handle to manually decouple the tow cable. It popped free of the hull and slapped onto the ground.

"Get him out of there!" Jeff yelled over his shoulder. He tossed his helmet onto the half-open ramp and jumped to grab the lip. He pulled himself up onto his stomach and swung his legs over the edge. The twins were standing again. Shurri's leg was fully bandaged. "And don't touch anything!" he added before sliding down the ramp, into his ship.

Can I skip down here, so close to the surface? Jeff wondered after he collected his helmet and stumbled in the dark toward the cockpit. *What if there's a mountain in the way? Would I pass through it or stop inside it?*

That grisly image gave him pause.

What if there had been a physical object between the two spots he skipped through? Did he pass through that space in a straight line, or did he disappear from the origin and pop out at his destination? The planet had a curvature. Could he follow that in one long skip, or would he have to do multiple little skips so he didn't end up in the lower atmosphere or below the surface?

The tangle of thoughts made him want to bang his head against the wall. He put on his helmet and slid the chin lock into place just in case the urge became too overpowering.

The controls responded blessedly fast after he was strapped into the pilot seat. He told the nav computer to follow Ayani's beacon. It calculated his arrival time at max atmospheric velocity and said it could get him there in less than half an hour.

I'll skip over the ocean, Jeff decided. *Small skips, well above the water.*

The prospect of popping out kilometers below the ocean's surface made him uneasy, but not nearly as much as the continuous flashing of Ayani's homing beacon from his wristpad.

I've never died underwater before, he thought wryly.

Jeff's "deaths" were what he called situations he'd survived that would have killed someone else. He was as susceptible as anyone to a painful physical demise. If the shield cube rolled over atop him, for example, he'd be flat as a pancake.

Yet he had survived hours of open exposure in space, a decidedly political situation where a rival had vented all the oxygen from his stateroom on Sunrise Station, and more than four-hundred years of daily human life.

What's one more for the list? he thought with a resigned grin.

A few moments later, the rattling bulk of the *Celerity* was skimming low over the surface, heading for the Equatorial Ocean — and the continent which lay beyond.

MERRITT

The sun was setting when they came for him.

He coughed against the metal floor of the utility shed, sending a cloud of dancing dust particles into the warm yellow light that sliced through a crack in the wall. Almost every piece of the shed had been salvaged from wreckage of the *Halcyon*. Merritt helped bolt it together.

That means I'm back on Lysette's farm, he thought groggily. The colonists had built as many sheds as they could between farm plots, using scraps too small for their houses. Lysette's was the only one with a metal floor. The rest were packed dirt.

He couldn't recall how he got to the shed. The last thing he remembered was running along the base of the hill, a half-dozen soldiers with big rifles in pursuit. He dared not risk so much as a glance up at the hospital to see if Gavin made it inside, for fear Vola would realize his plan.

Strange how few fifty-one people seem when they're all lined up, he recalled with sadness, thinking of his fellow colonists standing in bedraggled rows on the hill. Sadness gave way to anger when he remembered the terrified looks on their faces as he ran to distract the guards — and yet his anger hadn't stopped him from noticing several missing faces in the crowd. *Safe and hiding,* he hoped with great yearning for it to be true. *Hiding or already gone.* He had glimpsed neither Skip nor Lysette, but Ahmed was in the back, staring forlornly at the ground. Perhaps Vola had put the other two in the hospital to recover.

Blue light had crackled through the air and fire licked up his back as he ran near the hill, etching the faces of his fellow colonists in his mind — then came darkness.

How long have I been in here? he wondered.

When he'd awoken on the floor of the shed, his back felt like it was covered with acid. He could smell his own burnt flesh. Merritt had tried to stand. A fresh wash of pain swept over him, and he passed out.

The next time he woke up, he didn't move. He simply stared at the fading sunlight through the crack in the wall — stared until he coughed, and a black boot kicked in the door.

Two men each grabbed an arm and hauled him into the sunlight. Merritt blinked and his head swooned from the sudden movement. He saw sky, then soil, then a blur of soyflower stalks before he shut his eyes to keep from being sick.

The men walked out of sync, and the burnt skin on Merritt's back seemed ready to split as he was pulled in opposing directions.

Thankfully, it was not a long journey. They dumped him on the soft ground, face-down. He groaned and rolled onto his back, caking his wound with fresh soil. The one on his chest was already clogged with dried dirt.

"You put me in an uncomfortable position,"

Alexander Vola said from somewhere nearby.

Merritt opened his eyes and slowly sat up. He was on the edge of the scorched patch of Lysette's farm. The air smelled of burnt plants and exhaust. He turned to find himself staring at a white table. Vola sat behind it in a high-backed red chair, a guard standing behind each shoulder. Behind them, Vola's ship pointed majestically toward the sky, as if ready to take flight at any moment.

The young captain still wore the deep red jacket, though he had swapped out his plain undergarb for black combat fatigues.

With a grunt, Merritt got to his hands and knees. He put a dirty hand on Vola's table, smearing its pristine white surface as he used it to help him stand.

Vola stared at the broad smear of brown, his jaw muscles working. Then his pale blue eyes drifted up to meet Merritt's.

"A *very* uncomfortable position," he emphasized.

"You don't look so uncomfortable," Merritt said weakly, swaying on his feet. He tried to inject more strength into his words, but none came.

Vola crossed his legs and looked away, squinting in the late afternoon light. His white hair moved in a warm breeze, and his high cheekbones and sallow cheeks emphasized a lupine quality that unnerved Merritt on a primal level. Vola smiled as fast as a single clap — there and gone again — the thin skin of his face pulling back to reveal a little too much of his mouth.

He's a wolf, thought Merritt.

"There are precious few of you as it stands," said Vola. "If you'd been older or weaker, I'd have strung you up in the town square as an example. I trust that little show between you and my compatriots was enough to keep your neighbors in line."

Merritt rapped a knuckle slowly on the table, staring at it as he nodded. "You really put a table in a field?"

"The closest thing you savages have to a proper town hall is your latrine tent."

"Did you try the one near the western hill?" Merritt asked innocently. "It doesn't get used as much."

Vola smiled again, but this time it stuck on his face. The corners of his mouth kept moving, wrinkling the white skin of his cheeks. Then it snapped away and he stood brusquely, clasping his hands behind his back. The material of his jacket creaked when he moved, leaving Merritt to wonder if it was real leather.

"Mr. Alder," he said, looking across the field at nothing in particular. "Is this going to be a productive meeting?"

At the question, his guards stood up a little straighter. Merritt took the meaning clear enough. He nodded.

"Excellent," Vola continued. He ran a white finger along the edge of the table. "This piece of furniture is a symbol of what my father intends to bring to this colony."

We already have tables, Merritt wanted to say, but he bit his tongue. A slight tremor had started in his left leg, and the muscles in his back threatened to spasm. He didn't want Vola to see him collapse again — nor did he want the guards to help him back to the ground because of his smart mouth.

"Civilization," Vola proclaimed, knocking on the table before walking slowly away from it. He raised his arms to indicate imaginary structures on the horizon. "My father sees *buildings*. 'Alexander, there will be *buildings*', he said to me. And I said, 'Yes, father', because that's what I always say. Do you know what you need between buildings, Mr. Alder?"

Merritt had heard enough. "What did you do with my people?" he asked.

"Roads!" Vola shouted, laughing. "You need *roads*. You need people to build them. *That's* what I'm doing with your neighbors, you *farmer*."

When he finally turned back to look at Merritt, his pale eyes burned with madness. The fire snuffed out when Vola took a deep breath and closed his eyes. When he opened them again, he was calm as could be.

"Yet those are my father's plans. Tell me, where is the one they call The Envoy?"

The question caught Merritt completely off guard. He took a moment to regain his composure.

"If I tell you, will you leave us in peace."

"You could find out what happens if you *don't* tell me."

"He's gone. Took his ship and flew off. I don't know where."

"Earth," Vola told him. "He just stole a bomb from a secure orbital facility. I could use a man like that."

"You...you already knew he was gone?"

"I wanted to see if you'd lie to me. I was curious since I can't use your son as leverage to keep you honest."

"My son?" Merritt stupidly repeated, feeling lost.

Gavin is safe, he thought, careful to hide his relief. *He's free.*

Vola looked up at the sky, as if to beg it for help dealing with such a lackwit. "I think you farmers truly are only meant for physical labor. My father's roads should be paved in no time at all. Your son, Gavin," he continued, directing his condescension on Merritt. "The one who's been sneaking off to that cave."

"Cave?"

Vola held up a warning finger and jabbed it toward Merritt. "Now you *are* making me angry. Answer me clearly or I'll put your people to work in heavy chains instead of electric collars. How long do you think they'd last?"

"I don't know about any cave," Merritt said truthfully. The setting sun beat against his brow. Beads of sweat streamed down his forehead and into his eyes. He wiped it away with dirty wrists.

Vola seemed to consider his answer a long moment. "You might be lying."

"I'm not. Tell me what you want with me so I can pass out somewhere more comfortable. My back hurts."

"Don't run from me next time," Vola shot back. He sighed and rubbed his temples as he walked slowly back to his table. "You seem like a man who's used to being listened to," he said calmly. "So is my father. It's easy enough to recognize when you're beaten over the head with it from an early age. You don't run a shipping empire without absolute obedience from everyone under your heel. So I will tell you *exactly* what I want from you." Vola sat back down in his chair and spread his hands out on the table. "I want you to keep your people in line while they build my father's roads, and I want the location of your son's cave."

"We're to be your slaves?"

"I was wondering when we'd get to that. You probably thought your crop-debt was forgotten when your ship crashed."

Merritt shifted uncomfortably on his feet, wishing this farce would end.

"You and your fellow dirt-grubbers owe a substantial chunk of twenty-two harvests to the farming initiative that made it possible to come here in the first place. That farming initiative is a trust owned by a corporation my father bought in solvency. He owns your debt, and the debt of everyone else with a plot of land on Galena."

"The debt means nothing now," Merritt protested. "We have food stores, but only going back three harvests. It doesn't keep that long."

"That's why you'll be working off your debt instead."

Heat rushed to Merritt's cheeks as anger threatened to cloud his mind. "Why didn't you come here *peacefully?*" he spat. "Why didn't you *ask?*"

He expected more of a reaction from Vola. Instead, the young man studied his face as if he were observing some curious animal. Then he *tsk*ed like he was scolding a child. "Mr. Alder. You've been on your own here for eleven years. Would you have me believe you'd stop digging in your gardens and start digging my father's roads simply because I asked you to?"

Merritt chewed his lip, struggling for any kind of

defense. "This is illegal. They'll send ships after you when they realize what you've done."

"I don't doubt it," Vola replied easily. "But they'll have a hard time getting past the sentries I left at both Rips. I will make this as plain as possible. You will build my father's roads. You will not disobey. If your people prove to be exemplary workers, they might be allowed to continue on to the next phase of development. My father owns you now, Mr. Alder. You and everyone else here. As to the legality..." He shrugged. "I see no law enforcement here. I see no judges, no courtrooms, no prisons. Might makes right, the way it's always been. I have the weapons. And if you think your friends in the shuttle can save you, think again. My drones shot it down halfway across the world."

He grinned when he saw the distressed look on Merritt's face.

"You weren't going to tell me, were you? Trying to keep it a secret?" Vola threw back his head and laughed, a sharp, inhuman sound.

Ayani, Merritt thought sadly. *Henry. No...*

The loss was a pain he couldn't bear. His knees buckled and he sank to the ground. The sun had just begun to dip below the horizon. He stared at it with tears in his eyes.

Vola stood, looking down on Merritt with contempt. "Get some rest, Mr. Alder. Tomorrow you and your farmers start digging." He turned toward his ship, then paused and looked back. "Look at me," he said quietly. Merritt did. "If anyone goes missing, if anyone tries to escape...my father's roads will be paved with bones. Do you understand?"

Vola didn't wait for an answer. He swept past his guards and up the ramp to his ship.

Merritt collapsed on his stomach in the soil, his entire body burning in pain. The guards moved toward him, but he didn't care what they did or where they took him. Gavin was safe. That was the only thing that mattered.

Gavin was safe.

GAVIN

A black vein crawled through the rocky tunnel wall, gently illuminated by a distant purple glow. His fingers traced it lightly as he walked, following the dawning light like a moth follows a flame. Like a moth, Gavin didn't know if the light ahead was a fire waiting to burn him, or a harmless lamp to help guide his flight.

From the entrance of the underground river at the surface, he had crawled down the boulder-strewn remains of an ancient cave-in, following a familiar path deeper into the dark.

His muscles were shaking from having carried Shurri on his back, and the descent wasted too much time. Gavin had to pause frequently until his thighs stopped cramping. The footing in the downward passage was treacherous; the stones wet and slippery.

That passage opened onto the waterfall cavern, where Gavin had once arrived in a much less ceremonious fashion. Water from an offshoot of the underground river cascaded into an icy black pool, where he had found himself sputtering and gasping for breath three years ago, upon his accidental discovery of this place.

Gavin studied the black vein as he slowly walked

the long, curving tunnel connecting the waterfall cavern to the next. It hadn't been there last time he visited...six months ago, or was it longer? He couldn't put a date to it. In the beginning, when he'd first found what lay waiting in the next cavern, he hadn't been able to keep away. Gavin was used to the unusual sights, sounds, plants, and animals of Galena, but there was nothing like this anywhere else in the universe, he was sure.

Another black vein scarred the opposite wall. When Gavin touched it, his fingers came back sticky. He sniffed it and made a face. It smelled sharply of burnt plastic and rotten soil.

Is this why the creatures have been acting so strangely? he wondered as he walked toward the blooming purple light at the end of the tunnel. *Is there some poison in the canopy?*

He rubbed his fingertips against his shirt nervously, trying to scrape off the foul odor.

The squid growing bold enough to crawl into the shallows to attack him and Shurri was one thing, but it was turning out not to be an isolated incident. The wriggling centipede-like creatures he used for fish bait had disappeared, and he had been especially disturbed to learn that the pit he and his friends were to drop into during their escape from the colony led into a worm tunnel. The worms were seldom seen or heard unless you were closer to the mountains, where they were thought to make their nests. What would cause it to burrow directly beneath a farm?

That's not to say Gavin wasn't ungrateful for a path away from Vola and his crew. It had been a hassle to get Shurri past the bulk of a slain worm that almost completely blocked their path, but beyond that, they'd neither seen nor heard a hint of another one of the ravenous blind beasts.

He'd had to pass off Shurri to Arthur after he stumbled to the ground a second time. Her brother had accepted her weight on his back without complaint, his eyes focused on the tunnel ahead, while Gavin massaged his own aching shoulders and thighs. The small palm-light clipped to the shoulder of his coverall swung its beam from side to side with each step.

Of the two twins, Arthur had grown the most over the past several years, Gavin reflected. His chest was filling out and his face had become leaner. He'd always had boyish features, but Galena had been sharpening them this past year, chipping away the soft edges. After the crash, he'd been inseparable from his mother. At seven years of age, who wouldn't be?

Me and Shurri, thought Gavin.

Their independence had been a stark contrast to young Arthur's, who often hid behind his mother's legs whenever someone addressed him. Like a slow-blooming flower, he had opened over the course of years. He was still quiet amongst the other colonists, but he had no reservations when it was just the three of them.

Gavin had been watching Shurri bounce lightly on her brother's back for several moments as they marched through the worm tunnels, searching for a path back to the surface, when Arthur said, "We'll make them leave. They have our mom."

And my father, thought Gavin.

He nodded and signed his promise. *We'll make them leave.*

Shurri had awoken then — just a soft moan and a flutter of eyelids. Gavin helped Arthur lower her to the hard floor. His hand brushed her wounded leg and a chunk of dried-out healing moss crumbled. He gently picked at the rest until it had all flaked away.

His heart ached when he saw the wound.

The top and bottom of the spiral laceration had been sealed with needle and thread — the parts where there wasn't enough healing moss to cover. The widest part of the cut, from halfway up her calf to where the wound disappeared beneath the hem of her shorts, was as wide as his hand, and a fleshy, raw pink that glistened in the beam from Arthur's palm-light.

The moss hadn't been large enough to fully seal the wound before it died. She was no longer bleeding, but it still looked as if a strip of her skin had been peeled away.

Gavin wrapped it gingerly with gauze, but it instantly soaked through with clear fluid oozing from the wound.

We need to change it often, he signed to Arthur.

"We don't have much gauze."

We'll find more.

She recognized him and smiled, then fell back into unconsciousness.

He carried Shurri the rest of the way after that, up a natural opening in the tunnel wall that led them to the edge of a field of sharp, rocky pillars. The rock bats were still sleeping, night still hours away, or else the three of them would have faced a different kind of challenge.

Gavin didn't like leaving them at the entrance to the river cave, but he couldn't have carried Shurri down the tumbled remains of the cave-in. Arthur had quickly agreed to keep her company on the surface, and to redress her wound. He had never liked Gavin's stories about what lay beyond the narrow tunnel, and he was in no hurry to see it for himself.

As Gavin stepped out of the tunnel and into the vaulted cathedral cavern, he remembered why.

It was vast space of many levels — natural platforms in the rock, almost like performance stages. Hanging stalactites and rising stalagmites surrounded most of them like teeth, their points meeting in the middle, creating large gaps in each enclosing wall. All of this was illuminated by purple crystals embedded in every rocky surface. The closest to the middle of the cavern were cracked. They were the ones spilling light onto the creature.

It hung suspended by long black tendrils which were anchored to the floor, nearby rock pillars, and the shadowy ceiling far above. The bulk of its mass, lost to sight as it rose toward the faraway ceiling, was a translucent black sac webbed in a muscular net of the same glistening black substance as the tendrils. Purple light from behind the creature revealed a wavy mass of thin filaments inside the liquid-filled sac, swaying languidly side to side in time with a loud, steady throbbing, like an amplified heartbeat.

A mound of steaming black tissue was heaped beneath the suspended creature. The cloying reek of rot it sloughed into the cathedral cavern tightened Gavin's throat and stung his eyes. Accompanying the stench was a dull vibration at the back of his neck, near the base of his skull. Each step closer to the creature intensified the vibration, until the edges of its shapeless mass blurred. His ears rang without sound, a high-pitched *skree* thin as a needle.

Gavin had experienced the sensations before, but this time it was worse. Something was different.

How long has it been here? Gavin wondered for the hundredth time as he approached, staring up at its looming bulk. *Decades? Eons?*

The creature never told him, though he'd asked. It had only ever answered his one question — his one wish to see the future of the colony. Eventually, he stopped asking. Then he stopped visiting the cavern altogether.

He stood below the central platform, above which hung the creature. Other platforms rose like broad arena steps all around him. Black veins crawled through many of them. Gavin looked down at his boots. He stood near one that originated from the stinking black mound of tissue beneath the creature. A dozen more corrupted veins thick as his arm etched jagged pathways from the platform and down across the ground, thinning as they burrowed through surface stone in every direction. One crawled up the wall of the narrow tunnel leading back to the waterfall cavern.

Are you sick? Gavin signed.

The cluster of waving filaments inside its translucent sac fluttered rapidly, then resumed their gentle back-and-forth motion.

His eyes were drawn to a brightly-lit portion of the wall. Canopy branches as supple as soft roots slithered across a crumbling stone, covering an exposed section of the cavern. As soon as they emerged from the soil, their thin skins peeled back, scorching and turning black as if burned. Then they withered and snapped, falling in pieces to the floor. Immediately after, fresh branches snaked out from the soil to reform the shield.

For that is what kept the creature here, in this cavern.

Its prison, Gavin thought.

Jeff had told him as much. The branch shield surrounded the entire cavern, and it held some alien power over the creature, forcing it into dormancy.

Yet part of it was still awake, or else Gavin wouldn't be able to communicate with it — to ask it for help once again.

I could go to Jeff for help, thought Gavin, *if he hadn't left for Earth.*

They'd only spoken a handful of times over the past three years. Jeff stayed on his ship, and didn't want visitors. He knew Ayani a little better, since she'd been staying at the colony for a while, but she was hardly ever there. She liked to help the rangers when they went foraging, or with Henry on his mapping expeditions.

They were gone now, too, though not so far as Earth. Henry told Gavin's father he wanted to finally scout the other continent, having spent all his time poking around this one and in its surrounding riverlands. He seemed especially excited about a set of maps over which he continuously pored, often giggling to himself when he'd forgotten he wasn't alone.

Since he and Ayani had taken the shuttle, Gavin could think of no other way to rescue his father and the other colonists.

He stepped onto the central platform of the cathedral cavern and placed his hands against the warm, prickly translucent skin of the alien creature — and he asked for help.

Gavin fell *into* the creature without resistance, as if he'd put all his weight against a holograph. He spilled forward, his head plunging, his feet leaving solid ground...

...and he landed flat on his back against nothing in a great empty void. He stuck there like a fly in a spiderweb, only there was no web.

The cathedral cavern and all inside it, including himself, had disappeared. He looked down at his body but saw nothing. His hands waved, or at least he thought they did, but he couldn't see them.

In the far distance, colors swirled to life. Red, blue, and yellow mists danced against each other, but did not mix.

The colors approached, growing visibly larger, melting around each other like oils. They flattened into a two-dimensional plane and rapidly expanded in every direction, giving the void a brilliant floor of blue, red, and yellow, now woven together like strands of light.

Gavin felt as if he were soaring above the floor, moving in a definite direction (though he couldn't say which). The woven light beneath shined up at him warmly. He was comfortable here, wherever *here* was.

A city appeared on the ever-stretching horizon.

Monolithic towers and domed arenas grew larger as Gavin soared. A long tunnel extended from one of the buildings, made a short run at an upward angle, then flattened out to terminate into what Gavin knew to be the Casmin Sea.

How do I know that?

Knowledge he'd never attained settled on his mind like a snowfall, illuminating possibilities flake by flake, slowly revealing a more complete picture of whatever the cathedral creature intended him to see.

Gavin's formless consciousness passed above the city. Looking down, he realized the tunnels were built in a ring, and nothing was between them. Strange light undulated across that central void, dancing like...

Sunlight through water from above, he realized.

This city was beneath the ocean.

And he'd been wrong about the space between buildings. It seemed like an empty expanse of sand on the ocean floor, but then he felt something else down there...something deeper. Buried.

Thick black snaking branches, slick with an oily sludge, reached down into the sand. They had grown all the way from the shore — all the way from the canopy.

Gavin already knew where they'd started that long journey underground. They grew from atop the base of the central platform in the cathedral platform, from the mound of retched substance piled beneath the creature.

In that place, drifting above the recreation of the underwater city as tri-colored strands pulsed brightly beneath it, his mind was not allowed to consider any other possibility than that the branches pointed the way to his salvation.

Gavin's plea for help awaited him beneath the sand. He could see that with absolute clarity, and the uncomplicated thought of it filled him with hope.

AYANI

I'm going to splat like a bug, she thought as she fell.

Her surprised scream had died in her throat seconds ago, long after she expected to hit bottom. *Now it's my turn.*

Henry had gone first, slipping into the square pit after the floor around them lifted to form a funnel. Ayani had managed to hang on to the angling stone floor a few short moments longer, but she soon followed after him, sliding into the open pit and falling...falling...

She could see only light as she fell — blinding, white-yellow light that filled the space through which she tumbled.

The air was dry and sterile, lacking the natural smells of the surface world. When the first organic whiff of mineral water registered in her mind, she tucked herself into a hasty dive and plunged into warm water, slicing into it like a knife.

The light was in the water, too, glowing from all around. Looking down past her kicking feet as she swam for the surface, she could see no bottom, only a uniform illumination far below.

Ayani broke the surface gasping for air. She wiped her hair back from her face and shouted,

"Henry!" as she tread water.

She'd landed in a wide, square pool — one of a hundred that covered the floor of the palatial room beneath the bottom floor of the pyramid above. Light that seemed to come from everywhere at once assaulted her eyes, making her squint. She blinked, and her vision slowly acclimated. Details materialized in the harsh glare.

Henry lay on his back on a narrow wall between pools, water still dripping from his coverall. One arm was draped over his eyes, shielding them from the light. He smiled weakly and raised his other trembling hand in greeting. Ayani swam to him with sure, powerful strokes, and pulled herself up out of the water to sit beside him. The water left a thin film on her skin. She rubbed her fingertips and sniffed them. They smelled of the potent mineral water she drank on the surface, but the odor was less a bouquet of elements than a distillation of several.

"Iron," Henry told her. "Magnesium as well, I believe, and maybe copper."

"A drinking reservoir?" she asked.

"A cleaning tank. The crabs fall down into these pools." He sat up with a groan and gestured at them all, rows and rows of them stretching from wall to distant wall. "A disinfectant, perhaps, for whatever microbes they pick up on the surface."

Ayani laughed. It came out of nowhere, bursting forth to echo into the vast hall. Henry chuckled.

"It's a bathhouse for hex crabs," she said once her laughter subsided. She wiped a tear from her cheek, still grinning. "Then what happens?"

"Maybe they sink to the bottom," he replied.

"Maybe they dissolve."

"Maybe something eats them," Ayani said warily, leaning over the edge of the pool to look into its illuminated depths.

She squinted upward. The ceiling was a grid of black squares, barely visible in the painful glare, through one of which she and Henry had fallen.

"There's a door," he told her, pointing.

They had landed in a pool near the middle of the room. The wall Henry pointed to was so far away that the door seemed no larger than a mouse hole. It shimmered in the overpowering light like a desert mirage.

She helped him up, his legs shaking, and made sure he was steady before leading the way across the grid of walkways that separated the pools. It hurt her eyes to look anywhere else for long besides the dark walkway immediately in front of her.

"This level of...of zoological engineering," said Henry as they navigated the grid. "It makes me wonder what else on this planet has been controlled with such precision."

"You think the crabs aren't native?"

"They might be, or not. They may have been created down here to act as some kind of cleaning crew for the surface. The way their legs oxygenate the soil during their migration, stirring the nutrients for the underground canopy...it reminds me of a sucker fish cleaning the inside of an aquarium. The sucker fish sustains itself on the scum that would otherwise choke out the other inhabitants."

Ayani squinted up at the ceiling again, then back down at the impressive number of pools that glowed with a more tempered light than the omnipresent glare that filled the chamber.

"Who made *this* aquarium?" she asked.

"Whoever made the underwater city, I presume."

She stopped and turned back. "Underwater *what?*"

He looked stricken. "Oh my. Did Jeff not tell you?"

Her eyes narrowed, but not because of the light. "What city?"

"Let's continue, and I'll tell you," he promised gently. "My eyes can't take much more of this glare."

They walked in silence a few moments, Ayani in the lead, before Henry continued.

"The oceans of this planet are treacherous, as you know," he began. "The unbreaking waves make sailing all but impossible, even if we had boats, and the leviathans of the ocean consume anything unfortunate enough to find itself in their territory, above or below the surface. But the lakes, rivers, and smaller seas like the Casmin are seemingly devoid of larger life. Perfect for exploring, if one could hold their breath longer than a few minutes. Several years ago, the colonists found a cache of space suits in the wreckage of their ship. Niku Tedani donned one of the suits and began exploring the shores of the Casmin Sea. Do you know him?"

"The microbiologist," she answered. He seemed an amiable man, quick to laughter, though she had spoken with him only a few times. Her wandering nature usually took her far from the colony, as did his.

"He found a tunnel...a rather unnatural tunnel...leading east, toward the Equatorial Ocean," said Henry.

Ayani frowned. "It's not a long walk between those two shores."

"Nor is it a long swim in the connecting tunnel," Henry agreed. "Several colonists discovered that the tunnel led to an underwater city, built by someone or something of which they found no trace."

"Why didn't I know about this?"

"Only a few of us do. It was decided to keep it that way because there are dangers, perhaps more than on the surface. The first team lost someone down there, and two others died when I last visited over a year ago. It is a place of many secrets, and I fear most of them are deadly to us fragile humans. Niku is the only one who still visits the city. I believe he's there now, unless he's returned to the colony. He sometimes goes for a week at a time."

"What's it like?" Ayani asked.

Henry considered a moment before answering. "Cold and hard, but magnificent. You can feel the water above you like a great pressure, wanting to get in, but it can't. The passageways have invisible walls, so it seems as if the water forming a tube around you could crash in at any moment. It is a true wonder." His voice shook slightly when he added, "Though the memory is tainted by what happened to my companions."

"Has Jeff been down to the city?"

"Not to my knowledge. We spoke of it sometimes, when I visited the Celerity. His questions were always focused on the creature in the cathedral cavern, as he calls it. He wanted to know if there could be any connection between the creature and those who built the city."

Ayani felt somewhat hurt that Jeff had kept so much from her. She had no doubt that, next time she saw him and asked, he would conjure up some excuse why the city didn't matter because it had nothing to do with the cathedral creature — that pulsing mass of tissue that had so consumed his thoughts ever since they'd arrived on Galena.

Without realizing it, she and Henry had arrived in front of the door.

It stood twice her height, and was more slender than a standard human door. There was no physical barrier blocking their path through it, yet the black rectangle that filled the space between the door's edges seemed deeper than the void of starless space — an impossibility considering the amount of light that should have been pouring into it from behind Ayani.

Her hand disappeared up to her wrist when she hesitantly reached out to touch the shadow. She withdrew it and studied her fingers.

"The water film is gone," she told Henry. Her hand felt dry and clean, while the rest of her body was still damp and sticky from the layer of film that stubbornly clung to her skin and clothing.

She looked at Henry, a question in her eyes, and he shrugged.

A gentle pulling sensation helped her through the door when she stepped over the threshold. It wasn't forceful — more of a bump as she moved between rooms of differing air pressures.

The large room into which she emerged was blissfully dim. Her eyes felt instantly soothed after the constant, glaring assault from the room of square pools.

Henry emerged from the door shadow a moment later, staring down at his chest. He patted his dry coverall and inspected his hands with a grin on his face.

"Remarkable," he said simply.

"Wait till you see this," said Ayani.

He looked up, and his breath caught in his throat.

A wall of water twenty meters high rose before them, touching the tall ceiling. Its edges stretched to the far walls of the room. It formed a wide rectangle as big as a skyscraper turned on its side, its surface a blanket of smooth, lapping ripples.

Faint blue-green light filled the deepness beyond the wall, casting a pale glow onto the astonished faces of Henry and Ayani.

She walked forward slowly, across the black polished floor. The floor's edge was beyond the wall of water. It extended a few meters beyond it, where it met the dark sand of the ocean floor. She could just barely see the water's surface high above, wind-streaked and glimmering in the orange light of the setting sun.

"The pyramid is nowhere near the ocean," Henry murmured as he stood beside her, staring up at the wall of water. Then he turned to look back over his shoulder. The other walls were the same polished black material as the floor. "That door..."

"Not just a door," said Ayani. She gestured to the water in front of her. Henry only frowned, confused, but she smiled. "And I thought you were a map maker."

She took another step closer to the water, her

face dancing with iridescent blue-green light, and traced her finger around the outline of a symbol that formed a shallow depression in its surface.

Henry gasped when he saw it.

"It's Galena."

The entire surface of the planet was represented upon the wall of water, as if someone had drawn it with their finger, stretched out in a wide oval. Continents and riverlands were bordered by wavering lines that moved along with the surface ripples, yet held their shape. It was not a map meant for tiny details, but instead offered a broad impression of the planet.

Two points on the map glimmered more brightly that the rest. They were both shaped like small doors the size of Ayani's hand. One floated on the eastern shore of the Equatorial Ocean. The other wavered like a broken reflection farther east, inland.

The little doors dissolved into the surrounding water. Henry and Ayani looked at each other.

A single step had taken them a third of the way across the continent, from the pyramid to the eastern shore of the Equatorial Ocean.

"This is why I explore," said Henry, his voice thick with emotion. "No human has ever seen this, Ayani. We are the first."

She was allowed a few moments to experience a fraction of what he must have been feeling before her mind, independent of her wishes, veered her back toward the reality of their situation. Ayani left Henry gazing at the water map to walk the room's perimeter.

At first glance, she'd seen nothing to indicate they

were in anything more than an observation hall. The walls and floor were seamless black, and the ceiling was far out of reach. Pale greenish light rippled across its smooth surface, revealing no openings.

The only way in or out was the door through which they'd passed. Returning the same way would only send them back to the pyramid.

"What's this now?" Henry said behind her while she was staring into the shadow of the door.

She joined him at the water map, but its rippling surface had changed. The map was gone. Three large circles had taken its place. A different grouping of symbols shimmered with their own light in the middle of each, made up of arcing lines with sharp points, some of which glowed brighter than the others.

"This one looks kind of like a ship," Ayani said, nodding toward the cluster of symbols in the circle on the left. The sharp lines comprising the largest symbol in its group swooped out to form something not entirely unlike wings. If she squinted at the symbols in the middle, she could force herself to see a hex crab. The symbols on the right made no sense at all.

She touched a fingertip to the symbols on the left. They flashed with light, then the water smoothed over, swallowing all three circles and the glyphs within.

The water surface tensed like a sheet snapped taut, becoming as smooth as a piece of glass. Henry and Ayani both took a step back. She could see across the ocean floor as clearly as if she were in the water with a diver's mask.

Dark holes pockmarked the sandy expanse. Above the ocean floor, far in the distance, a shape emerged from the gloom.

Ayani took another step back, pulling Henry by the sleeve with her. He grabbed her arm for support and allowed himself to be guided.

The shape swelled in size shockingly fast, rushing over the ocean floor — yet it didn't disturb the sand below.

Ayani had pulled Henry half-stumbling back to the threshold of the black doorway when the shape slowed to a stop just beyond the wall of water.

It was a vessel half as long as the wall, wide and flat like a stingray, with two broad wing-shaped protuberances and a rigid fin rising from the top. There wasn't a sharp edge on its smooth, sleek exterior. Ayani thought it looked as if it had been carved from the same stone material as the floor of the pyramid.

The vessel moved closer, gliding as if on an invisible track, without any apparent source of power, until a blunted extension like a sanded-down tail broke through the wall of water. Water cascaded over the stub, spilling across the black floor. Then it opened in four separate pieces like a stone flower, revealing an opening roughly the shape and size of the black door behind them. Beyond this opening, a warm yellow light beckoned.

Henry and Ayani shared a quick glance. He squeezed her arm and nodded, then followed her back to the wall of water. One of the stone petals had lowered like a ramp to the floor.

Ayani entered the stone vessel first, looking back

to make sure Henry had followed. As soon as he'd climbed the ramp, the petals silently closed, blocking out the blue-green light of the water.

The vessel's interior was dry and warm. Ayani led them down a tall, narrow passage, toward the light source. It was a cockpit of sorts, but without seats. Instead, a thin stone pipe descended from the domed roof and terminated halfway to the floor. It was capped by a stone brick with no distinguishing characteristics. There was no other ornamentation in the room — no control panels, no buttons, no switches.

At the front of the cockpit was a curved cutout — a window to the ocean beyond. Ayani approached it hesitantly, unable to see any kind of physical barrier between herself and the water.

"It's the same as the tunnels in the city," Henry said, noticing her hesitation. "Your fingers will stop against a hard surface if you reach out, though nothing is there."

"Maybe later," she replied, trying to keep her tone light. Too much was happening that she barely had time to process it all. She was tired of being underground. She wanted to feel the sun on her face and the soft soil beneath her boots.

Henry stood next to the hanging pipe, inspecting the brick attached to its end. He put his eyes against it as if it were a submarine periscope, then jerked his head back.

"I thought I was being funny," he said in surprise. "I was going to make a joke about feeling like Captain Nemo."

"What do you mean?" Ayani asked, frowning.

"Take a look."

She pressed her forehead to the brick and stared at it...

...only she wasn't seeing the brick. She was seeing the ocean around the vessel in a wide field of vision. The view was distorted at the edges, as if she were looking through a wide-angle lens.

The ocean floor was moving, sliding beneath the vessel so fast it was a blur, the dark pits she'd seen elongating to streaks.

It's not moving, she realized. *We are.*

There was no vibration in the floor to indicate engine power. There had been no lurch as the ship began its journey. All momentum imparted by the vessel's movement was dampened to the point of negation.

"Where is it taking us?" Henry asked.

"To the city?" guessed Ayani.

Henry chuckled. "An underwater transit system."

Ayani watched the blur of the ocean floor slide beneath them. "Why not build another door?" she wondered aloud. "The same kind that took us from the pyramid to the shore."

"Perhaps it's too great a distance. Or perhaps they don't always want to go to the city when they depart the pyramid."

"Not much else out here," she said quietly, studying the emptiness of the ocean beneath the surface.

"Not that we can see."

Ayani rolled up the sleeves of her coverall and put her hands on her hips, acutely aware they should each be in some kind of suit with its own independent air supply. She prided herself on her lack of claustrophobia when so many others began to twitch, but she was starting to feel the weight of all that water above her.

Then the vessel *did* lurch, sending her and Henry stumbling against the smooth stone walls.

A shape glided past the window, flashing dull gold in the light from above. The shape moved out of sight as the vessel drifted free of its invisible track, utterly powerless, rising slowly toward the surface.

"Leviathan," Henry whispered.

The shape reappeared, closer. With nothing against which to judge its size, Ayani couldn't be sure just how massive it truly was. She guessed at least three times the size of a blue whale on Earth, but more stout — thicker around the head and midsection, like a sperm whale. Its lower jaw protruded in a massive cone half as long as the creature itself, and the top plane of its body, from the tip of its cone to the end of its blunted, flukeless tail, was almost perfectly flat.

Four large, dull eyes, two on each side of the mouth that etched a dark line atop its flat head, regarded the stone vessel as it glided past using its four massive flippers and swam out of view.

"Seems like we picked a bad way to travel with those things in the water," Ayani said. She ran her palms over the walls, searching for any kind of hidden control mechanism.

"I doubt this is normal," Henry said thoughtfully. He sounded unconcerned, but when she glanced at him, she saw he was pale. Sweat beaded his brow. "I've been noticing unusual behavior in other animals lately. Breaks in the patterns they've exhibited since we arrived. Something is affecting them."

The vessel jerked upward harshly, sending Ayani and Henry tumbling sideways. She hit the wall sitting down, and Henry fell onto her sideways. His head cracked against the flat stone wall.

He moaned weakly as Ayani rolled him off her legs. Bubbles gurgled up past the cockpit window as the vessel somewhat righted itself, and Ayani saw the flick of a tail off to one side.

They were rising toward the surface more quickly. Dim orange light reached long fingers into the ocean depths.

Still without power, the vessel spun slowly, until the cockpit window looked down instead of up. The broad shape of the leviathan was down there, a smear in the darkness, rising quickly — far more quickly than the gentle ascension of the stone vessel.

Ayani searched the cockpit for a brace, but there was nothing to hold on to. Henry groaned when she told him to get up, so she scooped him up under his arms and dragged him toward the narrow hallway leading back to where they'd first entered the ship. The heels of his boots scraped across the stone floor. Ayani yelled as she struggled to haul him up a continually-slanting floor. It tilted...tilted...and suddenly she and Henry were sliding down it like they had the funnel in the pyramid, back toward the cockpit window.

She smacked against the invisible barrier on her stomach, face-to-face with the ocean beyond. Henry landed on her back, knocking the wind from her. He neither moved nor made a sound.

Her muscles wouldn't listen to her demands to push herself away from the window. She could see nothing but the rising leviathan, its features resolving as it came closer. Its front two flippers paddled down in unison while the two near its tail paddled upward.

Ayani's breath caught in her throat when it came so close she could see the kevlar texture of its four eyes.

She flipped over and wrapped her arms around Henry, tucking her head over his.

The leviathan rammed the vessel with its jaw cone, sending it spinning sideways in the water. Ayani screamed as she was thrown into the air off the window. Henry slipped from her hands when she hit the hanging pipe. It snapped off with a loud crack and clattered against the floor, where Ayani landed a split-second later.

Water poured in through a jagged split in the stone next to the cockpit window. The vessel was mostly aright in that moment, floating quickly toward the surface at a slight angle, spinning and venting silvery bubbles that roared up past the cockpit window.

Ayani got to her feet and fell sideways, disoriented. She touched the side of her head and felt blood.

Henry lay tucked against the wall, curled into a ball with his back facing her. She crawled to him and collapsed near his head. Gently, she whispered that everything was going to be fine. They'd be on the surface soon.

The gradual spin of the vessel angled the cockpit window down once more. Through the cascade of bubbles, Ayani saw the leviathan rising for another impact.

She closed her eyes and hugged Henry close.

GAVIN

The yellow tent had been exactly where he knew it would be.

Without ever having been to that particular spot of the black sand shore near the southern tip of the Casmin Sea, Gavin had known what awaited. The sand curved in a gentle arc, shying from the water. Large silver-gray boulders shone wetly in the failing daylight, lining the small cove in a crescent shape.

Niku Tedani's yellow tent had been erected with its back to the largest of the boulders, using it as a windbreak against the gusts that would swell out of the calm suddenly to rip across the Casmin's gray surface. Farther north, three of the towering unbreaking waves rose toward the darkening sky.

He had seen Shurri and Arthur share a quick glance when they'd all first spied the tent. Gavin had told them about seeing it in his vision when he first emerged from the underground cavern to find her awake and her brother inspecting her wounded leg with a frown.

They hadn't believed him, or they simply had been willing to indulge him out of loyalty, until they saw the tent. There were no skeptical glances afterward, not until he produced the three orange space suits from a large container and said they were going underwater.

She's moving much better now, Gavin thought as he followed Shurri through the tunnel. Dark water surrounded them as the tunnel descended deeper along the sloping ocean floor, held up by a phantom wall they could feel, but not see. The faint outlines of the city, which had been barely visible when they first entered the long tunnel, were now lost to the gloom.

His own slight limp never seemed to catch the attention of someone unfamiliar with his old injury, but he couldn't say the same for hers. She never uttered a word of complaint, but she shuffled forward, hauling her stiff, wounded leg behind her. Both Gavin and Arthur had offered to help support her. She had briefly agreed during a steeper descent, then shrugged off their arms just as quickly afterward.

Gavin wasn't sure if she was angry, sad, both, or something else entirely. He wanted to see her smile again, but he figured she was probably still thinking about her mother, trapped back at the colony. He didn't know if he should be trying to cheer anyone up given the circumstances, but the three of them had been grim long enough.

Do you remember when Willef danced for our dinner? he signed, barely able to make the words comprehendible through his thick gloves.

They hadn't been able to figure out how to activate the comms system between the suits, so Shurri had pulled off her helmet when they were descending in a stone elevator shaped like a big drum, taking them away from the Casmin Sea, toward the Equatorial Ocean. Arthur cried out and tried to stop her, then waited with a pained look on his face until he was sure his stubborn sister wouldn't choke to death on poisonous fumes. Only then did he hesitantly pulled his off as well. It didn't matter to Gavin either way with regard to communication, but he liked the earthy, mineral smell in the tunnel better than the canned air out of his suit's power pack. The helmets now dangled from a looped cord below their packs. Willef's sheathed machete hung beside Gavin's helmet by a strap he'd cut from the pack he left behind on the surface, clacking lightly against it as he walked.

He asked us if we'd ever had roast rock bat, Gavin continued, his gloved hands forming the words for the others to see.

Arthur smiled, but Shurri kept her eyes on the tunnel floor. Her sandy hair was wet with sweat, tucked behind her ears. Gavin thought she might be feverish.

Then Arthur hopped forward on one foot, slid to the side on the other, and clapped his hands. It was a poor rendition of the dance Gavin referred to that lured rock bats from their pillars. Arthur spun and hopped again, but lost his balance and pitched forward. He managed to turn at the last second and land on his dangling helmet instead of his head. He made a pained face as he sat hard upon it and slipped off to the side.

Shurri giggled.

Gavin's smile threatened to split his cheeks.

The moment passed after he helped Arthur to his feet, and they walked on in silence.

When they reached the stone door at the end of

the tunnel, Gavin didn't hesitate. He depressed a small square in the middle with his thumb, and waited as a palm-sized section slid back and to the side. Reaching in, he felt the handle he'd known would be there without ever knowing it.

The knowledge imparted to him by the creature in the cavern was frustrating in that sense — he couldn't access it like a manual as he could his knowledge of other things like fishing or repairing the hydro dam. This new knowledge didn't reveal itself until he needed specific information — yet he seemed aware of its sheer volume on a subconscious level all the same.

The room beyond the stone door filled the entirety of the cylindrical building into which they'd crossed. Water dripped like rain from a source out of sight far above. Arthur flicked on his palm-light, piercing the dark. The light wasn't strong enough to bleed beyond its own beam, or perhaps the gloom was simply stronger. The three of them followed its thin path across the wet floor, and through an identical stone door.

Another water tunnel awaited them. Shurri greeted it with a heavy sigh.

Not much farther, Gavin signed.

He led the way by stepping into one of four cutouts aligned in a square in the stone floor. It was too large for his boots, but he knew that didn't matter. Shurri and Arthur joined him, standing in two of the other cutouts.

Lean forward, signed Gavin over his shoulder.

The cutouts glided forward silently, moving like shadows across the floor — except these shadows were *part* of the floor, sunken into it, sliding through it without the slightest hint of momentum or friction, and Shurri let out a surprised, "Oh!"

Lean, Gavin signed.

They all tilted forward, and the platform shot ahead, blurring the ocean floor outside the tunnel.

"You're sure you know where we're going?" Arthur asked.

Gavin didn't answer. He leaned even farther, but felt no wind on his face.

We are close, he knew.

He held up a hand to let the others know to lean back. The platform slowed to a stop as they stood up straight, delivering them to a third stone door.

The massive dome room beyond was filled with wonders.

Invisible walls held the crushing ocean waters at bay. Red coral structures rose from the floor, softly glowing in the darkening dome, twisting as they climbed for the ceiling and cast their soft light onto every surface. Blobs of water the size of farm sheds floated lazily among the twisting coral, and would shudder in unison every few seconds, as if disturbed by a tremor.

Holes large enough to crawl into pitted the entire floor. Two pools of still water lay near the center of the room, surrounded by flat tables formed from the gently rising and falling stone floor. They were arranged in groups of three and four, almost as if they'd been built for gatherings.

A man sat at one of the tables, staring into the depths of a silent pool, frowning. He wore one of the same bright orange space suits as Gavin and his friends.

Niku Tedani noticed them, and stood. His helmet rested on the table beside him, along with a crate of supplies.

"Gavin," he said, surprised. "Shurri. Arthur. You found the suits."

He had a broad, kindly face and black hair that brushed his neck. Gavin's father once told him he used to drink too much, especially before the crash, but Gavin hadn't seen him touch a drop afterward.

Gavin led his friends to Niku's table, avoiding the holes in the floor. He gazed into the nearby pool, but it seemed empty. It was a pillar of water with rock walls that appeared to descend through the sand under the dome.

Slowly at first, then with increasing speed as he reached the end, Gavin told Niku all that had happened in the colony...and in the underground cavern.

Besides Gavin's father, Uda had been the first to communicate with him on the *Halcyon* during their journey from Earth. They'd taken a farming orientation class and she had surprised both of them by kneeling down to use Gavin's own language. Niku had picked up much of it after years of living with Uda and watching her interactions with Gavin, so he knew he wouldn't have to pantomime the actions. Even then, when it came time to relate his vision in the cavern, Gavin had to resort to spelling out many of the words he knew Niku wouldn't understand given the context.

He finished by explaining the next part of his journey through the underwater city.

Niku's face had grown grave as the story progressed, taking on an air of despair when Gavin told him Uda and their son, Toma, were among those held captive.

"I realized long ago the buildings formed a ring," he said softly. His eyes danced with rage, but he kept them trained on the pool. "But there is only sand between them. I've been through every building in the city twice. There are no doors leading inward."

We're not looking for a door, Gavin signed. Then he spelled out the word *Niku* to get his attention. Niku's eyes slowly peeled away from the pool. His face softened when he saw the others. *Our path leads back to the colony,* Gavin signed. *But we need to hurry. Will you come?*

After a long moment, he nodded. "If there's a chance of saving my family, I'll take it."

You'll need your helmet, signed Gavin.

A soft noise escaped Shurri's lips, and her knees buckled. Gavin caught her before she hit the floor.

"What's wrong?" Niku asked, kneeling down.

"A squid," Arthur said, and Niku paled as if he'd seen a ghost.

On the shore, Gavin quickly signed. Then he pantomimed a tentacle shooting out to wrap around her leg. *Tore her leg open,* he finished.

Niku went to the table and rummaged through his crate of supplies. He tore the side of a plastic packet with his teeth and spat it aside. A syringe and two pills slipped out when he upended it into his palm.

Shurri's eyelids fluttered as he pushed the pills into her mouth and moved her lower jaw with his hand, forcing her to chew. Then he uncapped the syringe and injected clear liquid into her jugular vein.

"What is that?" Arthur asked, his voice shrill with worry.

"It will help," Niku told him, placing his palm on her pale, clammy forehead. "For now. But she needs proper care."

Her eyelids opened and she offered Gavin a weak smile.

"You go," she whispered.

Only then did another page in the cavern creature's manual of knowledge illuminate within the darkness of his mind.

The surface was too far away. He couldn't take Shurri back to the colony...but there was another way.

You have to come with me, Gavin signed, looking into her eyes. *It's the only way to save you.*

"Save her?" Arthur balked. "What do you mean, *save* her?"

Niku and Gavin helped her to stand, and they followed his lead to a portion of the invisible dome wall that looked out over the wide sandy expanse between the ring of underwater buildings. He stared into the dark waters for a moment, then took three steps back and turned in place.

A hole opened in the floor at his feet, wide enough to crawl into.

Here, he signed.

Shurri hung limply between Arthur and Niku. Surprisingly, she smiled, as if to say, *You're crazy.*

"There?" Niku asked with a frown, staring at the hole.

It's the only way, Gavin signed.

Then he hopped into the hole, hoping they would follow.

It dropped a meter, then sloped sideways, becoming a steep slide. Red light from the coral in the domed room vanished as the slide turned again. Arthur whooped from somewhere above.

Good, thought Gavin. He just hoped he hadn't doomed them all to a painful death. He was trusting his instincts now — though they had been continuously stretching the limits of his own believability since he'd seen that yellow tent from his vision on the shore.

I have no choice, he told himself. *Shurri needs help.*

The tunnel he half-slid, half-fell through was pitch dark. A roaring noise of wind and rushing water blew up the tunnel to greet him, carried on a gust of hot air that burned his cheeks.

Rigid claws scratched at his space suit.

Branches, he realized. *Canopy branches. Do they grow this far into the ocean?*

They had broken through the tunnel walls like a tree root seeking water in a pipe. At one point they grew so dense he slammed into them with a loud crunch, stopping suddenly. Arthur rammed into him a moment later, his boots stomping down on Gavin's shoulder. If he had a voice, he would have screamed. The branches screamed instead, groaning against the added weight until they finally gave way, snapping loose to send Gavin and Arthur farther down the tunnel.

They spilled out onto soft ground, one after the

other, and lay on their backs, breathing hard. Shurri tumbled out half a minute later, groaning, and Niku followed shortly. He sat up, rubbing the back of his head. His helmet popped out of the tunnel and whacked him in the temple.

They were in a low cavern, its ceiling not much taller than Gavin. An orange glow emanated from a lake of water in the middle of the gray, muddy ground. The cavern walls and ceiling were dirt and branch, mixed in with the occasional jagged boulder. Even in the dim orange light, Gavin could tell the branches were not gray like the ones just below the planet's surface, but a slick, oily black — the same as the ones he'd seen in the creature's cavern.

Water trickled in small streams from the ceiling, crawling over the walls and feeding into the lake in the floor.

"There are no supporting structures," Niku said as he stood, reaching up to touch the ceiling. "The ocean should crush this place."

Shurri's breath came rapidly. She stared at Gavin, but her eyes did not see.

Helmets on, he signed, emotion seizing his heart. *Help her, Arthur.*

Gavin yanked on his own helmet and jogged to the edge of the lake. It widened as it deepened, expanding to the point its walls were no longer visible — wider than any lake they'd mapped on the surface.

In its depths, three shapeless behemoths glowed like smoldering orange coals. They floated thirty meters down, anchored to the muddy lake bottom by thick umbilicals.

Arthur and Niku soon joined him, Shurri hanging between them. They all had their helmets on.

Will these suits handle the pressure? he signed.

Niku said something behind his face shield, then realized he couldn't be heard. *By design,* he spelled out with one hand while he held Shurri up with the other.

Gavin jumped into the still water, sending ripples across a surface that most likely hadn't been disturbed in eons.

He gestured for the others to pass him Shurri. After he lowered her next to himself in the water, Arthur caught his attention.

No weights, he signed.

Gavin waved him toward the water, then pushed off from the loose shore, kicking for the middle of the lake. Niku jumped in and followed, but Arthur stood at the edge, his gloves picking at the sides of his suit legs.

Gavin let go of Shurri with one hand and waved his arm with urgency, and finally Arthur shook his head, then jumped into the lake.

They gathered in the middle, circling around Shurri.

Okay, Gavin thought, exchanging wary glances with the others. *Now would be a good time to show them I'm not crazy.*

Below their feet, the three orange embers waited.

Then they started sinking.

As if standing on an invisible elevator, their helmets dipped below the surface, and their bodies were carried deeper by a slow but steady current that connected them to the soft, muddy lake bottom, where their boots thumped softly to send up slow-moving clouds of dirt particles.

Before them, the three orange behemoths glowed.

On the Starliner *Halcyon* — the ship that carried Gavin, then just eight-years old, and the other colonists from Earth — he had once snuck away from his bunk while his father was off working his maintenance job. The mile-long vessel had been built for pleasure cruises, then retrofitted to take tourists through the Rip. Business flagged, then nearly died altogether, and so most of the shops and restaurants along its expansive promenade were closed. Entranced by the colorful posters peeling from the cloudy windows of a theater, Gavin had snuck behind a loose panel and squeezed inside.

It was a cathedral hall of sorts, with many levels of ratty cloth seats, all facing a dusty stage. Yet Gavin had never seen anything so big other than the buildings on Earth. Those buildings on the street his father always hurried past were forbidden to him because he couldn't be seen. His father told him that someone who wasn't able to have children of their own would snatch him up. Gavin had sat in the theater for a long time, marveling at its emptiness.

A single orange behemoth *might* have fit inside that theater, but only just.

The three were identical to each other. Their exteriors were bulbous in places and had a rock-like texture in others. Orange light glowed from the bulbous sections; soft lantern-light that silhouetted lightning-bolt veins of some darker substance. The first image conjured in Gavin's mind's eye was of a floating brain, where each behemoth's stem was the umbilical connecting it to the lake bottom.

He trudged across the lake bottom, guiding Shurri alongside him. Arthur and Niku followed close behind, trusting him, trusting the vision he'd been shown. There was a current here, too. It kept him pinned to the bottom and moving toward the behemoths.

At first glance, one might think they were but fruits of some strange and enormous alien plant. Much like the bulbs of the bitterbell plant, these might simply be adornments of a native snaking vine — food, perhaps, for a larger beast not yet discovered.

Except Gavin knew the truth. He knew they weren't just another part of the canopy, or the vestigial growths of some underwater plant. They were separate from this world — born not of Galena, but of the creature in the cavern, and they were alive in their own right.

Thick branches lined with black veins crawled across the lake bottom, tangling together to create a vast carpet of woven limbs. At three points, those limbs twisted upward and connected to the orange behemoths, where the branches separated once again to cradle them like a chalice of antler tines.

It was below the nearest of these umbilicals that Gavin stood, looking up. He gripped a thick branch and was pulled upward along it, much as he and the others had been pulled along the walkway in the underwater tunnel. His hand glided up its length as their boots had slid through the solid stone floor.

The behemoth loomed above him as he pressed

Shurri to his side, carrying her with him. It swelled in his vision, until all he could see was a wall of orange.

It might not have been a bitterbell fruit, but its skin had the consistency of one. Gavin and Shurri were pulled up into it, and its flesh slipped around them like jelly. The inside of its skin moved them upward with gentle contractions. Viscous gel aglow with orange light smeared Gavin's faceplate.

He emerged from the floor of a hallway and stuck there at his waist. The floor of the hall was the same membrane-like skin they'd been sucked into on the exterior, and he could see the dark shape of Shurri's suit down by his boots. He plunged back into the floor and hauled her up by her power pack. With a wet suck, he pulled her free. Bracing his hands on the soft floor, he wriggled himself the rest of the way out.

I know this place, he thought, looking around as he slung Shurri's arm over his shoulder and started walking.

He could see the blueprint in his mind clear as if it were his own home.

The hallway had an organic look to it, as if it were the hollow inside of a giant's artery.

Their helmets knocked together as they walked, so Gavin hastily stripped them off, knowing the air was safe to breathe. Somehow he was able to ignore Shurri's deathly pallor, or the fact he couldn't tell if she was still breathing.

There was a wet sucking noise behind him as Niku or Arthur emerged from the floor, but Gavin didn't look back.

He could feel the panic building in him now, feel its icy hands clawing between his thoughts, trying to choke them. He stumbled and fell, crying. Then other hands were on him, pulling him up, lifting Shurri, too — carrying them.

"Tell us what to do," Arthur said, and Gavin pointed.

So tired, he thought, his inner voice a fading whisper.

His muscles wouldn't respond. It wasn't that the suit was too heavy for him. His mind had finally rebelled, refusing to carry out his orders.

They stopped suddenly.

"Dead end," said Arthur.

He started to turn but Gavin shook his head. Niku helped to ease him to a sitting position against a wall, which Gavin knew to be the front of the cockpit. It held the basic shape of a squashed sphere, and had the same organic-tissue look as the hallway, as if the four of them were crawling around inside the drained corpse of something long dead.

Gavin couldn't even lift his arm, so he lifted his finger to point at a natural cutout in the wall at the back of the room. There was something of a shallow seat formed from the tissue-like material of the wall.

"For Shurri?" Niku asked doubtfully.

Gavin's head dropped in a nod.

Niku and Arthur carried her to the wall and gently placed her on the shallow seat, facing the room. Her feet dangled just above the floor, which glistened with moisture.

She gasped and snapped back against the wall, rigid as a board. Her eyes flew open, wide with terror, as a thin branch whipped out from the wall and pinned her forehead.

Arthur cried out and ran forward. Gavin lunged. The strength had all but fled moments before, but Arthur had to *wait*. He *had* to, or she'd die.

Her brother fell to the ground with a shout, then flipped onto his back to kick at Gavin, who held his ankle in an iron grip.

Niku seemed uncertain what to do. Gavin signed *M-U-S-T* with his free hand, and Niku understood. He grabbed Arthur's other ankle and hauled him back.

Arthur kicked and punched and clawed and yelled, but Niku held strong.

Shurri's soft voice broke through the clamor.

"Brother," she whispered.

The rest of them froze. Gavin's hand released Arthur's ankle and dropped boneless to the floor.

Supple branches slithered around her torso like thick ropes, ripping holes in her orange space suit, covering her body from waist to shoulders. Yet she was smiling. Her smile grew wider, and wider still, until it became a leer, twisting her face in a grimace of pain and fear.

Gavin suddenly believed he'd made a terrible mistake. He flopped onto his stomach and pulled himself across the wet floor hand over hand, his entire body shaking from exhaustion. His vision darkened and he realized he was close to passing out. It felt like ten tons of pressure had settled on his skull. Black walls pressed in at the edges of his sight, quickly closing together until he could see nothing more than faint pinpoints in the middle.

No, he thought as he plunged toward unconsciousness. *Nooooo....*

Through Gavin's choked vision, he saw two

slender branches wrap around Shurri's neck and slither up to the holes of her ears, and she screamed. Arthur had Gavin's machete in his hand, and he was rushing toward his sister.

The scream became a fading echo as Gavin's world fell away.

THE ENVOY

He sat in the pilot seat of the *Celerity*, thinking of Kate as he flew his rattling ship low over the Equatorial Ocean. Its waters were dark in the twilight, like his mood.

During the three and a half centuries since his wife's passing, memories would flood into his mind, triggered by some random event, and then fade into the background once again. At first, the experience brought only a knife of pain — the deep, stabbing hurt of loss after a lifetime shared. Decades passed, and the sharp edges of that knife dulled. Jeff shaped the blade into a familiar coin he could turn over and over again to stare at without crying.

The detail on that coin had long since rubbed away, but the emotion had seeped into the metal, becoming a part of it. Jeff could pull it out whenever he wanted to feel the warmth of Kate's smile or the soft music of her laughter.

He turned in his seat to look toward the back of the ship, and felt the sharp knife twisting in his guts all over again.

Ayani's arm was visible in the passageway of the crew compartment, hanging limp from the bunk where she lay unconscious. Blood trickled down to her wrist and off the tip of a finger.

Henry was on the other side of the passage, in his own bunk. Yet his arms couldn't slip off his chest because of the black bag Jeff had sealed him in. They'd shared some conversation over the past three years, and were always pleasant with each other. Yet for Jeff, it had always been business: Had Henry seen anything out of the ordinary relating to the creature? Was anyone gossiping about it in the colony? Did they know about the underwater city? Did Gavin ever talk about the creature? Did the creature come to him in his dreams?

The creature, the creature, *the creature*.

Jeff was tired of the whole ordeal. He wanted to get back to the hypermass and shove it down the monster's throat. Maybe then he could get a solid night of sleep.

He glanced back at Ayani's arm, and the knife of pain stabbed him yet again. It was for her that he mourned. Even though she was still alive, she had given up so much to be guardian to The Envoy, and he felt a poor excuse for such a sacrifice.

She had graduated top of her class from the academy, and had already seen combat around the globe by the time she signed on to his sector. There was a good chance she'd already have her first star if she'd stayed back home.

She knew what she wanted, he tried to convince himself. *You're an old man, but that doesn't mean she was too young to make her decision.*

He stewed in his own discontent and rechecked the autopilot course back to the other continent.

Skipping had brought him and the *Celerity* right on top of their listing vessel as it bobbed on the ocean's surface — but not before he had to backtrack across a third of the continent when her homing beacon suddenly blinked out of existence and reappeared a hundred kilometers back the way he'd come, near the shore.

He dared not skip now. It had no negative effect on his own physiology, but he wasn't about to trust the experience would be the same in Ayani's weakened state.

It wasn't long before he felt himself starting to doze. His head bobbed and snapped up when he heard a noise behind him. Turning in his seat, he saw Ayani kneeling next to Henry's bunk. She had unzipped enough of it to reveal his face, peaceful in its rest. Her hand gently stroked his forehead as she whispered soft words.

Jeff looked away, giving her privacy.

Minutes later, she appeared beside him, staring out at the darkening sky.

Then she put a hand on his shoulder, and squeezed. He patted it gently.

"Nice ship you got here," she said, her words dripping sarcasm.

Several wall panels hung by a single bolt, and a rat's nest of wires had spilled from beneath the control panel.

"You should see the other guy," he told her.

"Why, did you blow him up?"

"No, but you should see him. He has a really nice ship."

She squeezed his shoulder harder, then quickly let go and leaned against the wall near the window, arms crossed.

"I guess you had plenty of time to improve your wit on Earth."

His jaw clenched, and he nodded.

"I'm sorry," he said, meeting her eyes. She looked away. "I didn't expect to make it back."

"That's why you should have taken me."

"I got lucky. The Weaver...it helped. I would have died without it. You would have, too."

Her gaze lingered on Henry's body bag before slipping down to her feet.

"There was nothing I could do," she whispered. "We were tossed around in there like rag dolls."

"Leviathan," he said, and she nodded.

Jeff had seen the shimmer of wet, golden flesh amidst the enormous splash that swallowed their broken vessel moments after he'd gotten Henry and Ayani aboard the *Celerity*. If he had arrived a single minute later, they would have been dragged under as well.

"I'm sorry, Ayani," he said again, though for a different reason this time. "I liked him."

She wiped a tear from her cheek. "So did I."

"Where'd you get the submarine?" he asked.

Ayani took a deep breath and wiped away more tears, then told him everything.

"Drones," he said, chewing on the word. "That was Vola."

She looked surprised. "Luciano?"

Jeff shook his head. "The younger."

"You mean *Alexander?* What is he doing here?"

"Subjugating the colonists, according to two teenagers. My guess is that his father sent him to build a city, and he's forcefully enlisted the local populace to his cause. It wouldn't be the first time."

Jeff remembered the elder Vola's short-lived attempt to start his own mining operation on Mars. He wanted to cut out his shipping company's middle man and be his own supplier. The only problem was that he lied to the miners working the Newton Outpost and shipped them halfway across the planet to an unnamed crater. He pleaded ignorance when the mining guilds tracked him down, searching for their missing workers, and got away in the end by merely paying a fee that would have crippled any other business. Luciano laughed it off as a trifle.

"Once a crook..." Ayani said quietly. "How long until we get back?"

Jeff looked at her, confused. "We're not going back. We're going to detonate the hypermass I brought back through the Rip."

"*I'm* not. I'm going back," she declared, her voice rising. "I won't leave those people to that madman. You know the stories."

Jeff nodded. "I know them. Entire crews gone missing if the captain is caught stealing so much as a chunk of ore. Rival shipping vessels arriving at their destination with no cargo and a terrified captain who claims it was pirates, but he can't recall what the ship looked like. And every time, Alexander Vola was near, patrolling the lanes under orders from his father."

"So we'll go."

"If we don't blow the thing in that cavern into a million pieces, it won't matter *what* Vola does to the colonists."

Ayani glared at him. "It's been three years since you found it! You think it's suddenly going to crawl out and fly away."

"That's *exactly* what I think!" he shot back. "I've wasted too much time already!"

She stepped closer and jabbed a finger in his face. "You *will* drop me at the colony, or I will force the hatch open and jump out of this rust-bucket."

Then she went to the back of the ship, leaving Jeff fuming and shaking his head, his lips forming soundless words of anger.

His fingers moved briefly over the control panel, and the twilit horizon line outside the window shifted slightly. A few moments later, Ayani returned to stand next to his seat.

"Thank you, Jeff," she said, squeezing his shoulder before walking away.

"If you get yourself killed, don't complain about it to me," he called over his shoulder, though there was no venom in the words.

A short time later, the ocean slipped away to be replaced by solid ground. The *Celerity* then passed over the Casmin Sea, and long, electric rope of blue light appeared in the dark distance.

Jeff took back control of the ship and slowed, squinting at the flickering blue line. He ran a quick scan. The ship told him it was an energy source, but couldn't elaborate. It warned him that it might possess EMP capabilities and to keep his distance.

"It's going to be a quick drop," he told Ayani when she joined him.

"I'm used to those."

"My weapons aren't responding, or else I'd torch whatever's down there. Vola's ship won't be far away, either."

"Stop making excuses," she said gently. "I can handle myself."

He looked up at her. "I know you can."

Jeff flew toward the barrier of blue light, passing low over the trees.

Nasty piece of work, that Alexander, he thought. *If I hurry at the cavern, I'll have time to come back before Ayani's finished with his crew and introduce him to my engine wash.*

When the *Celerity* passed above the electric barrier, a streak of blue energy licked up toward its hull, and the ship veered sideways in an auto-defense maneuver. Ayani grabbed the sides of the flickering control panel to keep from falling. Her hands left bloody handprints when she stood upright after the ship stabilized.

"Might want to wash those off," Jeff suggested.

She smiled wickedly. "Why? I'm about to get them dirty again."

Jeff cycled through the panel menus until he found what he needed. "Opening the hatch in five. It might only pop down halfway," he warned. "You be safe down there."

"Likewise," she replied, and then she was gone to the back of the ship.

Clear of the barrier, Jeff swung in low to the ground, aiming his nose back the way he'd come. The control panel beeped that someone had jumped from the hatch, and there was only one person left on board.

He thought of Henry as he piloted away from the colony, heading south into the night.

It was a short flight to the mouth of the

underground river cave. Jeff wondered what the hypermass would look like when it detonated. A mushroom cloud? An implosion?

Henry had told him what it looked like when Kellan detonated a string of hypermass pills in orbit to create the new Rip. Jeff doubted he'd see anything close to the fireworks show Henry described.

Well, he consoled himself as the ship set down near the river. *It won't be for lack of trying.*

He was pleased to see the shield cube containing the hypermass pill was right where he'd left it. If the best he could do was pop the box open and detonate the pill where it sat, then that's what he would do.

Maybe I can use the ship to nudge it into the cave, he thought hopefully as he walked to the back of the ship.

He jumped down from the half-open ramp to land on spongy ground. The stars were out in multitudes above him, and the twin nebulae spread their purplish fingers across the western night sky. Purple-green light was smeared like a hazy iris around the black pupil of the new Rip to the east.

Jeff paused a brief moment to allow his life-light to bloom — the first time since he'd arrived back on the planet, he realized. Beams of multicolored light extended from all the living things nearby, illuminating the surface in a rainbow of vitality.

This place is nothing if not beautiful, he thought, his heart full of longing for simpler times. He squeezed his right eye shut, willing the extrasensory vision away. When he opened it again, the world was dark once more.

Give me an engine to fix, he grumbled silently as

he paced around the shield cube. *Give me a space station to build. A wrench to turn. Anything but this.*

It had been so long since he'd been able to ply his engineering trade that he doubted he'd remember which end of a bolt went into the hole.

You're doing alright, Dolan, a more level-headed version of himself told him. Curiously enough, it sounded a lot like his old friend, Tag Riley. *You just need to do a little demolition work. Then you can play.*

Jeff smiled ruefully. He knew that wasn't true. As long as The Weaver was imprisoned in Shipyard 6, he must attend to his duties as The Envoy. That was the promise he made.

He linked his wristpad to the broken screen of the shield cube so he could access its system, then looked toward the black mouth of the river cave. Water rushed white in the starlight as it spilled forth under stone teeth.

A monster waited below, and The Envoy's duty said it must be destroyed.

Dawn broke in the east when he finally finished preparing the hypermass.

It floated above the flat walls of the shield cube, the individual square segments of which could be the foundation of a corporate skyscraper on Earth.

The hypermass pill was void-black, the size of a city bus oriented vertically, hovering perfectly still five meters off the ground. Static electricity crackled on his black space suit with every step he made. The ground emanated a strange warmth, powerful enough to seep through the soles of his boots.

Visible ripples of radiation washed over him, pulsing from the monolithic pill, but he was unfazed.

He knelt down on the wide platform that had once been the bottom of the shield cube, and began constructing the detonator, pulling its pieces from a series of storage panels.

Phobis was a solid disc above the horizon, and he was halfway finished with the detonator, when he heard the ship.

It flew in low to the ground, straight for his position. Even nose-on and back-lit by Phobis, he knew it was the *Morning Sun*.

Jeff glanced up at the pill, scowling, and stood. He wouldn't have time to finish the detonator before they arrived. *Three birds with one stone,* he thought. *And a proper send off for yours truly.*

There was a small pistol clipped to a side panel of his chair on the *Celerity*. Jeff opened and closed his right hand, regretting not taking the time to retrieve it.

The *Morning Sun* angled skyward as it set down between Jeff and his ship, blasting the ground below. Its polished metal hull gleamed with daylight.

Alexander Vola was first down the ramp.

He had donned a long red jacket over black combat fatigues, and was in the process of pulling on black gloves as he stopped to admire the hypermass pill, an easy smirk on his lips. His skin looked especially pale in the wan morning light, and his eyes seemed the color of faded stone. A black strap crossed his chest, and Jeff saw the four-pronged nozzle of a rifle hanging behind his back.

Kellan descended after, holding on to the ramp piston with his remaining hand and grinning at Jeff when he saw him.

"We lost your signal!" he shouted as he hopped lightly off the ramp. "Took us all night to sweep this area. We were on our way back to the colony when Alexander spotted the pill in the distance."

The signal interference was likely a result of exposing the hypermass. Its myriad emissions had been shielded by the cube walls until then — but Jeff saw no need to tell them that.

"You want to blow it up," Vola said.

Jeff noticed neither he nor Kellan approached any closer.

"You don't even know what 'it' is," he replied.

Vola's hand moved to scratch the back of his neck. Jeff tried to flick to another instance of the many stacked versions of that field he created when he first arrived, but the radiation blocked his fold space ability, just as the rad-soaked shielding of the *Celerity* had blocked him near the Rip. Vola, Kellan, and the *Morning Sun* would have blinked out of view. Instead, they remained, and Vola casually swung his rifle into his hands and fired.

There was a deep-sounding *blert*, but nothing shot from the nozzle. Jeff felt the attack all the same. His spine seized and his biceps constricted, twisting his arms behind his back. He screamed as he fought to keep his bones from snapping. Then he went numb all over. The attack passed. He pitched forward like a stiff board and landed on the side of his face in the soil, unable to twitch a single muscle.

"Let's find the cavern," Vola said. "Drag him to the river."

Jeff couldn't see him, or his ship. All he could see was the bottom of the hypermass pill and a distant mountain, half of it lit by the sun.

"I don't have a hazard suit..." Kellan protested.

"I don't care," came the cold reply.

There was another long moment of hesitation before he heard Kellan's boots tromping quickly over the ground in his direction. Kellan grabbed Jeff's shoulder and rolled him onto his back. Waves of shimmering radiation pulsed over them both, sloughing from the pill.

Grunting, Kellan dragged Jeff toward the mouth of the cavern with one arm, the stump of his other hanging uselessly at his side. Drag, pause, drag, pause.

He was sweaty and breathless by the time he collapsed beside the cave mouth. Water mist rolled over them, glimmering like ice crystals.

Vola stood on a rock, looking into the dark cave. Then he shoved Jeff onto his stomach, bound his wrists behind his back, and stabbed his neck with a syringe. Jeff's skin was still so numb it felt like a dull jab.

Then his muscles began to relax, and sensation flooded back into his limbs. He tried to access fold space again but a sudden tidal wave of dizziness crashed from one side of his skull to the other.

Vola tossed aside the syringe and roughly hauled Jeff to his feet.

"Show me," he hissed close to Jeff's ear, then shoved him toward the river cave.

Jeff's tongue felt swollen in his mouth, blocking an acid reply. He stumbled over rocks, pausing often to lean against the wall of the tunnel.

His awareness slipped away. Once, he blinked to

find himself halfway down the jagged ramp of broken rocks, remnants of a cave-in, with no memory of the journey up to that point. His wrists were still bound, and words would not form in his throat. He choked on their fragments, coughing. His foot slipped on a wet rock but Vola's hand shot out and grabbed his arm. After Jeff regained his balance, Vola pushed his arm away.

He passed through the waterfall cavern in a daze, stumbled through the illuminated passageway connecting it to the next chamber, and delivered Vola and Kellan to the creature.

It awaited them above the central platform, bathed in purple by the crystals.

Vola and Kellan forgot about Jeff. They left him swaying on his feet to approach the creature, speaking in hushed, reverent tones.

Blissfully, Jeff was allowed to fall.

He landed on his side. His skull bounced off a flat rock and the cavern went dark.

When consciousness found him again, he was on his back, lying on his hands. He blinked to clear away his brain fog. Vola's eyes were closed. He pressed his open hand against the shuddering black membrane of the creature. Rippling purple light from crystals behind it reached through its bulk, and the dancing tendrils beyond the membrane cast wavering shadows over his serene face. A rushing liquid sound, like blood pumping through arteries, filled the chamber.

Kellan stood back from the central platform, mesmerized by the sight.

Jeff concentrated on the small black sphere at the

base of his skull, mentally prodding it so he could use fold space and flick to another instance of the cavern without the other two, but it would not stir. His thoughts remained a thick sludge, but he was able to get his feet beneath him to stand.

And the pain was slowly returning to his muscles, which meant Vola's drug was wearing off.

Kellan glanced back and noticed him. A faint smile passed over his lips beneath his small mustache as he crossed the short distance between them. Jeff squinted drunkenly at that mustache, trying to think of a way to rip it off. Then he noticed the thin sheen of sweat on Kellan's face, the paleness of his skin, and the dark circles under his eyes.

Radiation, Jeff thought sluggishly.

"Something tells me he's forgotten all about his father's master plan," Kellan said pleasantly, turning back to watch Vola and the creature. "The winds have shifted many times since I came here. You, Jeff, are the oak that won't bend. I am the leaf that follows the wind."

Jeff leaned away from him so he could build more momentum for what he did next. He rammed Kellan sideways, driving his shoulder into the shorter man's ribcage. Kellan let out a surprised yell as they both fell to the hard floor.

Jeff's muscles surged with life. Kellan scrambled backward, but Jeff crawled after him on his knees, his hands still bound behind him. Kellan smacked into a rocky pillar and raised his right hand and his left stump to protect himself. Jeff climbed to his feet and raised a boot meant for Kellan's cheekbone.

Vola grabbed the collar of his space suit and flung

him backward to sprawl on the floor, groaning. He gripped his rifle and drove the nozzle into Jeff's chest, sneering down. His white hair hung in strands past his forehead, framing his zealous eyes. A vein bulged pale green on his forehead. He leaned against the butt of the strange rifle, and Jeff howled in pain.

At least my voice is coming back, he thought when Vola eased the pressure.

"This place," Alexander seethed through clenched teeth. "This planet...is *mine.*"

His finger closed around the trigger. The black sphere in Jeff's brain twitched. He blinked, and suddenly he was alone with the creature, in a separate instance of the cavern from Vola and Kellan.

He collapsed in relief, staring up at the pulsing, impassive alien presence. Moving slowly, he worked his arms lower down his back, and eventually managed to slip his bound wrists under his boots. A minute of gnawing at the hard plastic cord was enough to free his hands.

I need to get back to the pill, he thought. Once Vola figured out there was no way to follow after Jeff, he'd probably head back to the colony. Whatever plans he'd formulated during his...*communion*...Jeff had to make sure the cathedral creature played no part in them.

Suddenly, like a light in the dark, it occurred to him to ask it.

He'd communed with The Weaver, which had never resisted their connection. Sometimes it ignored him, but it had never rejected him. The last time Jeff had tried to touch *this* one, its membrane shied away from his hand. Like a dog that can smell other pets on an owner, perhaps this creature could sense Jeff's connection with The Weaver.

For the first time, Jeff wondered if it was afraid.

He crawled up the platform and stood next to the reeking mound of black tissue. The membrane didn't shrink back as Jeff closed his right eye and spread his fingers just above the creature's translucent skin. He could already feel something: a promise of pain and torment, but also of knowledge — so much more knowledge than The Weaver had ever shared.

Jeff could sense it wouldn't be easily granted. He had to steal it from this miserable creature — and the theft would come at great cost. The Weaver communed with him willingly, sharing crumbs of revelation. To take such bulk knowledge by force would be no gentle experience.

The particles in his hand separated to become mist as his palm touched the warm, rough membrane. Jeff opened his eye and saw that his hand was still his hand, though it was sinking through the membrane.

Then he was yanked inside, falling faster than humanly possible, screaming as his body pulled apart like wet paper.

MERRITT

He awoke sometime before dawn, and knew what he must do.

The room was dark, and thick with silence. Merritt sat up in the cot, wincing as fresh pain burned across his chest where the electric barrier had kissed him. He raised a hand to rub the itchy edges of the wound but found that someone had covered it with gauze, then wrapped his ribcage with long strips of cloth.

I'm alone, he realized, looking around. *But...this isn't the hospital.*

Moonlight filtered through thin curtains over a single window, casting a hazy square upon the dusty floor. Swallowing a pained groan, Merritt rose from the cot. One of its metal feet squeaked, and he froze. The silence continued.

On bare feet, he padded to the window and gently moved the curtain enough to see outside.

Galena's large moon — usually twice the apparent size of Earth's own in the night sky — was a mere sliver above the horizon. A few moments later, it blinked out, bathing the black sky above in ghostlight.

A man from Vola's ship walked sentry beyond a field of soyflower stalks swaying lazily in a night breeze, his bulky rifle resting on one shoulder. He turned away and walked toward the neighboring farm.

That's Willa Chen's farm, thought Merritt. *And beside that is Johan Wendt's place.*

So close to the window, he could hear the nearby river to the west, just beyond Skip's field — and mingled with that pleasant sound was the grating crackle of electricity.

The barrier, he knew.

Merritt looked again at the room, trying to decide his situation. Beside his cot was a canteen and plate of soy jerky, with two crooked carrots. There was also a small cup filled with clear liquid. Merritt walked carefully with muted footsteps back to his cot and sniffed the cup.

It was Skip's vodka.

The floor creaked to his left as a square cutout in the floor hinged upward. Even though the room was dark, Merritt knew the unmistakable silhouette of the home's owner.

"You never seen this room," Skip said in a soft drawl as he climbed up into the room. Shadows made pits in the cheeks and temples of his thin face. He scratched absentmindedly at his wispy goatee. "I put the kids here when they're too rowdy, or the missus wants some private time with yours truly."

"Where are they?" Merritt whispered.

"Taken," Skip answered, staring at the window curtains. "Same as the rest. I woke up in the field and crawled to the stalks. They forgot about me. Come night, I scrambled back here, swingin' wide of the sentries."

"How did you get me up here?"

"Lysette helped. I found her in some bushes. You wasn't easy to lift, neither. I don't know if anyone's said so, but maybe lay off the bitterbell pie."

"Where's Lysette?"

"Back at her place now, or else she was caught. I told her to stay, but the first patrol come 'round and tore the place up. We was already up here, and I ain't ashamed to say I was cryin'. But the patrol didn't find us. You got to really look for the door to see it. I couldn't say nothin' to make her stay after that. They come through again not long ago, but I was relievin' myself in the stalks and crouched down quick enough." He turned his face in the darkness to look at Merritt, his eyes shining wet. "I don't expect third time's lucky. They know folks is missin'."

Merritt went back to the window and peered outside. "Where did they take them?"

"Up the hill. They got everyone crammed into the prefabs and guards on the doors."

"Is Vola on his ship?"

"He booked it a few hours ago," Skip told him. "Another ship came scootin' across the barrier an' tore off again. I seen its engines in the dark. Vola and the one-armed Scot chased after it."

At least those two aren't around, thought Merritt.

"Well," he said, "if we can't stay here..."

"...then we might as well go *there,*" Skip finished, and Merritt nodded.

"You mentioned bitterbell pie..."

Skip's look of disbelief was plain, even in the dark. "I know you ain't hungry with all that good jerky goin' stale by your cot. Did you hear me say it took two of us to push you in here?"

"It's the fruit I need," Merritt told him, "and some of that irresistible homemade vodka of yours."

Soon after, they waited on the bottom floor of Skip's spacious Pioneer Lodge, watching the sentry loop around the neighboring field and come back for another pass. He had bragged about his house all the way from Earth, while he and Merritt worked inside the walls of the *Halcyon* on the maintenance crew. It was one of two models in the Galena Farming Initiative catalog that had so enticed Merritt's wife to bring their family to another spiral arm of the galaxy, and was nothing short of exorbitant in both cost and presentation.

Skip loved it, though, as did his wife and children, who'd made the journey to join him eight long years after the crash. His "farm castle", he called it. Several of the smaller Wilderness Cabins had survived the crash, their pieces and parts neatly stacked in large metal containers, but Skip's was the only Pioneer Lodge to be recovered from the wreckage. Truth be told, it was probably the only one on board to begin with, as most of the colonists had barely been able to afford the tickets to get them here. That didn't stop him from bragging about it after a dozen or so sips of his own vodka.

The sentry passed out of sight, and Merritt tugged Skip's sleeve and gestured to the door. Skip wore a long-sleeved thermal shirt and black cargo pants that had been found with a hundred similar pairs in a dented supply crate on the shore of a river far from the crash site. His boots were faded brown, but he swore by them. He'd given Merritt a short-sleeved shirt to wear over the hasty bandages. Skip claimed he was saving it for his oldest boy, who was destined to be twice the size of his father. Merritt's padded utility pants were smeared with dirt and dried blood. His boots had been lost somewhere between Lysette's field and Skip's house, but he'd been unconscious when it happened.

Skip followed him out the front door. They kept low to the ground as they hurried into the field of soyflower stalks. Leaves whispered and settled in their wake. Merritt's feet sank into the warm, moist soil when he paused to make sure the sentry hadn't seen them. He was oblivious, humming quietly to himself as he walked the edge of Johan's farm.

They carefully made their way through the colony while avoiding the other sentries — taking a quick detour to Merritt's home for a special pick-up . A short time later, they crouched behind a well-placed wall of stacked supply crates at the base of the central hill. The first pale light of dawn bloomed to the east.

Peeking out from behind the crates, Merritt could see two guards milling about the earthen courtyard between the five low prefabricated buildings that ringed the top of the hill. They looked bored beyond belief, chatting idly and waiting for the sun to rise. One of them squinted into the barrel of his own gun, then yawned.

"Rest of them must be on sentry duty," Merritt whispered. He shifted the two stunner staves he'd picked up at home to his other hand so he could unsling his canteen.

"Or asleep," Skip added. "Someone's gotta work

the day shift. I only counted twelve."

More than fifty colonists against twelve soldiers — but the soldiers had rifles. The colonists were lucky if they had metal shovels and rakes.

Merritt handed Skip the two stunners and brandished the canteen, liquid sloshing within.

"Here goes nothing," he said.

Skip grabbed his forearm when he moved to stand up. Merritt looked at him, confused.

"You don't drink as much as me," Skip said.

"So?"

"So between the two of us, I'm more qualified to make a sale."

Merritt considered his friend's words, then nodded stiffly and took back the two stunners. He handed Skip the canteen.

"If they don't buy it, shout and I'll come running."

Skip flashed a half-grin. "Bullets move faster than you, brother, but I'll shout anyway."

He unscrewed the cap of the canteen and stumbled out from behind the crates, spilling vodka on his shirt. With dramatic flair, he gathered himself to stand up straight, then let out a tremendous belch.

Merritt watched the show through a gap between two supply crates, nervously twisting the long shaft of the stunner staff in his hands.

The guards came to investigate, rifles at the ready.

Skip waved a drunken greeting and tripped toward them. One of the guards raised his rifle, but the other one looked as if he wanted to smile.

"Noble guests!" Skip called up the hill. He gestured vaguely in their direction. "Allow me to use the latrine yonder and I'll dig two roads tomorrow instead of one." He capped off the statement with a hiccup, then stood swaying as he awaited their response.

He's convincing, I'll give him that, Merritt thought.

The guards exchanged a glance, then a quick word.

"What's in the bottle?" one growled.

"Thish?" Skip said, blinking at his canteen. "The besht vodker...vodkis...it'sh booze."

He nodded to himself and stumbled sideways, finding his feet again just before he fell.

"Give it here," said the one guard, approaching with his hand held out.

"Latrine," Skip said simply in drunken defiance.

The guard walked down the hill and scowled in Skip's face, who leaned back from the grimace.

"Go in the bushes," the guard hissed.

Skip made a show of looking into the forest, then shoved the canteen against the guard's chest and wandered off.

"Get him inside," said the other guard.

"After," promised the first as he stalked back up the hill. He sniffed the contents of the canteen, held it at arm's length for inspection, then drank for several seconds. He regarded it with appreciation, then handed it to other guard. "Better than anything we'll get from the commander."

The other guard took a sip and raised an eyebrow. "I thought this was a dry colony." He drank again, gulping loudly.

As Merritt observed the interaction, he rubbed his palm against his shirt where juice from the bitterbell fruit he'd squeezed into the canteen left a sticky residue.

A man had poisoned one of the company wardens using the same technique after the crash. The globe-shaped fruit of the bitterbell plant was toxic to humans if it wasn't boiled and properly treated.

The guard who'd taken the canteen from Skip went first, grabbing for his throat as he fell to his knees. His companion watched him in confusion, until he felt the same tightening in his own throat. Half a minute later, Merritt and Skip stepped over their sprawled forms and strolled across the courtyard under the stars.

"Quickly," Merritt urged as he hurried toward the hospital.

Skip nodded as he split off to visit the other, smaller prefab buildings.

The hospital was packed with his fellow colonists. Some of them blinked at him, confused, when he rushed through the door carrying two stunners. Most were asleep.

"Wake them quietly," he said softly as he moved among them, touching shoulders and offering what little comfort he could. "No talking, no loud noises. Stay low."

He repeated the orders over and over again. Some of the children sniffled and one cried out, but his mother cupped her palm over his mouth and quickly moved for the exit.

Merritt found the dark-haired, youthful captain of the rangers, Weston, near the back of the hospital, already repeating the whispered directions to old

Toph, who was hard of hearing.

Weston was Miles Turner's replacement after the former had been killed by one of the squids during the first exploration of the underwater city three years ago. The other rangers liked him, and he got on well with the farmers. Even Ayani seemed to enjoy his company, spending more time roving the countryside with his patrols than back at the colony. He breathed a sigh of relief when he recognized Merritt. He was in need of a shave, and dark circles hung under his eyes from lack of sleep.

Merritt handed him the stunner staves and told him the plan, asking that he give the second stunner to another of his rangers and guard the rear of what would most likely be a loose and undisciplined caravan of frightened colonists.

Once outside in the warm night air, Merritt led the front of the caravan down the southern slope. Skip directed others as they exited the smaller prefab buildings to join the line streaming away into the darkness.

Merritt's gaze drifted past the two guards on the ground. He knew they would not be rising to interrupt the exodus.

They walked unmolested through the farm fields beneath a dawn sky gradually growing brighter, until one of the sentries noticed that the soyflower stalks were moving by themselves, though the wind wasn't strong enough to rustle the leaves.

A flash of white-blue light accompanied a harsh *brr-ZAP*, and the sentry fell to the ground with a soft thud. Weston had apparently given the second stunner to a capable ranger named Dezza. She grinned down at the fallen sentry and flicked off her stunner staff. The small electric arc dancing in its pronged tip fizzled out.

Merritt halted them at the edge of the pit in the middle of the Cohen farm. He caught the Widow Cohen's eye after she looked back at her home, and she seemed as lost as the rest of them. Maybe she had been hoping to glimpse one of her children inside, safe and sound.

Merritt couldn't remember seeing Arthur among the colonists. He clung to the hope that Gavin had managed to get both of the twins beyond Vola's reach.

He hopped down into the dark tunnel, calling on several others to do the same. They began the process of moving everyone from the surface to the tunnel, though with some, the task was accomplished more gracefully than with others.

After only twenty were pressed down there with him, Merritt was forced to move deeper into the tunnel. He turned on the palm-light he took from his home and guided them away from the Cohen farm. When he reached the reeking corpse of the cave worm that killed Dale, he turned back to tell them how to get past it. There was a wider cavern up ahead, he said. Wait for Weston, and he would lead them through the tunnels, toward the mountains.

The worms always dig at least that far, Merritt knew.

Many of the colonists whispered their thanks as Merritt moved upstream, away from the worm and back to the pit. Many more did not. They walked as if the life had been struck from their bodies, moving one leg and then the other in a daze.

Weston was in the tunnel under the pit, helping the last of the colonists jump down.

"There's a wide spot past the worm," Merritt told him, "but I wouldn't stop there. I imagine you'll see the bottom end of a barrier spike eventually."

"We'll make for the mountain caves," said Weston. "Henry took some of the farmers there when Kellan showed up, and it seems safe enough."

"Lysette's still up there," said Merritt. "I'll find her and join you."

Weston shook his hand, squeezing hard and nodding his thanks, before following after the tail of the procession. Skip hopped lightly down from above, startling Merritt.

"That's all of 'em," he said, putting his hands on his hips. "We didn't do so bad after all."

"You should get an award for your performance," Merritt told him.

Skip shrugged. "Just a shame to waste good drink on the likes of them." He slapped Merritt's shoulder as he followed after Weston. "See ya soon, partner."

Merritt jumped and grabbed an exposed branch near the lip of the hole. The wound in his chest burned as he hauled himself slowly back to the surface to flop on his back atop the wet soil.

Some of the stars were still visible in the early morning sky, but the new Rip had faded near the horizon, becoming a hazy smear of purple-green light.

Despite the ache in his body, Merritt forced himself to roll to his side so he could stand up. As he rose, three soldiers emerged from the soyflower field not five meters away, rifles trained on his chest. He lifted his arms slowly, wincing as the motion pulled open a portion of the burn in his chest that had just begun to knit beneath the gauze.

At first glance, they looked like triplets, with identical buzzcuts, square jaws, and thick brows which no doubt deflected many important thoughts from their brains. Yet they were simply cut from the same cloth, punched from the same mold as so many others in their profession. Strong, hard, thoughtless men without a purpose until someone like Vola scooped them out of society's cage.

Two of them stopped out of arm's reach, but the other shuffled past Merritt and looked down into the worm tunnel.

"Where'd they go?" he barked. "What did you do to Tommy and Ishmael?"

Merritt answered with a small shrug, trying to think how he could buy Weston and the colonists more time. He wiggled his bare toes idly in the soil, wondering how fast he could run without shoes.

"In," the soldier ordered, twitching the barrel of his chunky white rifle toward the pit. "Now."

One of his companions let out a choking sound and dropped to the ground like a sack of bricks. Behind him, Ayani stood silhouetted against the rising disc of Phobis. The soldier beside her swiveled his rifle away from Merritt to the new threat. Her arm whipped out to grab the barrel. She wrenched it free of his hands and swung it like a club. Merritt ducked and the stock cracked into the face of the soldier who'd told him to jump into the pit.

It seemed to happen faster than he could blink.

Ayani aimed the rifle at the only soldier left

standing. He slowly raised his arms and took a step back. She lunged forward and jabbed him twice in the forehead with the nozzle. He blinked hard, shaking his head in confusion. Ayani flipped the rifle around to grab the barrel with both hands, then swung it like a bat against the man's temple. He crumpled next to his unconscious comrades.

Merritt's arms slowly fell to his sides as he surveyed the aftermath with approval.

"Thank you," he said.

One of the soldiers groaned. Ayani sent him back to sleep with a goodnight kiss from the butt of her rifle.

"Any time," she replied.

He stared at the rising sun a long moment, then looked at her. "I have to find someone in the colony. Mind keeping me company?"

Without answering, she fell into step beside him as he walked. She had pulled her long brown hair back in a ponytail. One leg of her dark blue coverall was torn open, and most of the rest was smeared with dirt or blood or both.

It wasn't long before they had to step over the prone body of another soldier, face-down in the dirt. Merritt arched an eyebrow at Ayani, and she shrugged.

"There are a few more," she told him, waving vaguely at the entire colony. "I hope you don't faint easily."

No, he thought. *I want to see them all.*

Merritt had never been a vengeful man. Personal slights faded easily, as did the few grudges he'd expected to hold against people years after an offense. Yet he couldn't deny the small rush of gratification when Ayani bested those soldiers near the worm tunnel entrance. They stood for something which would mean the end of the colony as he knew it. Some of the colonists might survive a transition to industrialization, but Merritt thought a man like Vola wouldn't tolerate dissidents in his new world order.

"Where's Henry?" he asked, fearful of the answer.

"Gone."

"Did you see Gavin when you were outside the colony?"

"No," she said, not without sympathy. "I'm sorry."

"And your Envoy?"

She didn't reply for a long time. They passed another of her defeated soldiers, his neck twisted at a sharp angle.

"Jeff's not what I expected," she said at last. "I expected nothing but bitterness and hatred. If I'd been alive as long as him, I doubt I'd be happy. Yet somehow, he manages."

Merritt frowned. *Alive as long as him,* he thought, the phrase giving him pause.

"After Kellan arrived three years ago," he said, "he showed me a grave that had no business being on Galena. It pre-dated both human colonies. He said that the grave belonged to a man that traveled with someone who had been brought back to life by a machine called a torus."

He watched Ayani's face as he spoke, but it was hard as stone.

"After he was brought back, he couldn't die by natural causes, only by physical trauma. That man died shortly after, burned up in a comet's tail. Kellan told me there was another like him…another one brought back to life, and he never said he didn't die."

"Whose grave was it?"

"Noah Bell's."

Ayani stopped him with a gentle touch of his arm. "Are you telling the truth?"

He nodded.

"That name means something to Jeff. Will tell me where to find the grave?"

After they resumed their walk, Merritt told her where she would find the crumbling torus and the small stone monument to Noah Bell.

They met no more soldiers as they walked to Lysette's farm, crossing the blackened field where Vola's ship had scorched her crops. The ship was gone, as Skip had said, and so was his table.

Lysette wasn't in either of the two storage sheds that marked the border between her field and Ahmed's, nor was she in the house. Merritt and Ayani checked inside every cabinet and storage crate, under her bed, and in her crowded closet made from corrugated metal shoved against the corner of her bedroom.

Merritt didn't want to be on Lysette's property when Vola came back, so he and Ayani agreed to search the nearby farms before heading back to the tunnel to follow the other colonists.

When they stepped outside, Narienne and Henrik were waiting for them on the scorched field, their bald heads shining in the bright morning sunlight. Henrik was bare-handed, but Narienne wielded the same make of rifle as Ayani. They raised them at the same time, but Narienne squeezed her trigger first.

The first shot pelted the ground but the second caught Merritt in the left shoulder and spun him around.

Ayani leapt in front of him and the next bullet from Narienne's rifle ricocheted off the hard white shell of Ayani's.

How...? Merritt managed to think before he fell on his stomach. The blackened ground smelled like smoke and tar.

Narienne flicked a switch on the side of her rifle and a pressure wave slapped the ground at her feet, sending out a circle of dust. Her next trigger-pull produced a thick beam of blue energy that cut down through the air like a laser.

Ayani dodged sideways as the beam tore into the soil. Black smoke billowed angrily and the air crackled with electricity. Ayani swept her rifle in a sideways arc through the smoke, firing as she ran into it. Henrik dove out of the firing path but Narienne was stubborn. She aimed carefully and pulled the trigger...and missed. Ayani had anticipated the shot. She rolled sideways and came into a crouch, the bullet leaving her rifle while she was still in motion, sliding over the charred ground as smoke trailed from her clothes.

The projectile thumped into Narienne's chest and knocked her on her back, where she lay staring up at the sky with unseeing eyes.

Henrik wasted no time.

He fell on Ayani as she tried to stand, knocking her onto her stomach with a two-fisted hammer blow. She spun on the ground and tried to sweep his legs, but he stomped down on her shin with brute force, and she screamed.

Merritt tried to stand, but his legs buckled…so he crawled, his bare feet dragging behind him.

His left shoulder bled onto the hard ground as Henrik and Ayani fought each other, and he felt his energy bleeding away with every drop. He had no idea what he expected to do if he made it to her in time, but he had to do *some*thing.

Henrik picked Ayani up by her thigh and swung her like a doll. She beat at his thick hands with her fists, but he didn't seem to feel it. With a loud grunt, he let her fly. Sweat glistened on his bald, scarred scalp while he watched her fall. His hands closed into fists, and he ran for her.

He shouted and jumped as she lay coughing on the ground, extending his knee in a ramming lunge.

She kicked her legs up at the last second, and her heels caught him under the jaw with a loud *CRACK!* His head snapped back so violently it almost smacked between his shoulder blades, and he fell limp to the ground.

Ayani brushed the dirt from her hands as she stood, sunlight limning her body and shining through her long ponytail. She crossed the charred field to Merritt, limping on the leg Henrik had stomped.

"I may need to swing by the hospital," he said weakly, and she smiled.

GAVIN

He would never be alone again.

Long after the trees of Galena withered, after the oceans dried and the mountains crumbled to dust — after his colony faded to a distant memory — he would endure, and so would Shurri and Arthur.

The ship promised.

Veilship.

The word tumbled around in the vast web of consciousness Gavin now shared with the alien vessel, along with a million others he would one day speak.

Yes, he and the ship thought together. *Speak.*

Gavin was in the nerve center of the veilship — the same round room with walls of living tissue where he had watched supple, leathery branches emerge from the mottled brown flesh of the wall to wrap Shurri from head to toe. He had told Arthur and Niku to place her on the shallow seat in a vertical depression set into the moisture-slick wall.

The Reaver told him that was the only way to save her.

Gavin now sat on a shallow seat in a similar depression, but on one of the other two veilships he'd led his friends to deep beneath the ocean floor. The supple branches, slippery as snakes, roped around his chest and thighs. Two thicker branches emerged from the curved depression wall and spiraled down his arms. Their stubby ends brushed lazily over the backs of his hands while he gestured the commands that controlled his ship.

Reaver.

It was one of the many shapeless concepts that materialized in his mind the instant he joined his consciousness to the veilship, a name that was neither appropriate nor inappropriate. It fit the creature the way the word water fit water — there was no why, it simply was. Knowledge of the great feud between it and The Weaver was illuminated all at once, as if a thousand lights had been simultaneously angled onto a long mosaic inside a dark cave. There was no preamble to these instances, nor to the thousand others that crowded his mind.

The same was true for the way he now saw Galena — as a whole, instead of as a collection of parts.

There were no longer rivers and streams and oceans and freshwater springs. Now they were one — the lifeblood of the planet flowing in different forms.

He could *see* the underground canopy from within the nerve center at the heart of the veilship. It flowed like a river of light beneath the soil, and connected all things.

Gavin needed only to think the command, and his consciousness would extend like a bubble beyond his vision, revealing the secrets of his world.

He'd resisted at first, after hearing what happened when he passed out on Shurri's veilship.

She had screamed, said Arthur, so long and loud he thought her voice would break. He and Niku had pulled at the branches around her waist, but they were stronger than steel. Two branches slithered into her ears, and she'd gone instantly still. The branches gently pulled her upright against the back wall of the curved depression while Arthur and Niku watched helplessly.

When Gavin had crawled to her after he woke, the first thing he saw was her leg. The partially-healed spiral wound had been sealed over with healthy flesh, though the scar formed a puckered canyon in her skin.

The Reaver had only shown Gavin the path that would lead Shurri to the nerve center — the path to healing her wound. It never told him what came after.

But she did.

Gavin, Arthur, and Niku sat on the floor beside her as she told them her story. Soft orange light flowed in patches of varying brightness under the floor, casting a pale, shifting glow into the nerve center.

After she was finished telling them what it felt like to become a pilot of a veilship — the *only* pilot it would ever have — Arthur had been first to stand. At his request, his sister told him how to leave the veilship — the labyrinthine route through its hollow arteries that led to an organic airlock on its underbelly.

Gavin stopped him before he could pull on his helmet and leave the nerve center.

"She's my sister," Arthur responded simply after Gavin signed his protest. "I won't let her do this alone." His eyes slipped away from Gavin's for the briefest moment — a crack in his recently-found courage. "Besides," he added, quietly enough so only Gavin could hear. "I've always wanted to be a pilot."

"He must go," Shurri said behind him. Gavin looked at her, and she nodded. "He must."

After he'd gone, Shurri put her hand to Gavin's cheek. He closed his eyes when he felt its warmth. She had been so deathly cold before.

"You too, love," she whispered. "It must be all three of us."

Why? he signed.

Three ships, she signed weakly. *Three pilots, all or nothing. You'll understand, I promise.*

And now he did.

He had screamed just as long and hard as Shurri, though his scream was soundless. It echoed in his mind, flowing out from his consciousness and surging through the branches squeezing his chest and thighs.

The veilship felt it. Walls shuddered and water gurgled as the vessel thrashed on its umbilical, churning muddy sediment on the bottom of the underground lake.

He didn't fall out of the wall cubby, though. He felt it coming, as if the veilship wanted to spit out a seed, but he forced it to keep him, forced the branches to tighten around his chest once more.

In that moment, there was no longer *him* and *it* — there was only *them*.

Their thoughts bled together, as well as their histories. Gavin's past was simple, and the veilship had the whole of it in a nanosecond. It mourned his losses, cheered his victories, and nurtured his hopes for the future.

Then it spilled its own origin into Gavin's mind, and it nearly broke him.

The veilships were born of The Reaver, though they were sentient in their own right. By corrupting a fraction of Galena's underground canopy, The Reaver was able to inject its vile seed into the global organism.

For The Reaver could only create by corrupting, Gavin now knew.

Its seed sought out the cavern lake beneath the underwater city, where it spawned three invasive tumors which would grow to become the veilships. The lake was a perfect spawning pool, far from the reach of the hex crabs, which would have picked the malignant buds from their umbilicals and consumed them the moment they'd sprouted, as was their design.

Gavin was still processing that much and more as he piloted his veilship over the Equatorial Ocean.

The mottled orange-brown vessel had ridden a powerful upward current from the ocean floor and exploded from the violent surface next to a towering triangular wave, gray water sluicing from its bulging membranes in heavy sheets.

Another mystery solved, thought Gavin when he saw the wave.

His exit from the cavern lake had taken him deeper into the planet. Once unmoored, the veilship drifted in a steady current over the lake bottom, stirring the sediment. A perfectly round hole just large enough for the veilship had been drilled into the muddy bottom. The current sucked Gavin's ship into the hole and pushed it through a series of smooth-walled tunnels.

He had sensed no urgency as he drifted in his and the ship's shared consciousness, so he didn't think to fight the current.

It pushed him out of the tunnel high up in an immense cavern. The veilship managed the transition from submarine to airship gracefully, dipping once when it slipped from the tunnel before leveling out. It looked as small as an insect flying inside a hollow skyscraper.

Water from the cavern lake gushed out of the tunnel to join a hundred other falling rivers, all of them springing from their own tunnels, to disappear into a circular metal grate as big around as the base of a mountain.

Inside the veilship, Gavin could hear the thunderous roar that filled the immense cavern, though not all of it came from the rushing water. Factories of smooth stone as big as cities sat near the outer edge of the circular filter, emitting heat so strongly that the air above them shimmered in pulsing waves.

The veilship tilted down, and descended toward the filter.

Gavin's breath caught in his throat only once, as the ship joined a waterfall and plunged down to the grate, easily passing through its massive woven lattice.

The current overpowered any attempt to counteract it. Gavin and the veilship released control, and allowed themselves to be carried through a dark tunnel. Orange light glowing from the veilship's skin revealed polished rock walls and roiling silver bubbles, and nothing else.

Yet Gavin saw a map of the underwater tunnel system in his mind. It revealed itself to him like a forgotten memory suddenly remembered.

Dozens of identical tunnels led away from the circular filter, snaking through solid rock as they carried the supercharged currents of water higher, toward the surface.

One of the currents fed into and cooled a large black stone machine deep beneath the underwater city where he, Shurri, and Arthur had found Niku. Somehow he knew that without the machine and many more like it, the ocean would crush the invisible walls of the city and crash through its halls.

The tunnel he and his veilship tumbled through spat them out of a hole in the ocean floor, and the current carried them straight to the surface. The veilship erupted from the water like a bullet from a gun, narrowly avoiding a towering unbreaking wave formed by the constant upward current.

There was no damage to himself or the ship, but Gavin had spent a few minutes waiting for his heart to stop pounding inside his chest.

Outside of the dark cavern lake and surrounding tunnels, the veilship's soft orange glow was muted by the overpowering rays of Phobis. Thick veins of fibrous tissue crawled over its bulbous exterior, lashing the ship together. Free of its umbilical and the cradle of immense branches which supported its bulk in the cavern lake, the acre of constricted tentacle branches attached to its underbelly was allowed to unfurl.

They dangled like a twitching forest of sea anemone limbs as the veilship silently flew over calmer waters. Behind the veilship trailed a lumpy pipe of black smoke, dense as night, which hung in the sky like a hose frozen in ice. As the ship flew, fresh black cloud billowed from its aft end, and the pipe grew longer.

The ship's voluminous exhaust belched from a silent system of propulsion Gavin couldn't figure out. He probed their shared consciousness, his curiosity flowing like liquid through the veins of the ship. There was no hint of an engine — nothing that could make it *go*.

That's because you can't see the whole ship, he thought out of nowhere. The realization opened a new door in his mind.

His veilship existed in two places at once — some of it within the realm of Gavin's reality, and the rest of it somewhere else entirely. It was from this other place — this Great Void, as the veilship called it — that it drew its power.

Even saddled to the veilship and staring in the face of innumerable mysteries, he found his mind deviating toward thoughts of Shurri.

She wasn't in the pilot seat of her veilship when Gavin commanded his own to surface, but he had somehow known that Arthur was in his.

With the mere thought of Shurri's twin, glowing orange particles like liquid sparks drifted up from the floor of the nerve center in Gavin's ship. They flowed together to create a representation of Arthur's head and upper body.

Gavin didn't realize he'd thought a question until

Arthur said, "No, I'm staying here. Shurri needs me." He paused, then added, "Niku wants to stay as well."

Already he seemed a different boy than the one Gavin had known for a decade. Because of his own connection to a veilship, Gavin could *feel* inside Arthur's mind when he spoke; could feel a void where fear had once made its nest.

Gavin thought-projected what he meant to do. Arthur's image nodded, and the sparks fell like raindrops and dissolved into the floor.

A ship that straddles two dimensions, thought Gavin. *Command of it at my fingertips. So why do I want so badly to be back on the farm?*

His heart ached to think of it.

Where is this coming from? he wondered.

The veilship offered a freedom no one had ever known. He could go anywhere and do anything; see the wonders of the universe.

And then he remembered he'd never wanted to do any of it. He'd always been happiest with Shurri, as a simple colonist on Galena — his home.

Like his machete, the veilship was a tool. Powerful beyond belief — but just a tool in the end.

Time to use it, he thought.

There were no windows in his ship; no display screens to reveal his surroundings. Yet he saw it all anyway.

Half-sitting on the narrow seat formed from the soft wall of the pilot depression, his legs and chest held firmly in place by wrapped branches, Gavin tilted his head to look at the ceiling. Instead of seeing a glowing blob of orange matter drift past behind a thin wall membrane, he saw the blue sky outside his ship. When he looked down, he didn't see his feet, but the ocean. It gave way to a black sand shore, and then to a forest. Looking forward, he saw the path stretching all the way back to the colony.

And he saw the ships.

There were two of them, facing his direction, hovering over the colony. He breathed in sharply, surprised to realize he could sense the number of people aboard each ship.

Malice and predatory cunning seethed from the single occupant of one vessel.

Vola, Gavin and his veilship thought as one.

The other vessel, hovering fifty meters off the *Morning Sun*'s starboard wing, was crewed by eight. *Spitfire.* Gavin felt no specific anger or hatred from any of them, just a cold sense of duty.

The veilship cast a shadow that swallowed a grid of six farms as it slowed to a silent stop, dwarfing the two opposing vessels. Gavin looked down, seeing the colony below.

They're all gone, he realized, hoping that meant the colonists were safe.

Unbidden, liquid orange sparks flowed up from the floor and swirled to form the shape of Alexander Vola. Unlike Arthur's mental projection, Gavin felt as if he were seeing a copy of a visual signal Vola was broadcasting from his bridge. The sparks formed a perfect three-dimensional representation of Vola's command chair and Vola himself.

He was leaning forward in his chair, arms on his elbows, fingers interlaced under his chin.

"I want that ship," he said crisply.

His voice came through so crystal clear he could

have been standing right in front of Gavin.

"Leave," thought Gavin — except it *wasn't* a thought.

A voice he'd never heard had spoken. It was the disembodied voice of a young man of maybe eighteen years. The word was preceded and chased by a slight echo, as if it had been spoken in an empty concert hall.

Vola sat upright in his chair. "I was led to believe you were mute."

Gavin spoke without speaking, his veilship forming the echoing words. "You are not welcome here."

Vola lifted a finger ever-so-slightly, and Gavin felt the other ship drift to port. Without warning, it lifted and spun sideways, streams of projectiles spitting through the air. Gavin felt them puncture the front of the veilship, heard its cry of pain in his mind.

The vessel launched forward, following its projectile volley with a steady stream of tumbling kevlar chains which ripped into the soft flesh of the veilship.

Gavin didn't know what to do. The ship seemed separate from him then — two minds instead of one.

The *Spitfire* roared past his veilship, banking for another pass.

Closing his eyes, he reached for it.

Cold metal, burning engines, empty hallways, warm bodies, pumping blood — he felt all of this and more as his augmented consciousness swept over the *Spitfire*. The ship froze in midair under the assault, engines screaming as the pilot throttled up to escape the iron grip.

Gavin's own small ethereal presence was rolled into the tidal wave of another — the veilship's. Together, they crashed into the hull of the *Spitfire*, washing through it and carrying away the people inside, carrying them...elsewhere.

The smaller ship dropped like a stone, devoid of crew. Just before impact against the surface below, automatic emergency systems kicked in. The ship righted itself and landed behind Uda and Niku's farmhouse.

The glowing orange recreation of Alexander Vola seemed to consider what had just occurred. He tapped on the control panel of his arm chair, then frowned at whatever it had reported back to him.

"Your people are currently clustered in an underground chamber some five kilometers northwest of the colony," he said, leaning to one side of his chair. Gavin heard his leather jacket creak as if Vola were right beside him. "Surrender. Give me your ship, and let them live."

Give him my ship, thought Gavin. Such a simple concept — yet impossible. He knew that he was the only pilot his veilship would ever accept. He felt that in his bones the moment he opened his mind to the alien vessel.

What would my father do? he wondered.

At that exact moment, a presence made itself known in the hospital prefab, tapping on Gavin's mind like a spider taps on a single strand of its silken web to lure in prey. Gavin frowned, wondering how he could feel a sensation so specific.

He strained to extend his ship's consciousness deeper into the colony, pushing his field of vision along with it.

His father emerged from the hospital prefab, a bloody bandage wrapped around his shoulder. Ayani helped him limp across the courtyard.

Vola saw them, too.

The orange sparks forming his mouth twisted into a malicious grin.

"Think faster next time," he said, and his image cut out. The orange sparks fell like dead flies.

Ayani pointed to the sky, and Gavin's father looked up at the veilship.

A missile slammed into the hospital, and the courtyard was engulfed by a phosphorus glare. The pencil-thin shadow of his father was tossed through the glare like a rag doll.

Gavin lunged forward, but was restrained by the roots around his chest and thighs. The veilship screamed for him, the sound swelling in the nerve center until the walls shook. Under the ship, the forest of long whip-like branches shuddered in unison.

He was merely an observer to what he did next. His mind took over, and the mind of his ship, and he could only watch.

Through a haze of rage, he saw Vola's ship peel away in the opposite direction. Thrusters fired.

The veilship pursued, gliding silently forward, belching black smoke behind. Vola's *Morning Sun* was fast, but Gavin's veilship straddled two dimensions. It slid forward until the *Morning Sun*'s thrusters were near enough to scorch its orange-brown flesh.

Then it seemed to be in two places at once. A shadow version of itself blinked into existence directly in front of the first, surrounding the *Morning Sun* completely.

Gavin felt an explosion of pain from Alexander Vola in that moment, as if years of torture had been inflicted upon his mind and body in a single second. His soul shredded in the talons of the veilship, until there was nothing left but ribbons.

Only then, in the following silence, did Gavin draw a breath.

The *Morning Sun* was gone. Even its memory was quickly fading, as if soon it would have never been.

Gavin's veilship responded to his unthought desires and veered back toward the colony. The branches encircling his body slackened enough for him to step down to the floor of the nerve center.

The rest was a blur — his mad dash through the bowels of the veilship, his descent to the surface on one of the many tentacle branches dangling from the ship's underbelly — up until he skid to a halt when he saw his father on the ground.

Ayani knelt beside him, one hand pressed to a bleeding wound in her side. Her coverall had burned away in spots, as if someone had struck her with a fistful of burning embers — all except her right pant leg and the sleeve of her right arm. They had burned away completely, revealing charred flesh. The look she gave Gavin when she saw him was filled with enough grief and pity to last two lifetimes.

She slowly backed away as he approached. Gavin still wore his orange space suit, though now the top was pulled down to his waist, exposing a white shirt so filthy it was almost black.

He wiped his sweating palms against it as he

knelt next to his father's broken body.

The missile hit the hospital, but the blast radius engulfed the entire hill. Gavin couldn't tell which of his father's wounds had already been there when the fire washed over his body.

Gavin looked back at the waiting veilship, silent as the grave. Its lower branches hung just above the surface.

When he looked down again, his father's eyes were open.

Gavin grabbed the hand with the least amount of burns and held it in his lap. His father smiled.

"Nice ship," he whispered.

Dad... Gavin signed.

His father squeezed his hand and gently shook his head. "I'm going to see your mother. I can tell her..." Pain seized him, and his back arched. When it subsided, he let out a long breath. His eyelids fluttered. Then he saw Gavin again. "...tell her how proud I am of you."

Gavin wiped his eyes and started to stand, his hands moving quickly.

I'll get the LifeScan equipment. There's still time.

If he managed to scan his father's brain and collect a sample of his DNA, he could use the device Kellan left on Galena to bring him back — the device that was collecting dust under their work table at home.

Because it isn't a question of if, said a dark voice inside Gavin. *Just look at his body.*

His father grabbed his wrist and pulled him back down to his knees, shockingly hard.

"No," he said firmly. "Gavin, no. Please. I don't

want that. I want...I want to see your mother again."

His father's gaze drifted far away, as if he could already see her. Gavin picked up his hand again.

What does she look like, Dad? he thought. *Can you see her face? Can you hear her voice?*

Her voice.

The veilship drifted closer.

A voice spoke loud enough to be heard on the central hill — the disembodied voice of a young man, perhaps eighteen years of age.

"Tell Mom her boy misses her."

His father's vision snapped back to find Gavin. Tears streamed down his cheeks as he heard his son's voice for the first time. His body shook with sobs.

"I'm going to miss you too, Dad," Gavin said through his veilship, his mouth never moving.

Later, after all his tears had been cried out, Gavin picked up his father's body, and carried him home.

THE ENVOY

The *Morning Sun* was gone by the time he crawled back to the surface. Two starburst craters marked where its engines had scorched the ground.

That explains the tremors, thought Jeff as he emerged from the mouth of the river cave. The underground canopy had probably reacted when the ship's engines ignited, blasting the topsoil with concentrated heat. Jeff had been climbing up the treacherous, boulder-strewn passage leading up from the waterfall cavern, and had pressed himself flat against a massive stone as the rock walls trembled. Pebbles and loose dirt rained down from above, threatening another cave-in.

When the tremors subsided, he climbed the rest of the way up to the river mouth, the boots of his black Constellation Mark VIII space suit slipping on thin patches of red lichen.

The water rushed black and foamy in the dark cave, but turned brilliant blue once it spilled out into the sunlight, tumbling over rocks before calming as it snaked toward the horizon.

Kellan McEwan sat beside it some distance off, his back to the cave.

Jeff strode toward the hypermass pill, still hovering above the splayed walls of its shield cube.

His hair stood on end as he walked past.

Kellan sat with his knees hugging his chest, his left arm-stump draped around them while he picked at a clump of moss on the ground with his only hand. He squinted at the bright surface of the river, which gleamed like polished coins in the sun.

Jeff walked around him and stood by the river's edge, enjoying the fresh smells of mineral water and wet soil. It was a welcome change from the putrid odors in The Reaver's chambers.

I know your name now, he thought. *The name of your soul.*

Kellan looked like a risen corpse. Black circles rimmed his hollow eyes. His face was pinched and drawn, his cheeks sallow and bloodless from the effects of hypermass radiation.

"He left me," said Kellan. "I...I stumbled when the hatch was rising, and he didn't wait. I jumped to catch it, but..."

He waggled his useless stump.

Jeff looked away, toward two distant mountains awash with mid-morning splendor.

"You've made a lot of bad decisions," he said.

"Seems that way now," Kellan agreed sadly. "Though for a while I thought it might turn in my favor. You know I offered him my remaining few officers to bolster his ranks? Arrogant boy that he is, he rejected my offer in front of his men, and mine." He fell silent for a time, then added, "I hope they find their way back home."

"You should have adapted to this world instead of trying to change it."

Kellan snorted. "I should have left you under the

hypermass instead of listening to Vola. Now look at me." He held up his right hand, the skin pale gray and shot through with dark veins. "Vola wants to be you. Did you know that? He wants to live forever. I only ever wanted a percentage."

Jeff left him there, by the river.

He returned to the pill and waited as the shield cube walls rose around it, pushed off the soil by long pistons which nested back in their slots once the walls were in place.

After the tow cable was reattached to the *Celerity*, Jeff pulled himself over the ledge of the half-open ramp and used the manual crank to seal it tight against the ship's scarred and pitted hull.

The nose of the ship swung over the river as it lifted from the ground, giving Jeff one last look at Kellan, still sitting beside the river, holding his knees to his chest.

It seemed petty in retrospect, but Jeff had deliberately chosen to withhold the gift of satisfaction from Kellan by not telling him Vola was already gone — he would never be granted his wish of immortality.

Jeff had stolen that piece of information from The Reaver during their communion — that, and so much more.

Then the view out the window was of the way back to the colony.

The hypermass shield cube lurched in place as the cable snapped taut, then lifted on a cloud of shimmering air to trail behind the *Celerity*.

Jeff had been so close to detonating it before Kellan and Vola dragged him down to see The Reaver, never once thinking that it might instead kill the very thing that had been keeping the alien captive for centuries — the underground canopy.

When he'd first fallen into The Reaver's consciousness, he thought he was falling into an eternity of torture. His body was pulled apart and put back together so many times he'd lost count, screaming whenever his throat was remade in the great void through which he endlessly tumbled.

He soon realized The Reaver was fighting his presence — defending itself from an intruder. Jeff's communions with The Weaver had always been pleasant, and sometimes outright enjoyable.

That's because it wanted me to see, he thought. *The Reaver does not.*

Yet Jeff took the knowledge anyway. He overcame the pain and kept his mind from ripping apart by sheer will. The Reaver weakened, and Jeff became the dominant presence in their shared consciousness.

It was a dark place, and vast. Purple lightning streaked through black clouds above and below. Jeff drifted formless between them, his particles scattering and coming back together when an indigo bolt disrupted his thoughts.

The clouds parted to show him a primordial landscape of volcanic ash and spewing lava — the Weavers' homeworld. Several of them floated in the distance, little rocks on the smoky horizon. One of them was nearer, and it floated above a wide crater filled with ruddy lava and black cloud. Lightning crackled within, flashing against the jagged rock texture of The Weaver's underbelly.

Tendrils rose from the crater, long black fibrous ropes...searching. They found the edge of the crater and strained against it, pulling the misshapen bulk of The Reaver out of the roiling mass of lava and black cloud.

The Weaver created it, Jeff realized.

A flood of emotion washed over him — confusion and pain and loneliness and a great longing for purpose.

The emotions belonged to The Reaver in the first few moments after its birth.

Not birth, Jeff knew. *Not entirely.*

While the physical form of The Reaver had been engineered by its creator from the primordial goop of its homeworld, its true essence — its soul — had been ripped from elsewhere and molded into a physical form by The Weaver. Thus its creation was anchored in two realms — the physical and the ethereal — its mind torn in half between them, driving it always toward madness.

A lightning-streaked cloud swept over the memory, sending it back to the void. In its place, Jeff saw centuries of painful memories compressed into a single heartbeat: The Reaver put to work, made to haul mountains of raw material from the deep mines of the Weavers.

They created drones of us for such a purpose, Jeff remembered. The Weaver used resurrected humans to build a small city on Titan, and the larger one on Venus that was never finished.

The Reaver toiled for centuries, and was eventually forgotten in favor of newer creations which better interested its creators.

So it turned against them, drawing its power from the deep well of anger and resentment that had been slowly filling since it first crawled from its cradle. The poisoned water of that well solidified to anger, and it killed many of the Weavers during its years-long rampage, suffocating them with its long tendrils — choking away their eternal lives.

Aimless, it roamed the cosmos after narrowly escaping capture, until it discovered Galena.

It found a place to rest — and eventually, it found a purpose.

The planet was raw back then, wild and untamed. The Reaver sensed the presence of another sentient species beneath the waves, but the matter was of no concern. It nestled into a safe, warm cavern and secured itself to the inner walls glowing bright with purple crystals, and most of its mind went to sleep.

The rest forced a connection with the vast underground canopy. The Reaver slipped a corrupted finger into the pathways which fed life to so much of the planet. By the time it had worked out a way to spawn veilships by twisting the purity of the canopy toward a darker purpose, The Weaver had arrived.

There was meant to be a fleet of the dread warships, floating like balloons from every part of Galena's surface, anchored by braided umbilicals that burrowed into the soft soil to connect them with the canopy below. The Reaver would command them; would connect its consciousness to theirs and sweep across the stars, consuming everything in its path.

In its dormant state, it wasn't able to feel The Weaver's plan.

Its enemy made an ally of the sentient

underwater species, and raised them up from their primitive ways.

The Gardeners, Jeff knew without ever being told.

Centuries before they disappeared, the Gardeners abandoned their sprawling underwater cavern system for cities of stone on the ocean floor — yet they walked the surface as well — tall and slender, with crafty, delicate hands. It was on the surface that they cultivated the forests, engineering their borders to form a single globe-spanning organism.

Into the forests they released the hex crabs, which picked clean the buds of The Reaver's veilships before they could blossom. Every two years, hundreds of thousands of new-spawned hex crabs would crawl from nutrient-rich gestation vats and emerge from their pyramid to begin a year-long migration through the forest, following the underground canopy that nourished them.

The Gardeners tended the trees and the canopy, and the beasts of Galena as well.

They cleared the rivers and seas of a four-legged aquatic beast which would have decimated the hex crabs as they slowly traversed the equator. The beast laid thousands of eggs at a time along the muddy river banks, which fed smaller creatures. With the eggs gone, the rivers and streams soon became barren.

The rock bats in their jagged pillars hunted the hex crabs as well, but only in small numbers. Their droppings fertilized the soil over the canopy, enriching it to the benefit of the other crabs, and so the Gardeners did not interfere.

Jeff saw all this and more in the span of a few

breaths.

When he finally spilled from its consciousness and rose coughing from the floor of the cathedral cavern, The Reaver was straining against the tendrils cementing it to the inner rock walls.

It wanted him to detonate the hypermass. Jeff had seen that in the void. Most of the knowledge exchanged during their communion had flowed one way, from The Reaver to Jeff — yet he'd felt his secret of the hypermass slip away, siphoned into the clouds by another will. The hypermass was more likely to peel back the canopy prison that kept The Reaver at bay than it was to destroy the creature itself.

"You can't escape, can you?" Jeff said hoarsely. His throat was bone-dry. "Not so long as the crabs migrate. As long as they tend the canopy. And now someone else has the veilships."

He had seen that as well: Gavin, Shurri, and Arthur in their pilot cubbies, their minds one with their ships. Jeff wasn't sure he'd be able to scrape his way through a confrontation with all three of them.

Part of him dreaded going back to the colony for that reason.

He called up a localized map to check how far out he was from the colony, and from Ayani's homing beacon — then he frowned.

Her beacon wasn't anywhere *near* the colony.

After a quick course adjustment, the ailing *Celerity* banked, heading south.

Hold together a little longer, Jeff urged his ship. *I could have skipped,* part of him conceded. *And your ship could have fallen to pieces when it jumped through the space between,* said another.

Jeff wouldn't risk it. Ayani's homing beacon was embedded with simple vital readings — simple, but detailed enough to report that she'd been injured, though not critically. Jeff weighed the data against the possibility his ship might break apart if he skipped, and had decided to fly traditional.

A dozen new alarms had gone off when he tried to silence the dozen that popped up when he'd first set down, and there was a persistent rattle from inside the starboard hull.

She was waiting for him near a shaded freshwater spring, sitting against an enormous house-sized silver-gray boulder at the edge of the forest. Jeff set down in a nearby sunny field and hopped down from the half-open ramp, watching the shield cube land itself behind the ship.

Vivid red healing moss of varying sizes loitered near the bubbling mouth of the spring. The corner of one rectangular critter dangled limply in the trickling stream winding away into the forest, lazy tendrils soaking.

The moss was everywhere: crawling up tree trunks, resting on the ground near the spring — even stuck to the sides of the boulder.

Two pale red rectangles of moss smothered Ayani's right arm and leg. She opened her eyes and offered Jeff a weak smile when she heard him approach. When he sat down beside her with his back to the cool boulder, he noticed the smaller patch of moss stuck to the side of her ribcage. Dried blood traced a dark line on her stained coverall from whatever wound it was healing.

"Your eye," she said. "The light is gone."

Jeff had suspected as much.

He had tried to access the life-light several times since his communion with The Reaver, but had been unable to see the multicolored beams which burst from all the living organisms on Galena. He sensed that the knowledge he forced The Reaver to unwillingly surrender had come at a price — that he would have to leave a part of himself in the void as payment for what he brought back.

He sniffed and said, "It's nothing."

"I have a question," she said. "Why is there just one Weaver? Why didn't it make more?"

"That's what it was trying to do on Venus," Jeff answered. "It was terraforming to make a new homeworld. There would have been a spawning ground for more of them, but they captured it and hauled it back to Earth before it could finish."

"The Weaver let them take it?"

"It was dormant at the time. It seems to do that in cycles. Otherwise they wouldn't have been able to get close."

She frowned. "So what's happening on Venus now?"

"Everything stopped when they imprisoned The Weaver. Frozen."

Jeff remembered the images General Trager showed him of the surface. Large black structures swept toward every horizon, most of them only half-finished. Human drones hung in the air like flies in amber. Massive black pillars that were meant to be arches rose from the surface and terminated before they could curve back down, their open ends a jagged mesh of shimmering alloys.

It had looked like that for more than three centuries, Trager told him.

Jeff forced his mind back to the present. He tried to lift the corner of the moss covering Ayani's right leg, but it was cemented to her skin.

"What happened?" he asked.

"Burned," she answered. "Vola's gone. And Merritt. Gavin, he..."

She swallowed hard, choking back emotion.

"I know," Jeff said gently. "I saw."

She looked at him curiously, but didn't ask him to explain.

He sighed and made a show of checking the moss again. "I expect you waded right into those soldiers without so much as a weapon."

Ayani held up a fist, showcasing her weapon, and grinned.

He leaned his head back until it touched the rock, then said, "I should have gone with you. I'm sorry."

She shrugged almost imperceptibly. "You're The Envoy."

"You're my friend." He looked around the shaded oasis. "This isn't exactly close to the colony."

"Missile hit the hospital. No moss there anyway."

"And the colonists?"

"Safe."

They sat in silence. Jeff listened to the gentle trickle of the stream, and Ayani's deep, steady breathing. He thought she'd fallen asleep until she said, "I didn't come here just for the moss."

She groaned as she stood, bracing herself against the boulder.

"Ayani..." he warned, standing with her, ready to

catch her if she stumbled.

She waved him off. The moss was wrapped like thick sleeves around her arm and leg. The smaller patch on her side crumbled away in dried-out chunks when she poked it. A ragged hole was beneath, and inside it was a fresh pink scar in the shape of a starburst.

"It's not far," she said, and started walking. Her right leg wouldn't bend at the knee because of the moss, so she swung it out with each step.

Jeff followed her into the forest, staying close to the stream. The pale yellow sun made long pillars of the trees' shadows. Ayani veered from the stream and walked away from the sun, eventually leading Jeff to a different raised spring. Patches of moss larger than the ones at the other spring crawled slowly over the moist ground.

Near the spring, a void-black arch rose from loose soil and came back down a short distance away, burrowing into the ground. A lichen-covered chunk of the same material lay beneath the arch.

Ayani waited as Jeff approached the arch, reaching for it with a trembling hand. Its surface was so dark it seemed to soak up the light.

"This is a torus," he said as he pressed his palm to the arch. "How did you know it was here?"

"Merritt told me. He and Kellan found it three years ago."

Jeff's gaze drifted down to a lead sulfide headstone leaning at an angle from the ground. He knelt before it and rubbed a film of grime from the etched letters *N.B.*

"Noah Bell," Jeff whispered. "So this is where you

ended up."

Below the letters, someone had scratched a rudimentary diagram of Earth's solar system, with a small arrow pointing at Earth.

Jeff stood slowly and looked around the shaded glen as if seeing it for the first time.

"Riley was with him," he said. "He dug the grave."

Jeff had parted ways with them before they embarked on a galactic tour, jumping between tori on different planets. The tour must have ended on Galena. Riley returned to Earth, but Noah never did.

He turned to talk to Ayani, but she had left him alone, making her limping way back toward the ship.

Jeff looked down at the headstone, and bid farewell to his old friend.

When he got back to the ship, Ayani was leaning against one leg of the landing gear with her arms crossed, staring at the shield cube. The moss from her arm and leg lay scattered in dried-out flakes at her feet.

"You didn't blow it up," she said.

"Didn't have to. The canopy surrounding the cavern creates a prison cell. If I'd detonated the hypermass, I might have destroyed the prison instead of the prisoner. It can't escape."

"Huh," Ayani said thoughtfully. "I'm sorry you didn't get to use your bomb."

He shrugged. "Never say never."

Ayani gestured at her bare arm and leg. "What do you think?"

He inspected the raw red skin. "I think the moss works fast. Maybe you should have left them on longer."

"What are you trying to say?"

He smiled as he walked past her, toward the ramp. "I hope you have a good moisturizer."

"You could use it on that thick scar of yours," she called after him. "It might soak through and soften your skull a bit."

They were agreed that the time was right to return to Earth. Ayani had years of field reports she wanted to submit to the Seattle office, and Jeff wanted to commune with The Weaver as soon as possible.

"Do you think Trager will let you anywhere *near* it after what you pulled?" Ayani asked him as the *Celerity* lifted off.

"One way to find out," he replied, sounding more confident than he felt. In truth, he was terrified he'd be arrested the moment they went back through the Rip — not because of the time it would cost him, but because he wanted to share all that he'd learned with The Weaver.

It won't be the first time I've had to appeal to the general's empathy, Jeff thought as he set a course for the colony. He only hoped the man's limited supply of it hadn't run dry in the time Jeff was on Galena.

Ayani frowned at the control panel when she noticed the ship was still flying parallel to the surface. "The Rip is up *there*, not down here."

"We'd never make it in this bucket of bolts," he said. Then he patted the side of the rattling control panel. "Nothing personal, sweetheart. You've been great."

The electric blue barrier was still crackling when the *Celerity* passed above it.

Jeff trusted the memory he'd seen while sharing

a consciousness with The Reaver — a memory which had traveled through the space between, passing from the veilship to its creator.

It was a memory of an empty ship coming to rest in the middle of a farm field after a failed attack on the veilship.

Minutes later, Jeff landed the *Celerity* next to the empty *Spitfire*. He transferred the tow cable while Ayani moved their personal effects to The Envoy's new ship. She limped on her right leg, but was already looking stronger. He apologized about the moisturizer comment in passing. She punched his shoulder in response and told him he was going soft.

Maybe she was right. Later, she caught him admiring the darkwood embellishments on the bridge when she returned.

"Going to keep it?" she asked as she took a seat at the control station next to the wide view screen at the front of the bridge.

"It'll work," he answered. "Thank you, Marco."

"Gavin is a natural with mechanics," said Ayani. "Maybe he can patch up the Celerity."

"He's welcome to try."

Jeff sat in the pilot seat in the middle of the dimly-lit bridge and set a course for the Rip — leaving time for one small detour along the way.

A single kevlar chain was enough to rip through one of the barrier darts surrounding the colony. It exploded in a cloud of metal shards and the barrier blinked out.

"Always good to leave a place better than you found it," he said as he angled the *Spitfire* toward the sky. It was a much more agile ship than his *Celerity*.

The brilliant blue sky had almost completely transitioned to the black of space when an alarm bleeped on Ayani's panel. She seemed confused for a moment as she studied the interface, then slid the pulsing red box to the side.

The view screen flicked on, showing a wide landscape view of Galena as the ship flew away from it.

Behind the trailing shield cube, a veilship grew larger in the center of the screen, thick black smoke billowing in its wake as it rapidly gained on the *Spitfire*.

"Look who came to say goodbye," Jeff muttered under his breath.

The image of Galena was replaced by an orange-tinted monochrome representation of Gavin Alder. The details of his face and body were sketched by crude lines made up of what looked like a million magnet shavings — tiny gray needles that danced and reformed with his every movement. They briefly trailed a ghostly image of his head when he nodded a greeting.

He stood in a curved depression aboard the bridge of the veilship, seemingly pinned there by a dozen thick ropes or vines wrapped around his chest.

"I'm sorry to hear about your father," Jeff said.

Gavin looked down for a moment, the myriad dancing gray lines shaping his face blurring with the quick movement. Then he looked up, and his voice filled the bridge of the *Spitfire*, though his mouth never moved.

"Thank you for your help." A faint echo chased after his voice. "Ayani, Weston's going to miss you."

"Tell him to make sure he clears his corners. I'll come back someday and check."

"No," said Gavin's voice, heavy with sadness. "No one comes back."

Jeff and Ayani exchanged a wary glance.

"The Reaver is on Galena," Jeff reminded him.

"And here it will stay. I know about the other one...the one in your shipyard. I don't trust anyone from Earth with the future of our colony. My father trusted Kellan, and look where that got him. He—"

Gavin's voice broke off, thick with emotion. The sketched outline of his face on the view screen looked away.

"Gavin," Jeff said carefully, "it's *Earth's* colony."

"Not anymore. You tell them no one comes back through the Rip. No one comes back, or we'll be waiting. Let us be farmers, or whatever else we want to be...not what *they* want us to be. Let us live without looking to the skies in fear of another ship."

"Think about what you're saying," Jeff said. "Think about what it means to be cut off from Earth."

"It means no big cities," Gavin's voice replied. "It means no failed crops, no low birth rates, no snatchers."

"It's never that simple."

"I will *make* it simple!" shouted Gavin's voice, his calm facade cracking to reveal a burning anger. The sketched lines of his face vibrated with his words. "You have already destroyed one planet. You will not destroy ours."

The silence that followed stretched painfully.

"I will tell them," Jeff said at last.

Gavin looked to the side, the conversation

finished.

"Henry is still on the Celerity," Ayani blurted. "Gavin, please..."

Gavin hesitated, and in that moment Jeff saw a hint of the boy he'd met in the cathedral cavern three years ago — a boy filled with curiosity, still clinging to an innocence that had been ripped away along with his father.

"Was he alone when he...?"

"I was with him."

Gavin nodded, and the view screen switched back to the image of Galena, shrinking slowly as the *Spitfire* left it behind.

"Trager's not going to like that one bit," Ayani said to break the silence.

"Not just him," Jeff added. "I doubt Luciano Vola is going to be happy to learn his son disappeared on a planet no one's allowed to visit."

"Do you really think Gavin would attack us if we came back?"

"I think he's been on the wrong end of other people's progress all his life," Jeff replied. "And I think being the pilot of a ship made by something called The Reaver is asking to be corrupted."

"So what do we do?"

Jeff let out a slow sigh and sank back into his comfortable, high-backed chair as he watched Galena recede on the view screen. He absentmindedly ran a finger up the scar over his left eye patch.

"We go back to Earth and relay the message," he said at last. "And sleep for a *very* long time."

"You old man," Ayani teased. "Just sleep on the way. We have five months."

"Think so?"

She gave him that curious look again.

Jeff let the deep hum build in his skull until his vision vibrated. He imagined a point near the Ceres Rip. His fingers tingled, and he skipped.

The *Spitfire* appeared in deep space, facing the tall purple-green iris of the Rip. Jeff grinned, savoring his personal victory. He had reached farther than ever to see if he could make the journey in a single skip.

"What..." Ayani said, staring at him. "...was *that?*"

"Something I learned from The Weaver. That's how we're going to get home in a day instead of five months."

The dim bridge lights glowed brighter and took on a red hue as an alarm blared throughout the ship.

"Sentry wall," said Ayani, her hands working the control panel. "Looks like we're not going anywhere except back."

Jeff's chair had smaller control panels in each armrest. He tapped out a quick command, then magnified the view screen until the sentry wall was in clear focus. Its metal walls unfolded to reveal its city-sized arsenal.

A dark object shot toward it from behind the *Spitfire*. A heartbeat later, a new star appeared in front of the Rip, swelling white, its surface crawling with whip-like flares, before shrinking to a pinpoint against the darkness. The pinpoint blinked out, and the alarms on the *Spitfire* went silent.

Ayani turned around slowly in her chair to face Jeff. "Well, well, well," she said primly. "You got to use your bomb after all."

"You never doubted me for a second," he said, and she laughed.

He set a course through the Rip, eager to test the *Spitfire*'s engines over a long stretch of space on the other side.

EPILOGUE

The bait worm wriggled beneath the surface, dancing on the hook that impaled its body. Ripples of late afternoon sunlight glinted off its shiny black carapace and segmented legs half as long as a finger.

They were hard to spot against the black sand, even with nothing but shallow, crystal clear water above, yet all you had to do was dig your hand into the sand up to your wrists, and you'd pull up a fistful of them.

A flat round fish with a ribbon of fin around its gray-black body drifted below the twitching worm, the four eyes on its flat back regarding it coldly.

Emily sighed.

"They're not *hungry*," she pouted, sticking out her bottom lip and wrinkling her nose. She gave her pole a shake. The worm dangling from the hook at the end of her line spasmed, then went still.

Gavin ruffled her short, sandy hair and stood up on the raft to look at the sun as it dipped closer to the horizon. They would need to head back to the colony soon.

A roar of laughter followed by a loud splash drew his attention toward the shore, where Toma and his mother Uda fled from Niku through ankle-deep water, kicking up fans of foamy water.

Toma is growing fast, Gavin thought, smiling as

he watched the mock-chase. Eight years old, the boy was more than twice the height of Gavin and Shurri's three-year-old Emily, and threatened to grow taller than his father.

Most colonists enjoyed the western shore of the Casmin Sea closer to home when they were in the mood for a swim or a bit of sunbathing, but Niku and Uda always brought Toma here, to the ocean. He still made camp on the western shore of the Casmin while exploring the underwater city for a week here and there, but he claimed he liked to keep work and play separate.

Farther up the black sand beach, wiry Skip and his stout wife, Janey, basked on their backs in the sun, holding hands. They had left their six children on the farm, the elder in charge of the younger. Even still, Lysette was always willing to swing by to make sure they hadn't burned the place down.

Skip had taken the death of Gavin's father harder than anyone other than Gavin himself. His face still grew solemn at the mention of his name, and he could often be heard toasting his good friend Merritt after a few too many pulls at his "special" canteen.

After three years, the sharp pain of his father's passing had blunted to a dull ache in Gavin's heart. Sometimes Emily would look up at him and smile, and Gavin would see his father's eyes and chin. The memories would often come flooding back in moments like that, and he'd have to fight to keep from crying as he kissed her forehead.

"I got one!" Emily shouted suddenly.

She stood up on her short legs, rocking the raft. In the shallow water below, a disc-shaped fish thrashed at the end of her line. It pulled too hard and the strip of dead tree she'd been using for a rod slipped from her hand and plunked into the water. The fish swam off, trailing the rod with it.

"Hey, give that back!" she shouted.

A tinkle of distant laughter drifted over the water.

Down the beach from Skip and Janey, Shurri was returning from her walk, barefoot in the sand. She wore a loose linen blouse that came down to her thighs. The deep, pale scar winding up her left leg from her ankle stood in stark contrast to her tan skin. If you knew to look for it, you'd catch a slight limp on that side when she walked, even less pronounced than Gavin's own.

When she became the pilot of her veilship, the vessel had stitched her up, finishing the job the insufficient supply of healing moss had begun.

Dale died because I gave all the moss to Shurri, thought Gavin, remembering him on the cold metal table in the hospital, already dead, while Uda fussed over Shurri's leg.

There hadn't even been enough moss to cover the whole terrible wound, but Gavin had dumped it on anyway, terror-blind at the thought of losing her.

Uda told him that such a meager amount wouldn't have made a difference for Dale, either. He'd already lost too much blood. Yet that didn't ease Gavin's tortured mind. He still felt responsible for robbing Arthur and Shurri of a potential stepfather, and their mother of her future husband.

The wind pulled at Shurri's blouse and the short, sandy hair she'd passed to their daughter. Her hands cradled her pregnant belly, so swollen Gavin expected the baby to arrive at any minute.

Arthur had gone with her, but now he was nowhere to be seen. Gavin wasn't surprised. He usually went off on his own whenever his twin sister talked him into going to the beach. Sometimes he'd be gone for days. When Shurri asked him about where he went, he would shrug and say he just needed time to think.

Yet Gavin knew the truth. He knew Arthur went to his veilship.

Gavin's own veilship called to him, as Shurri's and Arthur's ships called to their pilots. Shurri hadn't sat in her command seat since she learned she was pregnant with Emily. Gavin spent far too much of his waking time willfully ignoring the gentle but insistent beckoning of his veilship. Every time he shared its consciousness, he came away feeling like he'd left part of himself behind. Besides that, there had been no need. He had revisited the lake cavern in his veilship and excised the corrupt branches, yanking them from the mud in gouts of oily discharge.

He'd done the same in The Reaver's cavern, though that time with one of the energy rifles Vola's soldiers bequeathed the colony upon their deaths. The crackling blue beam sliced through thick black branches that crawled from the reeking mass of tissue beneath The Reaver. The walls shook and loose rock tumbled from the walls, but the canopy prison surrounding the cavern remained intact.

No more veilships would spawn from corrupted branches. Gavin returned to the cavern every few months to make sure no fresh corruption had leaked from the dormant Reaver.

He could feel its sleeping anger whenever he visited; could feel the eons-long grudge it nursed against the uncaring universe. Gavin hadn't communed with it since he first joined his mind to the veilship's. He saw its memories sometimes, floating in the consciousness he shared with his ship. They seemed connected somehow — the creator and its creation — yet on some plane Gavin couldn't access at will.

Whenever he was in the cavern, he inevitably thought to turn the blue energy beam on The Reaver. Knowing it would do no more than scorch the creature's membrane, he would then think about coming back with his veilship — and finally he would be left wondering why his mind had veered toward thoughts of killing it in the first place.

The Reaver had told him about Vola. It had shown him where to find the veilships, without which most of the colonists would probably be dead. Gavin always found himself reluctant to leave The Reaver alive to fester in its chamber, yet fearful that it wouldn't be there if he needed it again.

It wasn't long after he torched the corrupted branches that the animal life of Galena began to behave itself once again. No more squids had crawled onto the shore (though he'd stashed two rifles near the shoreline, just in case), Emily now had worm bait to tempt the frustratingly cautious fish, and moss was once again growing in the patches close to the colony. After Vola's missile vaporized the hospital, it took the moss gestation tanks with it. The colonists had to travel to nearby springs when the need arose.

Gavin had a lot to keep himself occupied. Between working the farm and repairing broken machinery, he even found the occasional hour to tinker with the *Celerity*.

There were only a few quiet moments, usually just before falling asleep, where the call of his veilship grew too strong to ignore.

Occasionally, his resolve faltered.

Six months ago, he had left his home in the middle of the night and made the short trek to the veilships. They hovered at the edge of a forest, in a sunken field near Compass Rock — a monument so named for the tall, thin blade of lead sulfide that thrust from the ground to point north. The trees and boulders surrounding the sunken field provided cover from passing eyes.

The veilships seemed to prefer being close to the underground canopy. They drifted just above the soil, their tendril branches piled in loose coils on the surface.

Gavin set foot in the nerve center of his veilship for the first time in over a year.

He found a pile of bones waiting for him.

They were heaped at the base of the pilot cubby. One of them had been broken in half — an old break, long healed over. It was someone's partially-amputated left arm.

Kellan.

No one had so much as caught a glimpse of the man since Alexander Vola and his entire ship vanished. Gavin and many others assumed he'd vanished with him.

When he joined his consciousness with the

veilship's that night, he relived the ship's memory of Kellan emerging from the floor of the nerve center and standing before the pilot cubby, eyeing it greedily.

He turned and sat on the narrow seat within the shallow depression, and the same branches that wrapped around Gavin wrapped around Kellan, too. On Gavin, they constricted just firmly enough to support him. They squeezed Kellan until he burst.

Standing on the raft by the shore, Gavin closed his eyes against the memory. The veilships wouldn't allow anyone else to pilot them other than himself, Shurri, and Arthur. He knew that now. It was a marriage of sorts — they were bound to each other, body and soul.

The three of them had a discussion about it not long after they became pilots. It was agreed they would only use the ships for the colony's defense, should Earth ignore Gavin's warning and send people back through the Rip.

In three years, no one had come — yet Arthur seemed to spend as much time on his veilship as he did back at the colony. It troubled Shurri whenever Gavin brought it up, so he hardly ever did. She was so happy in her pregnancy that he didn't want to spoil it by rehashing old concerns.

Shurri waded out to the raft, smiling, the water coming up to her thighs. Fish scattered from below the raft as Gavin helped her climb up.

"They were down there the whole time!" Emily declared, kneeling to peer into the water.

Shurri stood on her tiptoes so Gavin could kiss her forehead. They wrapped their arms around each other and looked out to sea. On the shore, the other families were preparing to leave.

Emily giggled when a fish splashed water onto the raft, then scolded it in the same breath when it vanished. It had come to inspect her fingers below the surface, then jetted away when she yanked her hand back.

"She has your fishing skills," Shurri teased.

And your temper, Gavin signed, smiling.

Shurri batted his arm playfully. "She does not."

For no reason at all, he looked in the direction of the distant veilships. Shurri cupped his cheek and drew his gaze back to hers.

"We're safe here, right?" she asked quietly.

Gavin stared into her eyes, and nodded.

She took his hand and placed it on her swollen belly. *Soon,* the gesture promised. He smiled down at Emily while she hummed a song and trailed a finger in the water, hoping to lure another fish.

Sunlight glimmered on the ocean surface as the pale yellow disc of Phobis slowly descended from a cobalt sky to kiss the horizon.

Gavin's mind saw shapes in the flashing ripples where there were none. The shapes were letters, and they formed a single word.

Home.

Want to read the trilogy that takes place 400 years before the events of *Galena*?

https://mybook.to/titanchronicles

<u>More Books by Samuel Best:</u>

The INFINITE SKY Universe

Titan Chronicles

Mission One
Deep Black
Last Contact

Galena Chronicles

Another World
Third Colony
Galena

Pantheon

Forthcoming

You can find more info on the author's website
<u>https://sam-best.com</u>

About the Author

Born in Cape Canaveral, Florida, Samuel grew up a mile from the gates of Kennedy Space Center. His grandmother built space shuttles, his father designed scientific equipment that flew on them, and Samuel watched the launches from his rattling front porch, dreaming of the stars.

His best-selling novel Mission One, a near-future first contact odyssey, is the book that launched his career as a science fiction writer.

He recently spent three years traveling the world with his wife. They welcomed their son near the end of that journey and are now spending their days exploring the United States while Samuel works on his next book.

Printed in Great Britain
by Amazon

22873469R00172